PRETTY LITTLE TEASE

PRETTY OBSESSIONS
BOOK ONE

AJ MERLIN

Pretty Little Tease is a dark romance that contains some content that may be problematic for some readers including murder, graphic violence, serial killers, kink, sex work, coercion, and consent that isn't always given properly.

The men are morally terrible, at best, and not fit to be brought home to meet your parents.

CHAPTER 1

"So what's the catch?" I can't help the question slipping out as I stand in the small foyer of our new apartment, and it's hard to stop myself from chewing my bottom lip as I look around this small space of our apartment.

"Hmm?" Juniper slides her backpack off her shoulders and blinks at me, confused. "What do you mean 'the catch?'"

"I mean that, last time I checked, we aren't in the uh, financial bracket of people that get *foyers* in their apartments. It's like a tiny little greeting hall." I sweep a hand toward the other end of the small hallway, where a door into the rest of the apartment sits ajar. In this small, already decorated space, a long sideboard hugs the left wall, a rack on the other to hold... whatever we might come home with that we don't want to take further inside.

"It's considered college housing." Juniper shrugs. "We got a bit of a discount to live here. Enough that it was still in our price range, and not even at the very top."

I shift, slightly uncomfortable at the discussion of money. I don't have a lot of it, and I don't have a job lined up like she does for after the year is over. A potential one, anyway. It's always been Juniper's plan to work at her mother's company, and her entire college education plan has always revolved around that.

On the other hand, being that I'm a history major minoring in folklore and Ancient Roman Studies, I do not have a solid life plan of my own. Hopefully, at some point, I get the *Night At The Museum* treatment and get whisked away by Teddy Roosevelt for nighttime shenanigans.

That or I learn how to time travel and ask my college freshman self if we're *sure* we want to go through with a questionable course of study.

"Some college housing. Did someone die here? Is this part of the St. Augustine ghost tour on Saturday nights? That's totally why there's a foyer, right?" My voice is light, the tone playful, and even though it's clear that I'm joking, I can't imagine doing this with someone I don't know as well as Juniper. After all, she's been my best friend since freshman year, intro to roman studies. If anyone can tell when I'm joking and not take my inappropriate, nervous giggles seriously... it's her.

"Yeah, and your bedroom is their first and last stop, Blair," Juniper agrees, teasing. She glances at me, her dark hooded eyes solemn as she tries to keep with the joke. "Totally should've told you that before we picked rooms off the online pictures. Oh, well."

"Guess I'll die," I reply, following her as she pushes open the door that takes us into the apartment proper. It's a good thing she can't see my face, or the way I'm sawing at my lip. This *is* in my budget, but when I was on my way back from Tennessee this morning on the bus, it had suddenly hit me.

I don't have a life plan.

I don't have a career picked out.

I don't have a job or a huge savings account.

I'm not related to the Rockefellers or Bill Gates.

And I'm not in a relationship with a sugar daddy who takes care of all my wants and needs.

I can afford this apartment without hurting myself, honestly. Especially because of the student housing discount we're getting. It would've been almost as expensive to live in a single room on campus, as there was no way in hell I was moving in with anyone other than Juniper, and she's wanted *out* of the dorm for a year.

The rest of the apartment is just as great, because of course it is. The furniture looks new, and the place smells like fresh paint and cleaning supplies. Surely we aren't the first ones to live here, though for the life of me, I can't see any other signs of someone having moved out a few months ago.

"Someone died here," I assure Juniper, opening the door to the bathroom that's more spacious than I would've thought it would be. There's even a small washer and dryer stacked in the corner by the door, giving us a reason to never have to find a laundromat or do our laundry on campus two miles away. Not that I'd want to do my laundry at Wickett University of St. Augustine. No offense to the school, but some of its accommodations are a little less than inspiring. It's one reason so many students prefer to live *off* campus, rather than on.

My eyes flick over the square, glass-walled shower in the corner before I step back out, looking at the shiny kitchen before passing by the kitchen island to get a look at the open living room. Nothing separates the two, other than the island with three stools slid under it. A long, L-shaped couch sits in the living room, a coffee table perched on a dark blue rug on the faux-wood flooring in front of it, and on one wall a large tv hangs, screen a bright and shiny black.

It looks so much better than my dorm room that I could die.

Instead of dying, I peek out onto the balcony where two wicker chairs sit, barely noticing the view of the water I can see a half mile away. How in the *world* is this actually student housing?

Maybe a whole family was murdered here, and their bodies were used in some kind of dark summoning ritual that nearly leveled the city. It's so cheap because every month or so the *Ghostbusters* have to show up, with the exorcist from the *Poltergeist* tagging along, so that the apartment building can be made clean again.

Or something similarly displeasing and inconvenient to the tenants.

"Have you looked at your room yet?" Juniper asks, the door to hers ajar. They're on opposite sides of the apartment, and it takes me a few seconds to stride over and open the door to my private room.

It's been awhile since I had one. Even before living in a dorm room with Juniper, I was sharing a bedroom with my younger sister back home whenever she was at Mom's house instead of her dad's.

My hand finds the cold metal and I turn the knob, peeking inside like I'm going to find the grisly remains of a dead, sacrificed body. Maybe it'll be like in *13 Ghosts* and a body will be rolling around in cellophane.

Maybe I should just stop watching horror movies while I fall asleep. Or at least stop letting them play on repeat, allowing them to infect my dreams.

The room is about as large as our dorm room, give or take three square feet in my novice opinion. A full size bed sits against one corner, the bedside table is white and minimalist. A desk sits in the opposite corner, and across from both the bed and the desk, set into the walls on either side of the door, are two shallow closets with shelves marching from the top to about knee-height. My bags are in here, where they'd been left by the employees who had helped us sign the last of our contracts. I still can't believe our apartment building basically has a *bellboy* service.

Had they helped the residents of the other nine apartments?

Being on the third floor, we're at the top of the building, and there are two apartments on our floor apart from ours. I don't mind, and I like the view, frankly. Besides that, there's a window in my bedroom that overlooks the street and at least if I'm stupid and walk in front of it naked, I have less of a chance of flashing the entire world. That's what I hope for, anyway, though I'll clearly have to do some street-level scout work to see for sure.

Footsteps herald the arrival of my best friend and room-mate, and seconds later Juniper presses her hands against the doorframe as she looks around. "This is really nice, huh?" she asks, her dark gaze flicking from one piece of furniture to the other. "I don't want to admit it, but maybe you've a point about the ghosts and death."

"And the grisly murders," I remind her stoically. "All of which clearly happened in our apartment."

"Clearly," she agrees quickly. "Anyway, I guess now we just unpack and wait for the undead to seek their revenge?"

"It will be swift and mighty." I fight not to yawn, and I cover my mouth with my hand as if she doesn't know from the sound of my voice what I'm doing. "Maybe we'll get drowned, or possessed. Maybe drowned *and* possessed."

"You want pizza?" Juniper asks, breezing past my warnings of woe. "There was that place down the street, kind of where the bus dropped you off."

"God, ugh. Don't say '*bus*.'" I shudder. "I'm striking it from my vocabulary until two weeks before winter break on the exact day I need to schedule a ticket back home for Christmas."

Juniper snorts. "Canadian bacon and pepperoni?"

"Pineapple?" I ask hopefully, going to sit on my bed with my laptop out. "Please, o great apartment-finder. Hero of my life. Moon of my heart. *Pineapple?*"

"Drop dead," my best friend replies oh-so-sweetly... and disappears from my doorway.

I snort and pull my legs up under me, glad I get the chance to sit down even though I know I need to be unpacking. When I grab my laptop, my new tattoo, which still looks darker than it will in a few more days, catches my eye.

It hadn't hurt more than, say, the one just over my collarbone, but getting the back of my hand tattooed hadn't been the greatest experience of my life. Flowers litter the skin just behind my fingers, draping along the sides of my hand as they work their way back to my elbow before stopping. Twined between the blooms and only visible in a few places on my arm are the coils and shapes of snakes. On my hand, a snake's head is actually visible, and I flex my hand as I look at the design.

I hadn't planned this part. Not that I've told anyone other than Juniper that, but I had thought I'd just get more flowers to match the ones on my thigh. Even the tattoo on my left upper arm and shoulder, which features a twisting fox with wide, sightless eyes and a mouthful of fangs, is buried in a background of flowers.

But I'd never thought to get a *snake*. Still, it fits. I love the design, and I love the contrast of the black to the flowers against my pale skin.

Absently, I open my laptop, hands going up to push my thick, blonde hair back from my face as it boots up. I try not to scowl at my hair, because that'll just give me something else to be pissed about, but it really is wild that after just a few hours of not brushing it, my hair gets tangled like it's been days since I've touched it.

One of these days, I'm going to take it from waist length to chin length and never look back. Hell, maybe I'll even get a damn pixie cut if I'm feeling frisky enough.

My brain short circuits when I see my computer screen, and I realize that it's a damn good thing I hadn't tried to use it on the trip today, since *someone* had forgotten to close out of all the eighteen plus browsers she'd had up last night.

That someone is me, and I'm surprised the muted videos haven't decided to spontaneously start moaning at me.

Studiously I click out of them, pretending that I'm not scrutinizing every single one to see if I want to throw it into my favorites. But they were just filler. Just things to watch while passing the time, and most of them aren't even my thing.

Even the camsite, which features less scripted porn and more people talking to their audiences while they fuck or get off, doesn't appeal to me that much. Though, according to Juniper, that's because I've never found someone to connect to.

Before I click out of it, I hesitate, refreshing the screen instead as I glance up at the door. I'm certainly not about to watch porn in the middle of the day with my door open but... I scroll through the thumbnails until one of a guy in a white, almost handmade looking mask with a drawn-on smile catches my attention. He tilts his head to the side, like he's amused or questioning, and I click on the thumbnail while turning my volume up just enough that I'll be able to hear him but I won't be blasting out my roommate's ears with his sexy sounds.

Besides, I'm not about to watch this, anyway. Cam shows aren't normally my thing, and while he looks attractive from what I can see, I doubt I'll like watching him.

Whatever he's saying, he breaks it off when my username comes up in the chat, and he leans forward just enough to read it, his cock gripped lightly in his fingers and drawing my attention as it, too, gets bigger on my screen.

Okay, so, judging from his appearance outside of the crudely made mask... he's definitely my type.

"You're a little late, *finalistgirl*," he greets me with a low chuckle, reading my username out loud. "I've just finished up."

Damn. But, I remind myself, this is probably better. I'm not going to watch porn right now. I need to unpack and go get the pizza if Juniper doesn't want to do it herself. Sighing, I go to close my laptop, only for his voice to pull my attention back to the screen.

"Aren't you going to say sorry?" His tone is goading, and more than a little flirty. "You missed what I worked so hard for... and now I'm missing the joy of your company."

Is he talking to... *me*?

"I'm talking to you, *finalistgirl*. I know you're still here with us." Messages of support start popping up in the chat, and I freeze, not knowing what to do. This isn't what I expected, and no camboy has ever said anything to me before this.

"Tell me you're sorry, and maybe I'll let you leave." His sultry purr of a voice sends shivers up my spine so I do what any reasonable, rational citizen would do.

I close out of his stream... and slam my laptop shut. My cheeks burn with embarrassment and I force my thighs to unclench, eyes wide as I stare into my empty closet.

Forget my apartment being haunted. Now I'm going to have to relive this moment every day for the rest of my life and wonder what would have happened if I had typed out the words *I'm sorry* like my fingers had itched to do and hit send.

CHAPTER 2

I let out a sigh as I walk down the outdoor hallway that connects the campus center to the liberal arts building, absently chewing my lower lip. By now I've been doing it so long that my mouth is sensitive and my bottom lip feels like it might be starting to swell, just a little. Almost forcibly, I remove my teeth from it and run my tongue along my lips, thinking to myself as I walk.

I was supposed to have photography with Juniper. That had been the plan when my roommate and best friend had coerced me into taking the class with her, but now that she's dropped out because of a last second conflict in her schedule, I'm the only one here.

And from what I know about our professor, who's a famous photographer in his own right and sometimes works with the local news, I really could've used her help here. He's supposed to be an absolute hardass; a jerk, with no consideration for things that happen outside of his class. I've heard it's impossible to do well, unless you spend your entire life working toward his expectations, and that's not something I'm interested in doing.

I don't want to *be* a photographer after all. I'm just here because I needed an elective and, when Juniper would've been here too, it probably would've been fun. But with all the other art electives full and me not wanting to overbook myself on credits next semester, this is my only choice.

Not that I'm afraid of a strict professor, but Professor Solomon, along with having an intimidating name, has the reputation of being pretty unpleasant to deal with most of the time.

Silently, I walk into the classroom, noting that the desks are lined up like a 'U' instead of sitting in lines. A soft breath of disdain leaves me, and I wish I could throttle Juniper. Or at least send her a stern glare. This is yet another reason I didn't want to be in here alone. I have two options, it seems to me. Option one is that I take one of the corners of the U, and if I do that, then I'm as close as possible to Professor Solomon's desk or where he'll probably stand to teach.

If I don't, then I'm going to be trapped between two people I may not know. So far I haven't heard about any of the acquaintances I have in my arts major taking this class, and with a professor that has a reputation like his, why would they?

So I hesitate, only to scoot to one side as two girls walk in and rush to the tip of the U closest to the desk, like they're dying to be as close as possible to our professor. Have they had him before? Or maybe they're really interested in what he has to teach?

All I know about him are the rumors I've heard.

After another moment of hesitation and three more students walking in to sit at different parts of the U, I realize that class is about to start. Even though Professor Solomon hasn't shown up yet, I lunge forward and take the seat at the other tip of the U, closest to the door. It's not because I want to sit near him, or that I want to escape.

Well, okay, it might be that one.

But because I don't want him to come in and see me just *hovering*. He might think I need help. Or that I'm an idiot. I'd at least like to get a jumpstart on the semester before having one of my professors hate me.

Laughter from the hallway catches my attention and I turn slightly, not enough to see the door, and certainly not enough to see the person breeze in who dumps his things on the table beside me. I flinch, surprised, and look up into the friendly face of a guy who might be a few years older than me. Not that I'm surprised by that, exactly. Wickett offers multiple masters programs, and sometimes those students audit lower level classes, according to Juniper. Her brother had done that when a class had come around he was interested in.

That, or I'm just really bad at guessing ages.

The guy smiles broadly, sitting down hard in his seat with a sigh while he does. "Want to trade seats?" he asks, catching me off guard. "I don't mind. He's yelled at me before."

"...What?" I ask, barely listening to the low buzz of conversation outside the door.

"Oh, too late I guess. Next time?"

I don't get the chance to ask him to clarify or figure out what in the world is going on. The door *slams* shut, and I clench my teeth so hard I'm surprised they don't crack.

"Color me surprised," a low, disappointed voice sighs, and I have the distinct feeling I'm being glared at. "I thought you'd be the one looking for an escape, Oliver."

Who the hell is Oliver?

I don't turn around. I don't want to look afraid, or like I've done something wrong. But embarrassment rises in my chest as I look down at the smooth fake wood of the table under me and let out a long, low breath.

I hate this class already.

"She was just trying to be nice to me," the guy beside me chuckles. "She heard about how rude you are to me every semester and thought that I deserve a break."

"Oh yeah?" My professor prowls around the side of the tables, not even looking at me. Finally, I have a chance to scrutinize him, my heart still pounding from his words.

He's younger than I thought he'd be. His hair is brown, though its shade is somewhere between my light, almost blonde hair and Oliver's dark auburn beside me. He's tall, probably six feet, though to my five-foot-five, a lot of people are considered *tall*.

Unlike some of my more formal professors, he's dressed in snug jeans, a long-sleeve shirt, and dress shoes. Frankly, he looks like he's just stepped out of some magazine. Especially when he leans against his desk, rolls up his sleeves, and takes off his sunglasses so he can look all of us over. All in all, the class numbers maybe thirteen, and I endeavor to make that *twelve* by the end of the week.

I don't need to be in a class where the professor is a dick just because I sat near the door.

My nails tap lightly on the table in front of me, and somehow that draws Professor Solomon's attention again, making me still. His eyes flick down to my hand, then immediately to the female student nearest him, who can't help but hide her smile at his nearness.

How could anyone have a crush on him?

"As this is an elective, I'm assuming most of you are just using it to fill that requirement," he sighs, like this job is beneath him. Hell, maybe it is. In that case, I wish he would've found someone else to teach it. "But I'm going to pretend you're all enthusiastic photographers and you're aiming to shoot for either journals, the news, or fashion. If that's not the case, I don't really need to know. In fact, for this semester, pretend it *is* the case. Who knows?" He lifts a brow. "Maybe I'll convert some of you and see you next semester as well."

Count me out.

Beside me, Oliver's leg brushes against my thigh, causing me to flinch, and I fight the urge to do anything but stay still. I don't want to look at him, or see him, or do anything. In fact, it is absolutely my goal to make this professor forget I'm here so that, at the end of class, I can slip out of here and run straight to my dorm so I can unenroll from this class immediately.

It shouldn't be hard, really. It's not like he knows me and I'm not a photography major who's taking this class for more than side-credit. Not to mention that while he talks, I find myself only half-paying attention. Unlike my other classes, he actually reads through the syllabus, ignoring the looks shot towards the door by the other students who clearly thought that we'd get to leave early.

"AND THAT'S ALL. You're free from my clutches and if you're upset that I didn't end class early after handing out syllabi like other professors..." He shrugs. "You know where the unenroll button is just as well as I do. Don't hesitate to use it."

He looks pointedly at two guys sitting near the back of the room, who had seemed particularly disgruntled at having to stay the whole hour today. They avoid his look, pretending that he's not clearly talking to them as they shuffle to their feet and head for the door *fast*.

The two girls get up as well, though they crowd at Professor Solomon's desk, leaning over it to speak in low whispers to him. I can't help but frown. Can't they pick a better professor to swoon over? At least someone who isn't so, well, mean?

Though degradation is certainly a kink, and maybe these two are into it. Who am I to yuck on their yum?

"Sorry," Oliver says again, arm sliding against mine as he gets his stuff together. He's sitting closer than I feel like he needs to, and my stomach twists every time I get a hint of his spicy-sweet cologne in my nose. It's not unpleasant, that's for sure, but I don't know anything about him, and I'm on the opposite side of the spectrum from *extroverted*.

"For what?" I murmur, hurrying to get my shit packed up. I should've tried doing it sooner, but when someone else had, once it was close to class ending, our professor had made an unfriendly comment that had frozen the other student in their tracks and caused everyone to sit perfectly still for the rest of the time.

Well, except Oliver. *He*, on the other hand, seems like someone who never stops moving, never stops fidgeting. Even when Professor Solomon had glared at him for clearing his throat or making some kind of noise, Oliver had just fucking *beamed*.

"I try to take that seat since I know how he gets about it. Obviously you aren't trying to escape or anything, but he's just..."

A dick, I want to say. A jerk, an asshole.

Not my problem for much longer, either.

"But give it a chance, okay?" It's as if the older boy can read my mind, and I turn to look at him in surprise.

"What?"

"Give. It. A. Chance. He's..." Oliver glances at Professor Solomon, who's currently looking like the two girls trying to flirt with him are causing him to be in physical pain. Good for them. "Okay, yeah. He's an ass. I've audited this class three times, so I get that. But he's a really excellent teacher. Like, insanely good. You might end up finding you're into photography."

Doubt it.

"I didn't catch your name, by the way. I'm Oliver Greer." He doesn't stick out a hand, but he does follow as I get to my feet, like he's prepared to bar me from my grand escape.

"Blair Love," I say after a second's hesitation. "I, umm. My friend was supposed to take this class with me," I explain, as if he'd asked. Students filter out around us, but I barely notice as Oliver grins sympathetically.

"Do you think she quit because of him?" He tilts his head towards the other side of the room.

"No. I don't think so. There was a scheduling problem with one of her science classes. Anyway, she can't fit this in her schedule now, and I..." I let out a sigh, holding my iPad tighter in the crook of my arm. "I really need the elective, since I'm hoping to take it easy next semester before I graduate."

"Then I guess you'll just have to grin and bear it, and wallow about with us photography peasants, won't you?" The voice behind me makes me close my eyes hard, my teeth clenching so much that the muscles in my jaw ache.

Oliver turns, still smiling, and doesn't appear perturbed to see our professor leaning against the wall behind me. I look as well, wishing I could do something to stop him from glaring at me like this. What did I even *do* to irritate him? Is he really so upset that I sat in front of the door?

"I'm... sorry about sitting in front of the door," I apologize. "I didn't know that... umm." I tuck my hair behind my ear, heart in my throat trying to choke me. If this were Juniper, I'd make stupid jokes about escape and running for the ocean, but it's not.

Instead, it's a professor that already makes me uncomfortable and a student who radiates friendliness so strongly I'm afraid I'll burn from it like a vampire doused in holy water.

"She didn't know you had such a weird *thing* about it, or she would've run out of class beforehand instead of sitting here while you called her out," Oliver supplies, smiling sweetly with glittering brown eyes like he thinks he's helping me.

Immediately my gaze goes back to our professor, my lips parted as I look at him. There's no humor at all in his green eyes that are fixed on Oliver, and before I can say a word, he turns to look at me instead. "You're an art history student," he states, not phrasing it like a question. When I make a noise of surprise, he adds, "It's on my class paperwork, in case you think I'd bother to research my students before the semester started."

"I'm an art history major with minors in Roman Studies and Folklore," I force myself to correct. He is *not* going to leave out all the work I do to make those one cohesive thing, even if I have to drag the words out of my throat when he looks at me like I'm a speck of dirt.

Well, at least his eyes are pretty.

"All right," he shrugs. "I was only saying it because Professor Carmine speaks highly of you... and she never speaks highly of any student. I was curious about who you were when I saw your name on my roster, and..." He looks at Oliver, then back at me, and my heart skips a beat. "You're not really what I was expecting."

Yeah, that feels like an insult.

"But at least you have good taste in seating partners. He's good at this. Though, I guess he should be, given the training he's had with me." Oliver grins at the compliment, but doesn't say anything before our professor goes on. "If you want to be good at this, too, you should listen to him. Sometimes." He goes toward the door and halts without looking back. "Unless you're going to unenroll and I never see you again," Professor Solomon remarks offhandedly, before breezing through the doorway and into the hall beyond.

I stand there, confused as hell, as I listen to him go.

"You good?" Oliver asks, moving to stand in front of me again. "He can be a lot. I get it."

"I think I'm... uh, insulted? Offended? Maybe I'm flattered." I blink a few times, trying to sort through his words. "I don't know yet."

"Ah, yeah, he's good at that. Something to look forward to if you don't drop the class, huh?" Oliver chuckles. "Anyway, I'll see you on Monday, I hope?" I realize that this class is a terrible way to start *and* finish the week, and frown. "Have a good weekend, Blair."

"You too," I say, when he's already halfway out the door. I almost add that he *won't* see me on Monday, because I'm about to go home and get out of this damn hellhole of a class that I don't have to put myself through.

I'm not a *masochist*, after all.

CHAPTER 3

I t's only a little after four when I get back to the apartment, and I pause in the foyer, listening for sounds of life within. Though, since Juniper has class until seven tonight, if I hear something, then it's probably a ghost.

We're in St. Augustine, though, I should probably just take that as par for the course. Is property value raised by the presence of the dead? Since it feels like that's the whole point of tourists coming here?

Letting out a soft sigh, I go to my room and thump my backpack down on my desk. It's absolutely time to get out of photography. I can't deal with that attitude all semester, even if he is nice to look at and Oliver, while also gorgeous, is actually *nice*. If Professor Solomon was a little less bad, I'd think it would be worth staying.

But he isn't, and it's not.

Before going to my bed, I close my door on a whim, laptop in my hands so I can lay it on my comforter. I hesitate, and decide that it's not going to kill me to change out of my school clothes first. They're uncomfortable. Especially since, for the first time in my life, I'm trying to dress like a real person instead of a zombie that crawls out of bed, hits class, and crawls right back *into* bed, thanks to my friends asking me if I'm doing my best, continuous audition of a modern *Sleeping Beauty*.

Shimmying out of my snug black jeans and red tee, I kick off my shoes as well and go to my bed, pulling on a pair of comfy, ripped sweatpants that are at least two sizes too big. On the left leg of the black fabric, WICKETT is spelled out in big, blocky letters, while the other leg is just black. Once my bra is off, I drag on a much looser t-shirt, this one purple and black tie-dye. It's not like I'm going anywhere else tonight, unless it's to get takeout, so I'm safe to be comfortable. On the off chance that Juniper wants to go somewhere, I'll put jeans back on and complain about it for a while.

When I bring up my browser, I immediately go to my saved links, finding the one that will log me into my student portal for classes. I click through the info, get to my page, and immediately find what I'm looking for.

My schedule loads instantly, popping up before my eyes. It's not bad, as far as semesters go. My sophomore year was worse when I added Roman Studies as a minor. Back then, I'd had to take eighteen credits in one semester, and I'd definitely prefer not to do it again. Though, if I drop Photography, then next semester isn't looking so great.

God, I don't want to do eighteen credits again. Especially during my last semester as a college student. Already I'm working on my senior project, or at least planning it out. My idea has been to incorporate folklore and art history together to do a report on it, and some dumb little part of me had thought about applying some photography to it as well when I'd signed up for the class. After all, I have a camera now, thanks to enrolling and getting a student deal on a nice one.

It seemed like a great idea at the time.

So great, in fact, that I'm having trouble dropping out of the class now. It would be a waste. A total waste of money, credits, and effort. There really aren't any other electives open that will fill the gap, and I've already bought the damn camera.

Could it really be so bad to just stick around? Professor Solomon will take up two hours of my week, sometimes three, when we have a project to turn in and work in the darkroom. But it's not like he can do anything other than look disapprovingly at me and be shitty.

He isn't some kind of real life monster, after all. Just an unhappy, dismissive college professor. I can handle that. Instead of taking myself out of the class, I sigh and close out of the browser, leaning back against the head of my bed. There's no homework for me to do, and it's becoming more and more apparent that I'd really like a nap. It's quiet, and nice, and the view into the city of St. Augustine from my window gives me something to look at other than my phone screen.

Absently, I return to my favorites menu on my laptop's browser, pausing when I see what I'd added last night.

The camsite. It's never made it to my favorites before. It probably doesn't deserve to be here now. But the guy from last night gave me weird, questionable dreams that weren't completely bad... and he was hot.

Plus, the way he'd talked *to* me? I haven't been flustered by porn in a long time, and I hadn't thought I would be now.

Curiously, I click on the link to the site, *funxcams*, and end up firmly on the home page. Damn. I realize now that my mistake from yesterday is going to haunt me today.

I never found that guy's name. With hundreds of people streaming at once, the best I can do is click on the menu for guys that are live now and scroll through it, hopefully landing on him. At one point I do end up checking my history, but when I click on the link from yesterday that isn't just the base site, it takes me nowhere.

Damn it.

I blink, scrolling to the second page, and then pause.

Did I just see...? Curiously, hopefully, I scroll back up, just in time to see a shirtless, masked guy sit down in a fancy office chair. Still wearing jeans, he sprawls back in the thumbnail, lifting his hand idly like he's talking to his viewers.

Yeah, it's definitely him.

Will he notice if I join? The viewer count is going up by the second, so I know he must be popular, and surely he has to have more important people to talk to than me. Better tippers, too, since I haven't given him real views *or* real money.

Refusing to overthink it, I click on the thumbnail, watching as his specific stream opens up in my browser. Now I can see that there's a tip list in the top corner, listing the top tippers for the show and the top tipper of all time.

Both first place spots are held by the same person with the username *framed_failures*. Feels weird, but who am I to judge? My username, made on a whim as I was watching *Scream*, is *finalistgirl*.

"Oh hey, look who's back." That purr is unmistakable and I freeze, figuring he can't be talking about me. "It's my friend from yesterday, *finalistgirl*. Say hi to our shy new friend, everyone."

Fuck. His viewers are literally telling me hi in the chat like this is some kind of roundtable discussion and not a stream of this guy getting off and talking dirty. Absently I check his name as well, noting that it's *letsplayjay*. Is that his name? Jay? I also notice that, despite getting over twenty people to tell me hello, none of the welcome messages are from *framed_failures*, even though he surely has to be here if he's already tipped.

"Don't be rude, finalist. This is where you say hello." A

shiver goes down my spine as his viewers agree, and again I consider slamming my laptop shut and never getting on here again.

But what can he really do? He's being fun and interactive. There's no crime in that, and since it has me flustered, clearly it's working. I bet he does it to a lot of new people, and it drags them in to be his lifelong fans.

I wish I could do that, I think distantly, typing *hi* into the chat and smacking the enter key to send it.

"There she is!" he chuckles when he sees it. "That's a good girl." Yeah, that does things to me that normal porn doesn't, and I press my thighs together as a shiver runs up my spine. After a few seconds, I tune back in, half-listening as he explains his tipping system and that anyone in the top three can request what they want or ask him anything. Except to show his face, of course.

I can't help but think that's an ingenious idea. Clearly no one here cares that they can only see his body, though I do see a few messages begging him to take it off. But he only plays with the idea, fingers skimming along the outside of his mask teasingly before dropping them to his upper body again.

And yet, his top tipper never says a word. Finally, someone does tip a significant amount, and my eyes widen when I see the person casually drop over a hundred dollars to *letsplayjay* so that he'll show the stream his cock.

"So soon? But we were having such a good chat." The streamer is flirty when he says it, though his deft fingers are already working at the button of his jeans. I watch, caught up by the movement, and notice belatedly that he has tattoos winding up his sides, though I can only see the hint of wings and maybe feathers from what has to be a giant back piece. "Now I'm scared you think my conversation is boring." He lifts his hips just enough to shimmy his jeans downward, revealing his cock slowly enough that people in his chat moan in anticipation until finally he closes one hand around it and moves it up and down slowly, clearly for his audience.

Even *I'm* into it, and it's definitely not my usual type of thing. The same person tips him again, begging him to use his other hand, and because of that, slides into first place on the tip chart.

Only to be immediately replaced with *framed_failures* in less than a millisecond. Meaning that his top fan *is* watching, he or she just isn't talking. They have to be paying attention to notice that and correct it. So why not make requests like everyone else is?

Off-handedly, I hit the tip button as well, feeling like he probably deserves it for being the one camboy in history to keep my attention. It's not much, not enough to compete with any of his top tippers, but still. At least it's something, right?

"Looks like I've converted you already, haven't I, *finalistgirl*?" He chuckles, though it sounds like more of a purr than anything else. I feel myself shiver once more and hold my breath as I wait. Will he say something else to me? I haven't tipped enough to get a request. Even if I did, I don't know what I'd ask for, honestly. I'm new to stuff like this, and not really the type to take charge in the bedroom. Or in the stream.

"Tell you what. Since it's your first time and you came back even though I teased you, why don't you tell me what you want to see?" the masked camboy urges. "As long as you don't tell me to take off my mask, I'll do it for you."

God, he already does it for me, truthfully.

Messages blow up the chat, telling me what I should ask for, or begging for *letsplayjay* to notice them too. Some people argue they tipped more, but I notice there's still no message from *framed_failures*.

Hesitantly, I lift my hands to the keys, typing out a message and hitting send before I can stop myself.

Can I see your tattoos?

He reads it quickly, head tilting to the side behind his mask like he's considering it. I cringe, wondering if that's not allowed, or maybe in the rules he went over before I started really listening.

But then he chuckles and nods his head, getting up enough so that he can turn around, his knees in the chair, and leans forward for his audience to see not only his back, but most of his ass as well.

It is a very nice ass, though I can't stop my eyes from being drawn to the tattoo that spans most of his back. It's gorgeous, with crows flying in and out of flowers, some of them more hidden than others. The more I look, the more I see, and when I finally glance back at the chat, I notice a message that is almost gone in the stream of requests.

Nice choice, finalistgirl. The sender is *framed_failures*, and I feel like I've had some kind of honor bestowed upon me, since he hasn't said a word to anyone else.

Once more I reach out, typing a quick *thank you* into the chat to be polite.

I don't expect *letsplayjay* to pause as he's reading. His hand curls around his length again and for a few moments he doesn't say a word. Then he sits back, gives a soft, rolling chuckle and continues on, talking to his other viewers instead of me as they tip him or engage with him.

His stream goes on for longer than I expect it to, and even though it's definitely interesting and fun to watch him tease and flirt, I tear my gaze away from his perfect body and shut my laptop. I had a plan for this afternoon, and I do still intend to take a nap before Juniper gets home so that I'm rested and ready for whatever she wants to do for dinner and after.

24

Not that I think there's going to be much of an 'after' in terms of going out. Juniper doesn't *love* parties and neither do I. Therefore, it's normally at least a few weeks into the semester before she gets the itch to go and drags me to some questionable frat house.

But just in case, I want to sleep and definitely not dream of *letsplayjay* and the way he spoke to me in his stream.

ONCE I'M AWAKE AGAIN, the sun is starting to set. I check my phone, unsurprised to see I slept for over an hour, and that Juniper is on her way back as of five minutes ago. That gives me time to actually wake up and check to make sure no teachers have left any announcements or assignments on the school's website.

Not that I think they have, but after nearly failing a class because of assumptions like that a few semesters ago, I don't take anything for granted.

I pull my laptop off of the nightstand and into my lap once more, combing my fingers through my long, tangled hair. Naturally I'd forgotten to close out of *letsplayjay's* stream, and I frown at the ended stream as I go to close it.

Or I would, if there wasn't a message blinking in my inbox. I'm not dumb, I know these sites send messages urging people to buy tokens for tipping or a subscription to premium streams. This one is probably offering some kind of special or sale, but if I don't delete it now, it'll bother me.

Except, it isn't what I think it's going to be.

The message is from *letsplayjay* and doesn't look like one of the 'official' ones showing their links and stream options. It looks like a real message, though the subject is just :] and nothing else. I click it anyway, and am even more shocked to see I was right. It isn't an automated subscription message at all.

Thanks for coming back. I hope you had a good time, finalist-girl. I stream mondays and fridays from 5 to 6 and sometimes on Saturday. Maybe I'll see you around? I think I can make it worth your while.

I snort and finally close the browser with a shake of my head. If he hadn't locked in my interest before, this has definitely done it. And while it's not my normal go-to, I can absolutely see myself making an exception just this once, for just this camboy.

Though, I can't help but wonder what it's like to be on the other side of the stream, talking to viewers, not showing your face, and getting paid to do it.

Could I do it? Or would I crash and burn like the world's saddest tree falling miserably down a cliff into lava?

CHAPTER 4

"I hate you," I tell Juniper lightly, no real enthusiasm in my tone as I mop up sour cream with my cheese quesadilla. While I'm not exactly vegetarian, meat has a habit of upsetting my stomach. Especially when I don't cook it myself. Besides, it's not like I mind eating what's basically cheese, spices, and bread dipped in *dairy*. Quite the opposite, in fact, as dairy is my favorite of the food groups.

"Do you?" Her finger runs down the lines of her syllabus as she reads. "Tell me all about it while I give you *all* of my attention." She doesn't look up, or stop reading, and it's clear I won't be getting even half of her attention, truth be told. Not that I need it for slightly insulting her.

I snort anyway, like she's hurt my feelings. "You quit photography, and now I'm stuck there. I need the credits, and I've already bought the camera."

"So?" She looks up at me, brows raised. "What's the big deal? You wanted to take it anyway, last time I checked. *And* Professor Solomon is drop dead gorgeous."

"And awful," I amend vehemently. "He's *awful*. Incredibly

27

mean. Talks shit about students while they're in class. I have never had a worse professor, and after freshman year, Mr. Porter, and earth and space science, that's really saying something."

"It is," Juniper agrees, nodding at me. "I didn't think anything would ever top Porter for you. Especially when that Christian student locked eyes with you and, what was it?" There's a smile growing on her lips as she pretends to forget what happened.

But she hasn't. Not only was she there, she's never let me live it down.

My mouth opens, but before I can speak, I hear my name and a person slides onto the bench beside me, grinning. "Hey," Oliver Greer greets, resting his face on his chin. "So, uh, it's not four o'clock yet." He throws a quick look at Juniper, who's looking at him like she's never seen something so offensive before. "I'm Oliver."

"I wasn't asking," she assures him. "Besides, I know who you are. You tutor on Thursday and I do too. You're a... criminal justice student, right? You're about halfway through your masters?"

Well, I was off in my calculations. I'd pegged him at twenty-three or twenty-four, but if he's halfway through, there's a chance he's closer to twenty-six, depending on whether he took a year off in between.

"Oh, right!" Oliver sits back, palms on the table. "I remember seeing you." I glance at him, surprised to see that his incredibly friendly grin is... different somehow. When he looks at Juniper, I don't feel as much of the friendliness or the helpful attitude.

It feels almost fake.

But it's also none of my business and I have a quarter of a

quesadilla left, so I just watch them instead of butt into their conversation.

"Are you guys in a class together?" Juniper asks, focused on him instead of me. I'm glad for it. I get nervous around strangers, and Oliver's attitude is enough to throw me off my pathetic game, even with his seemingly easy-going nature.

"We're in Basics of Photography together," Oliver nods. "Look, I was just..." He frowns, tapping his fingers on the table, and I bite my lip as he turns to look at me. "You didn't quit, did you? Like I said, I know Rook is awful, but—"

"Rook?" I ask, confused. Who the hell is *Rook*?

"Professor Solomon, sorry. Anyway, I know he's awful to be around, and a jerk. But he is a good professor, and most of the shit we do in here is independent work. He won't be breathing down your neck for long. Though, I guess it's probably too late, if you have decided to opt out, for me to convince you otherwise."

"I didn't, actually." Unsure why I feel almost excited about telling him. "I didn't quit, I mean. You're umm, still stuck with me, sorry to say." I match his voracious smile with a nervous one of my own, watching as he rakes a hand through his soft-looking auburn hair. I realize now that it's always tousled, as if he's constantly running his hands through it, and that it's a stark contrast to his pale skin that's only a few shades darker than mine.

Which is definitely saying something, since I could use white paint as foundation and get away with it from a distance.

Oliver opens his mouth to say something then stops, suddenly looking almost sheepish. His eyes narrow, fingers tapping on the table again, and the change is so sudden that it takes me a second to realize that he's no longer thrilled to be here.

"Uh oh," he mutters, in a much softer, darker voice. "Guess my fun's over." He gives me one more quick, effortless smile. "But I'm glad to hear you're not leaving class—"

"Mr. Greer." The unhappy, snappish voice behind me can only be one person, and I nearly choke on my quesadilla as I realize it's Professor Solomon.

Shit. *Shit*. There should be a rule that he can only terrorize my classroom hours, not my quesadilla eating time.

Not to mention he sounds angry, and I'm scared my name is next and he's going to call me out for eating cheese and bread or for how much sour cream I'm using. Sure, it sounds stupid when I think about it, but why the hell is my photography professor here to yell at Oliver outside of class?

Even Juniper looks confused, and stares unabashedly over my head where I know Professor Solomon is standing. She looks at me, eyes narrowed, then back up as he starts talking again.

"I need you to come to my office before class." His voice is tight and irritation bubbles through the words. "*Now*, Greer. Before class."

Oliver raises his hands in surrender, eyes widening. "Yessir," he agrees, getting to his feet. "Sorry. I..." He frowns, looking at me as I bite my lip. "I was just checking to see if Blair was still in your class."

I close my eyes hard and fight not to let out a sigh. That's totally what I need my professor to hear. That I was thinking of unenrolling.

But thankfully, Professor Solomon doesn't seem to care. He hisses out a breath and Oliver stretches lazily, as if to show he doesn't take orders.

I watch, captivated by his bravery, and see the tiny flash of skin under his t-shirt that feels more like a tease than anything else.

"Yeah, that was weird," Juniper admits, once the two of them have left the courtyard. She shakes her head and looks down at her syllabus. "Now I'm glad I'm not in your class. That feels like way too much to deal with."

"I want out. I hate it there," I inform her.

"So leave. Nothing bad is going to happen if you drop the class, except you'll have to make it up next semester."

Instantly, I'm shaking my head. "No, I don't think so. I don't want to have to overload my credits next semester, for one thing. And also? I want to learn some about photography so I can maybe incorporate it into my senior project next semester. Besides, nothing bad's going to happen if I stay. Except that I might die of embarrassment. Or Professor Solomon might scream me to death."

I'M NOT EXPECTING Oliver's absence in class.

Our professor, of course, doesn't mention it. He seems almost distracted in some ways, though still manages to snap at three students and glare at the rest of us. Then at the end, instead of sticking around for the two girls near his desk to flirt with him, he just... leaves. Grabbing his stuff from his desk, Professor Solomon breezes out the door without a look back, like he has somewhere incredibly important to be.

Still bewildered by it, I make my way home, forgetting until I'm there that while this is one of my early days, it's Juniper's longest. She planned it like this, I know, but I still don't see how she does it. I'd much rather get up early and be done with class early, so I have the evening to myself. But not her. Juniper schedules all of her classes for afternoon or night, and Mondays are when she has class until nine.

I mulled over photography all the way back to my apartment, and only part of that was about Solomon's weird behavior. I also can't stop thinking about what he'd taught, and I pull my photography textbook out of my backpack before sitting on my bed, legs crossed under me. Admittedly, it isn't long before I've tossed my textbook to the side and opened my laptop instead of doing any of the reading I'd said I might.

It's *Monday* after all. While he hadn't streamed on Saturday, this is the day that *letsplayjay* will be live again, hopefully. And it's just now five, so I have a few minutes before he starts. Still, I navigate to his page and wait, seeing the THIS STREAM IS OFFLINE text bright and clear on my screen.

If he doesn't stream, then he doesn't. It won't ruin my day at all. Especially now, while I'm thumbing through the book I haven't bothered to crack open yet. While it focuses on DSLR photography, there are a few references to film and how certain things differ from digital.

Not that I'd trust myself shooting with actual, valuable film any time soon. I'm more than willing to stick with the digital camera I'd bought for class, thank you.

My interest wanes quickly, however, and I move to my laptop, sighing. He's still not live, and maybe I'm obsessed if I'm going to just sit here and wait. Besides, having this stream up makes my other curiosity itch a bit.

Is camwork hard to do?

It doesn't *seem* like it. Sure, I'm betting there are a ton of nuances and skills that I could never fathom. But I'm not thinking about it in terms of getting famous. I'm just considering that it would be easier than getting another part-time job as a barista, or waitress. Wouldn't it be better to do something out of the comfort of my room? With Juniper's long hours and the fact that I have no neighbors above or to the side of my bedroom, I should be safe as long as I'm not screaming.

Plus, I don't have to show my face. *Letsplayjay* doesn't, and while it leads to thirsty simps in his chat, no one actually complains about it. If anything, his viewers seem to *enjoy* the mask, and the character he plays.

Why couldn't I do that?

Because you have no people skills, my brain hopefully points out, but I chase that thought away. Wouldn't it be easier to do if I had a mask like him? Or at the very least found a way to not show my face?

My eyes dip to my hands on the keyboard and I frown, recognizing the other problem with my scenario. My tattoos are noticeable and unique. They're easy to see, and it would be easy to identify me off of them.

Though, how many people see my arms that much in class? Usually I'm wearing a light hoodie if I can, or a longer shirt, and I could just start making an effort to do that. Besides that, how many people from my school would ever *actually* click on a link that was of me?

I'm not vain enough to think I'm some godly catch. Sure, my tattoos are great. I love all of them, even the slightly wonky flower on the inside of my right thigh. But I'm not thin enough, not blonde enough, not well-endowed enough to be a standout.

Still, if I could just make *some* extra money by streaming a few times a week, that would be more than worth it. Especially if I could make just a few hundred a week. Just enough to get by, and it's not like I'd need more than four hundred or so to be able to most likely put some back.

Would it really be so hard? My curious fingers itch to explore, and when it becomes clear that *letsplayjay* isn't streaming today, I let myself head over to the other, more feminine side of the streaming site to see just what exactly I'd have to do if I really wanted to make this work.

CHAPTER 5

I s it coincidence that *letsplayjay* streams on my least favorite days of the week, just after my *least favorite* class? It feels like a divine gift, if anything, and I'm thankful for it as I drag myself down the hall of the arts building toward the lounge that's just outside of Professor Solomon's classroom. Or at least, the classroom he uses for photography. There's nothing permanent in it, though I guess classes switch rooms every semester, and it looks like a generic arts room.

But what had I expected? Framed photographs on the walls? Medals? Awards or him standing with celebrities he's worked with? From what I understand, he's not that kind of photographer, anyway.

I'm early enough that the classroom door's shut, and the lights are off, so I go past the room and to the small lounge instead, staring at the vending machine to figure out if I want something to drink. With how my stomach feels, I'm sort of craving a ginger ale. But Professor Solomon has strictly outlawed food and drink from his class, so I'd either have to stuff the bottle into my backpack or chug it on the spot.

It's not worth it. I sigh internally, sinking down onto the sofa. I'm slightly hungry, but that can wait too. This is my last class, and I'll head home after this to the apartment that I'm really starting to love.

"Do you want something?" There's no mistaking the overly friendly voice behind me and I turn, spotting Oliver sitting on one of the couches with his face turned up to me.

When in the world did he get here?

"Oh... no," I tell him, going to perch on the couch nearest him. Dressed in a v-neck tee and dark jeans that hug his body perfectly, he's fantastic at edging the line between cute and hot. It's perfect, in my opinion, and he's the one good thing about photography class.

"Besides, I'd have to hide it in photography. And I don't want to chug a ginger ale in three minutes or throw it away, on penalty of death by glares," I admit ruefully, a half-smile on my face. He makes me nervous, like most humans do, but I'm starting to soften toward him and talk to him almost like I talk to Juniper.

Almost. I've even mostly put Monday's episode out of my mind, where he sat at my table in the courtyard and acted so... strange.

"Oh, hey. Where were you Monday?" I ask, remembering. "You came to see me when I was eating, but then you just didn't show up here. Did something happen? You umm. Had to meet with Professor Solomon, right? Did he, like, do something to you?"

Oliver, who's taking a drink from his water bottle, chokes suddenly. It's almost surreal, and I watch in surprise and confusion as he chokes on water, nearly aspirating in front of me. "Are you okay?" I demand, worried, my hands raised from my lap as if I'm going to do something like give him mouth to mouth or Lassie-run out of here for help.

He nods, working on getting himself under control. His face is red, water bottle forgotten in one hand, and finally he looks at me, eyes watering, with an incredulous look on his face. "I'm sorry," he laughs breathlessly. "I wasn't expecting that. What do you think Rook *did* to me, exactly, Blair?"

"Why do you call him Rook? Isn't his first name something with an A? Does he know you call him that? Because honestly he doesn't seem like someone who's fond of nicknames." I look behind me, making sure he's not in one of the offices at this end of the hall. I don't want him overhearing anything I say and taking it the wrong way.

"It's..." Oliver trails off, frowning. "It's his middle name," he says finally. "And it feels *disrespectful* to use it. So I do."

"That seems dangerous."

"Very." He coughs again, clearing his throat, before he wipes his eyes on the back of his wrist. "Anyway, no. He didn't do anything to me. I wasn't feeling well on Monday, and I knew what he was going over in class. So I skipped. It's not like I *have* to attend. I'm just auditing it for fun. I kind of like to think of myself as his TA, actually."

"Does... he think of you as his assistant?" I ask, skeptical about his take on it.

"Oh, absolutely not."

"Yeah, I kind of figured."

I glance at my phone and let out a breath through my nose. "I guess it's time to suffer. Or, not suffer for you. Since you're in this class every damn semester."

"What makes you think I'm not suffering too?" His eyes dance, a smile curling over his full lips as he walks toward the photography room with me. The door's open now, light on, and inside I see that Professor Solomon is already there.

"Why would you come here if you didn't like it?" I lower my voice as I ask, eyes on our professor as we walk in.

Only for Oliver to chuckle and say, loud enough for him to hear easily, "Maybe I'm just a masochist."

Professor Solomon's hand stills, pen going rigid as he looks up from the small notebook he's writing in. We're the only ones here, out of the eleven students remaining, and he looks both of us over with careful scrutiny.

Oliver still just fucking grins like we're probably not going to fail the class for this, while I wonder if an apology would help the situation.

But our professor just scoffs and looks back down, paying us less attention than if we were flies on the wall or specks of dirt on the desk.

As I get comfortable beside Oliver and try *not* to bump into him, even though he sits *so close* when I know he could move toward the empty table beside us, I freeze.

Oh no.

Oh, God.

I've forgotten my photography textbook. I know where it's at with absolute clarity: on my desk, where I'd been working through the first chapter like the professor instructed us to do. It's right there, with my neon tabs sticking out of the pages where I'd found information I wanted to mark for future use.

And that means it's not *here*. Where it should be.

"Uh oh," I whisper, mostly to myself as my stomach twists. In any other class, it wouldn't be a big deal, but this is certainly not *any other* class.

"What's wrong?" Oliver's quick to lean over, eyes scanning my backpack like he's going to see some kind of issue.

"I, umm." Quickly, I glance up at Professor Solomon, who's still writing in his notebook. "I don't have my photography book. Should I... leave?" Leaving seems like a better idea than sticking around and waiting for him to notice.

"He'd notice if you walked out," Oliver tells me. "No way you'd get away clean."

My heart sinks in my chest, and I prepare myself for the berating and embarrassment I'm sure is going to happen when class starts. My fingers tighten on my bag before I let it fall to the floor between my knees, face in my hands. *Fuck.* This is exactly what I'd wanted to avoid, and here I am creating a self-fulfilling prophecy of him being an asshole to me.

"He's going to kill me," I mutter against my palms. "I should've dropped this class last week." Lord knows if he rips me apart today, I absolutely won't be able to show my face here ever again.

"Nah, he's not." Oliver pulls one of my hands down, voice gentle, and presses something large against my fingers. "You'll be fine, okay?" I open my eyes and look down, heart twisting in my chest when I see what he's pressed into my hand.

It's *his* photography book. The soft cover feels worn, not smooth like mine, and the book is tabbed and dog-eared. The spine is worn, with duct tape holding the bottom part of it together, and overall it looks... very well loved.

Does Oliver really love photography this much? I still can't fathom why he keeps showing up to Professor Solomon's classes, but I suppose it's something he truly enjoys.

"But he's going to yell at you, isn't he? And he's going to know it's not my book," I point out, placing it down on my side of the table.

"No, Blair," Oliver chuckles. "Well, yeah. He'll yell at me. But he isn't going to know it isn't yours as long as you keep it open. You think he's really *that* observant to be able to tell the difference between our textbooks?"

It might be my imagination, but his voice rises as he says it, tone almost... goading? Like he *wants* our professor to hear. Nervously I glance up, but if he did, he isn't acting like it.

"And then I'll share with you, with the book in front of you like this..." He slides it more directly under my nose and scoots his chair even closer, which I wouldn't have thought possible, before draping an arm over the back of my seat and leaning in so he can look at it too.

For a moment, I can't breathe. My heart stutters in my chest, and when I look up at him, I realize I'm close enough that I can almost feel his breath on my cheek.

Oliver blinks and looks down at me, grin turning big and goofy. Right. I remind myself that this is just *him*. Just... Oliver. He's too friendly, too physically affectionate, even though we barely know each other.

Too intense for someone like me, who worries over personal space and tone of voice. It feels like I'm a mess when he's around me like this, even though it's clear to me that he's just doing it because he really is this nice and maybe a little unobservant of my personal comfort levels.

"Oliver." I hadn't realized our professor had gotten to his feet, and I jump at the tone of his voice, and the closeness of it. "What are you doing?"

"Oh, well, I forgot my textbook," Oliver lies, beaming up at our professor as he looks at us. "So I'm sharing with Blair. She told me I could, actually."

Professor Solomon's gaze slides to mine, the epitome of unfriendly, and I smile nervously. He stares at me, lips pressed to a thin line like he wants to say something, then looks at Oliver again. "You don't need your books today, so you can sit up, Greer," he warns quietly.

Oliver does, looking almost like a kicked puppy.

"And you can give him his book back, Love," Professor Solomon adds, taking a breath and launching into his discussion topic of the day: digital vs. film and how we might use each.

Sufficiently embarrassed and more than a little surprised, I slide Oliver's book back over to him and focus on the lesson, trying to fight the urge to curl up into a ball and pretend I'm not here.

When Professor Solomon's lesson ends, I'm surprised. Glancing at the clock, I see that it's time to go, and I feel almost... disappointed, in a way. He's a good professor, and he makes the material interesting. Even the details that I hadn't thought of, such as going into the details of DSLR photography, are more interesting than they have a right to be when he talks about them.

Sitting back, I push up the sleeves of my light-weight hoodie until they're at my elbows. I watch as Professor Solomon goes back to his desk, shoving his supplies into his fancy leather bag like he wants to be out of here just as much as the rest of the class.

I'm so focused on him that when Oliver nudges me, I jump, eyes flicking to his. "What?" I ask, unthinking, as I look at him, only to see a peculiar look fading from his face.

I don't recognize it at all. Just that it's not as friendly or enthusiastic as he normally is. But as I watch, it's replaced with his usual, overly friendly grin and he gets to his feet to stretch, my nose at the line of his jeans as I silently beg for his shirt to ride up as it had on Monday.

It does. His skin is pale here as well, though still not at the level of my own Tb-ridden-child complexion. I look away before he can catch me, shoveling my notebook into my backpack and getting to my feet as well, so I can sling it onto my back. At least now I get to go home, check to see if *letsplayjay* is streaming today, and maybe take a nap.

I do love my naps, after all.

"Blair." Professor Solomon loudly sighs my name and I look up at him, perplexed and maybe a little bit terrified. As I watch, he crooks his fingers at me, dropping them a second later as his eyes go back to his phone that's in his hand. The last few students, the two girls who clearly want in his pants, go out the door, whispering something I don't bother trying to catch.

Can I make it out the door too? Could I run and pretend I didn't hear him say my name?

"*Blair.*" His voice is firm, stern and sends a chill down my spine as he looks up and sees I'm not at his desk. "Come *here.*" God, I'm not a dog and I'd love to tell him that. But instead, I walk toward him slowly, dragging my feet like they're connected to heavy chains.

Professor Solomon looks over my shoulder, eyes narrowing. "Last time I checked, your name isn't *Blair*," he tells Oliver lightly, though there's not an ounce of friendliness in the words. "And this is a private conversation."

"Is... it?" I ask, looking back at Oliver. "Did I do something wrong?" I'd prefer him here as well, just for moral support, but our professor just shakes his head.

"No. *Out*, Greer." He points at the door and Oliver raises his hands in surrender, smiling apologetic as he makes his way to the open door. "And close it behind you," Professor Solomon adds.

Oliver hesitates, and as I watch, he turns to look at our professor with something like disdain, and disappointment on his face. But when he just gets a *look* in return, Oliver rolls his eyes and closes the door hard, almost a slam, behind him.

In the silence, I can clearly hear Professor Solomon's sigh. This close, I can also smell his cologne, that's a mix of citrus, sandalwood, and maybe cedar. Though, the sandalwood is more of an undertone and I wouldn't know if my mom hadn't loved to use it in her incense burner.

"So..." It's awkward to just stand here while he's on his phone, but he sure seems intent on making me do it. "Is there —" He holds a finger up at my words, and I go quiet.

"One moment, Love," he says, and for half a second, it's almost as if he's using my last name as a pet name, instead of just my surname.

God, it's so easy to see why so many students are in love with him. If only his personality wasn't as appealing as a trash can full of broken, dirty razors in the middle of an interstate.

"All right." He shoves his phone in his pocket and straightens, meeting my gaze. "Is Oliver bothering you?" he asks, throwing me off guard.

"What?" I blink, unsure of what to say. "What do you mean?"

"I've seen how he acts. I know he can be a lot. Is he *bothering* you, or upsetting you in any way?" He watches me carefully while he speaks, and it only serves to make me even more nervous.

I shake my head, and he frowns. Had he wanted the answer to be something different?

"No, umm. I like him." I shrug. "Well, from what I know of him, anyway? Oliver's really nice. He's a lot, and I'm not exactly used to that." I'm not about to do a deep dive of my personality and past to this professor. "But he's not being too intense, or whatever you're asking me. He's really, really nice. I'd tell him if I wanted him to leave me alone."

"If you say so," he says at last, looking away once more. "That's all, Love. You can go now."

"Thanks," I mutter, not sure what I'm even grateful for as I head for the door.

"What did you say?" The demand of his voice draws me up short. "I didn't hear you when you were *muttering*."

I look over my shoulder, surprised at his strict, firm tone.

"Umm. I said... thanks?" I repeat, hating how apologetic I sound.

"You're welcome," he replies, dark eyes narrowed as he lifts his hand and shoos me out the door with two fingers. It's fine with me, and I'm all too happy to get out of his room at breakneck speed.

I feel like I don't stop rushing until I'm back home, facedown on my bed, and letting out a tired sound of irritation. My hair is tangled, I can *sense* it, and I need to brush it before I nap or do homework or get food. It'll bother me if I don't, and at this point I'm probably going to put it back into a braid for the weekend so that I can just forget about it somewhat. At least for a little while.

Instead, however, I open my laptop, wondering if my favorite streamer, aka the only one I ever plan on watching, is live today. He hadn't been on Monday, and I'd checked a few times during the week to see if I'd missed anything, but I hadn't.

Am I destined to no longer get to swoon for him? Even though I only discovered his stream a week ago, that would be tragic.

Clicking on his name on my homepage, I wait as the page refreshes, bringing me onto his page instead, just in time for me to see that he *is* starting his stream.

The masked camboy, *letsplayjay*, sits back in his chair, twisting it this way and that as he waits for his viewers to pile in. Which, of course, they do. The viewer list updates by the second, and it's unreal that so many people join the instant he starts his stream.

I wonder how long he's done this, and how long he's been this popular.

"Am I having a good Friday?" he leans forward to read the messages, his slightly muffled voice is light and playful. "Oh, I guess. It was a little stressful, but it's over and now I get to hang out with all of you. Sorry about Monday, by the way." He raises his hands in apology. "Maybe you can all forgive me? I was having a pretty bad day, and I was... tied up. Not how you all are probably thinking, though. Or was it?" He puts a finger to his mask thoughtfully, and comments pour in, begging him to talk about it.

"Oh, I couldn't take up your time with something so boring, could I?" he teases. "Why don't you tell me about your day, hmm?" He checks the chat and calls a random username, asking how his appointment went as his fingers toy with his waistband.

He's so good at this, and again I wonder if I could do it too, if I had something to hide my face. Surely I could put on a persona, a character kind of, and it wouldn't really be *me*. Because it isn't the sex-work aspect that scares me.

It's the people being judgmental, or mean, or creepy. What if no one liked me? Or worse, what if they *did*? Could I handle the kind of requests or comments that *letsplayjay* seems to constantly get from his fans?

Well, in my case, at least I know I wouldn't have the same volume of audience he has. I don't even know if I'd want to.

"I just finished eating, actually," the streamer chuckles, answering someone's question. "What did I have? Teriyaki chicken from, uh..." He moves offscreen, shoving stuff around on his desk as he moves. Finally, a pile of books falls in front of the camera, obscuring the bottom few inches as he picks up the brown bag and reads the name on it, but I'm not listening.

I'm too fixated on the pile of books.

Or, more accurately, I'm fixated on *one* of them. The one that's closest to the camera, and the easiest to read the spine of.

An Introduction to Digital Photography.

That wouldn't be so bad... except that the spine is bent and cracked, and at the bottom, holding it together, is a line of dark silver duct tape.

I know this book, because I'd had my hands on it earlier today. It's *Oliver's* book.

And when Oliver chuckles again and says something sweet to his viewers, it clicks into place that I should've realized it sooner, since I've now spent time listening to his voice and the way he speaks.

Letsplayjay is definitely, unmistakably, Oliver Greer.

CHAPTER 6

S itting at my computer later the same night, I suck in a
breath. I don't know what's more surprising, honestly.
The fact that *Oliver Greer* is the only camboy that I've
ever actually wanted to watch, or that I'm about to overnight
myself a black, fox-like mask with tall ears and slitted eyes. It
won't cover my lower face, which I've decided is a good thing,
and as I hover over the 'buy now' button, I can't help but feel
like my heart is about to pound out of my chest.

Am I really going to do this? According to the site I'm on,
the mask is guaranteed to be at my apartment by noon tomorrow, and that's... that.

Can I actually do this?

Before I can talk myself out of it, I hit the button and push
my laptop off of me with a soft sigh. It slides back, tipping onto
its back cover as a picture of the mask stares up at me. I give it a
minute to sink in, still finding it unreal that I really just did that.

But now what to do? I could go back and watch Oliver, I
guess. Or... I could go do some market research. While I'm not

into women, watching their streams should be pretty helpful, right?

Yeah, that's what I tell myself as I get back onto *funxcams* and click through to the female side of the site. It takes me a minute, and nerves knot up my stomach as I browse through the thumbnails of streamers. Some have elaborate setups, and others don't. I'm definitely looking for someone that doesn't. Not to mention. I'd prefer someone who's sitting at a desk, instead of on a bed.

Finally, I stop, and when I click on the thumbnail and the link takes me to the streamer's page, I realize this is exactly what I'm looking for. She's still wearing a bra and leggings, and she's talking to her viewers more than anything. Sure, her hands go up and she plays with herself a little, and as someone gives her a huge tip, she laughs sweetly and takes off her bra so she can show her viewers more.

I don't take notes, but I do end up watching the rest of her stream, and another one, before I decide that it's too close to Juniper coming home to keep doing 'research.'

At least the mask was less than twenty dollars, I think as I hear her unlock the door. Then if I chicken out, which I'm absolutely going to do, I won't be out that much money.

SHE'S LEAVING *in five minutes.* Or less, my brain tells me as I hear Juniper pulling her boots on in the living room. My heart pounds in my chest as I sit at my desk, head tilted to the side so I can hear her better.

Am I really going to do this?

"See you in a few hours, okay?" Juniper asks, sticking her head in my open door. Her eyes narrow and she looks me over, gaze scrutinizing. "Unless you want to go."

"It's a date," I remind her. "I don't think Jesse would like it if I showed up, too."

"He'd be fine with it." Juniper easily dismisses me. "And you're looking pale. Like you haven't had enough sun lately."

I roll my eyes and sigh loudly enough for her to hear me. "Yeah, Jun. I'm always this pale."

"I know," she assures me, and disappears back into the living room. "Want me to bring you dinner?"

Oh, that's an idea I hadn't thought of. I pause, my hand on my keyboard. "Yes, please!" I call back. "You know what I like?"

"Beef fajitas, extra spice, no sour cream?" she asks, breezing out the door. It's the exact opposite of what I'd want, which she knows, and I snort instead of giving her a genuine answer in reply.

Besides, my mind is on other things right now other than bantering with my favorite person in the entire world. I give it a few minutes before I move, listening to make sure that she's gone and not coming back to get something.

By now, with the time alone I've had today, I've set up a streamer account on *funxcams* and gotten verified. Which is something I thought would take longer, but in reality it only took a couple of hours for my new streamer account to become unrestricted. I'd had the option to use my viewer account, *finalistgirl*, but that had made me nervous.

What if someone from Oliver's stream caught wind of what I'm doing? Worse, what if *Oliver* found out? The idea that he could stumble across my stream still terrifies me, and I'd struggled with the decision of possibly blocking his account from mine before deciding that wasn't necessary.

There are over six thousand streamers on *funxcams*, first of all. Meaning the chance of him finding me are one in a million give or take.

Getting up from my desk chair, I grab the clothes I'd

stashed under my pillow for when Juniper was gone, and I quickly strip out of my comfy sweatpants and long-sleeve tee to put them on. My heart pounds in my chest as I pull on the black, low-rise panties and the bralette with its collar-like top and straps that go from top to bottom. While it provides full enough coverage, the straps give it sex appeal, in my opinion. Over that go my black running shorts that I'd found hiding in the back of my dresser and a snug, thin white t-shirt that should probably never see the light of day again.

Do I look a little bit like a typical co-ed dressed like this and with my hair around my face? Yeah, maybe. But it's my age-range, and while doing my research I'd seen that it's a pretty popular tag that people seemed to be into.

Sitting down again, I take a deep breath and look at my computer, then pull the mask out of my drawer to place beside it. My stream is ready, and all I need to do is hit the green button on my screen to go live.

God, I don't think I can do this. My stomach flips and twists, trying its best to kill me with some incredible, impossible torsion that'll knock me on my ass right here and now.

I don't think I can do this.

But I put the fox mask on anyway, blinking a few times as I get used to the limited field of view through the narrow eyes. It makes me feel more at ease somehow, though I suppose it just goes to prove that old saying, right?

If I can't see them, then they can't see me.

My hands tremble as I place one on my trackpad, laptop open and new webcam on. Thankfully, I didn't have to buy this. My tech-loving uncle had gotten good webcams for all of his nieces and nephews last Christmas. This is just the first time I'm really putting mine to use.

What if they hate me? I think, feeling the slightest bit panicky. What if I freak out, or freeze up, or, even worse, vomit?

Though I've never vomited from nerves in my life... this would be a really bad time to start.

Finally, I let out a breath, closing my eyes behind the mask as I fight back fear. The worst, or best, thing that could happen is that no one comes into my stream. Or that just a few people do, and I'm only embarrassing myself in front of a person or two.

That won't be so bad.

"You are a strong, independent woman," I tell myself, body rigid. "You are playing a character. You can do this."

I always did love theater in high school. What's this, but a strange next step?

Before I can talk myself out of this incredibly terrifying idea... I click the button on my trackpad and, after a second or so delay that makes me nearly choke, my stream goes live.

It isn't as fancy as Oliver's. There's no custom tip chart in the corner, though I do see in the chat that my goal of fifty dollars is on display, along with the embarrassing '0' in front of it.

For a long moment, there are no viewers. One minute turns into two, and I sit back in my computer chair, arms up on my armrests and trying to look aloof behind my mask.

God, this is embarrassing.

That is, until I look down, and the number of viewers isn't zero anymore. First one, then two, then *four* people appear, two of them saying hello in my chat as I sit there like my heart isn't trying to pound out of my chest.

"Hello," I say, not bothering to try to seem overconfident or cocky or sassy like some of the other women I've seen on here in the past day. No way anyone would believe that of me, when I know that's not true to my personality. "I'm really grateful you're here for my first show. I'm kind of nervous, if I'm being honest." Nervous is an understatement, though I move my hand to toy at the hem of my shirt, showing a peek of skin above my crossed legs.

Three more viewers pop in, and one leaves, though that still leaves me at six. Another person says hello, and one asks me about my day.

Surprisingly, someone even throws me a two-dollar tip. That's... not what I'm expecting. Especially when I've barely done anything, but my smile grows. "Thanks so much *fiendham*," I gush, leaning closer to the computer screen. "You're my very first tipper."

Hopefully your first fan, the person, probably a guy, says in the chat.

I snicker. "I really hope so. But you asked how my day was? It was all right. To be honest, I spent a lot of time worrying over whether anyone would want to watch me or not. I don't know, I hope I'm not boring." Two of the guys in the chat rush to assure me I'm not and it's... strange.

So is the fact that when I look again, the view count is up to twelve. I bite my lip lightly, touching my mask when someone comments on it in the chat. "This? Well, one of my favorites on here has one, and he's so cool that I wanted to be just like him when I started," I lie, still grinning. It feels weird to say 'because I'm too afraid to show my face.' Absently, I drag my shirt up a little higher, noticing a comment asking me to take it off.

"Do you want me to? I'm only going to stream for an hour or so, but don't you think it's a little soon?" I drag the material up anyway, surprised I can be so nonchalant about this as I take my time pulling it away from my mask and tossing it to the floor.

The chat is appreciative, and someone new tips me a dollar. It's not the hundreds that *letsplayjay*, or rather, *Oliver*, gets. But it's something, and as I keep going, my fingers teasing the lines of my bra as I talk, I keep an eye on my viewer count.

It isn't awful. It fluctuates up and down, though by the time my shorts are on the floor, my matching black panties being commented on by viewers, I'm up to a whole fourteen with ten minutes to go in my stream.

Scratch that, fifteen. Then back to fourteen, before it settles at fifteen again. I say something offhand, then pause as I read a message in the chat that makes me bite my lip.

I'll tip you thirty if you take off the rest of your clothes. The username, *rob784*, isn't particularly original, and I don't like the way the message stands on its own in the chat, without anyone replying to it. Do I want the money? Yeah, I do. But I didn't want to go that far today, when I'd just planned on trying this out first.

But then someone agrees with him, and it makes me feel even worse. I'm glad that my face is mostly inscrutable behind the mask, and I tilt my head to the side like I'm considering the idea.

That is, until my screen lights up with the notification of money being sent to my stream, and I pause as I watch another follow it.

Sixty dollars, then eighty, puts me at a total of one hundred and forty. For a moment my heart stops, because I'm sure it's *rob784* and someone else giving me money to get naked right now, but then I see that the money *isn't* from them.

MalevolentMask is the first, the one who'd sent me sixty, and the other, who sent me eighty, shows up as *ThrillingTerror* in my stream.

"Thank you so much," I tell them, letting my enthusiasm color my tone. "You guys are making this a really great stream, umm. What do you want me to do for you before I end my stream?" For that kind of tip, can I really say no? Hell, I really *will* take off the rest of this in short order, for a tip of that much.

It takes a second for the message from *MalevolentMask* to pop up, and when it does, I can't hide my grin.

I want you to tell me what your favorite tattoo you have is, and to end your stream on a positive note instead of taking off the rest of your clothes. You're gorgeous enough, and they don't deserve to see more until they pay more <3

I blink once, then again, biting my lower lip. "My favorite is this one," I tell my viewers, showing the hand and arm piece that contains the snakes and the flowers. I trace along the scales, moving closer to the camera as I do and leaning forward so they can see down my bra. I'm not *stupid*, after all. "And, honestly, this is the end of the hour that I promised. You guys have made my first stream way better than I ever could've imagined."

A few other viewers congratulate me on my stream, and I try to look confident and *not* like I'm still terrified about this.

"My plan is to stream on Sundays for now, and maybe Fridays? I hope to see everyone again. Have a good weekend." As similar sentiments roll in, I hit the button to end my stream, looking over at the final figure for the day.

One hundred and sixty-eight dollars. That's about a hundred and forty more than I ever thought I'd get doing this. Not to mention, it's probably a one-time thing. I can't imagine those two will come back. I doubt I'm very interesting, after all.

I nearly have my laptop closed when I see the little exclamation point over my messages, and I stop. Is it spam? Is it *rob784* coming to tell me he's upset with me? If that's the case, I can't find it in myself to actually care.

It's not. Instead, *MaliciousMask* is in my inbox, and when I open the message and take off my foxy disguise, I smile.

It's sweet, to be honest.

You did so good for your first time! Don't be nervous. I promise, everyone loved you. Or everyone who mattered. See you on Friday. <3

Sweet is an understatement, actually.

Another message comes in just as I'm typing out a thank you, and I swap over to it once I'm finished.

This one is from *ThrillingTerror*, and it's decidedly not as sweet.

You're gorgeous, and you shouldn't let them scare you. Don't do anything you don't want to do.

I type a thank you to him as well, though I don't get a response from either of them as I sit back in my chair and finally close my laptop.

I need food. And caffeine.

And maybe a nice movie to watch to chill out a little before Juniper comes back.

CHAPTER 7

"You seem off," Juniper says, stirring her chopstick around the plastic bowl of noodles from the takeout place down the street. It's by far some of the best noodles I've ever had, though I doubt Jun is that impressed. She always says her parents make way better Chinese food, and since she spent half of her life in Hong Kong, I'm sure she's right. But for me, anything that isn't out of a plastic-wrapped container from the local supermarket is normally great. Tonight's meal feels like a step above.

I don't answer her right away. My fingers drum against the table, and I frown. Is it possible to still be so wired from the show I'd done over a day ago? It definitely feels strange, and I'm not about to tell her about my new source of income. Not yet, anyway. I love Juniper.

But this is something that I don't know how to bring up to her. Or at least, not easily.

So I sigh and scrunch up my nose, looking at her from under the stray hair in my face as I stir my own noodles thoughtfully. "I just *hate* photography," I admit at last, knowing if I use something that's true, then I won't sound so forced. I'm barely a good liar at the best of times.

Which is why I want to tell Oliver as soon as possible that I know it's him.

Right?

Every time I think of how that conversation will go, I cringe. How do I bring up the fact that I watch him get off in front of an audience? I certainly won't go so far to say he's inspired me to do it as well, though I'm sure I'll never net the audience size he does.

But there's no way in hell I can keep watching him. It feels like some kind of invasion of privacy, now that I know. Like it might be wrong and dishonest, since I have to face him three days a week in class. I'll tell him, eventually, that I know it's him and promise I don't watch him anymore. That's the right thing to do, in my eyes. The friendly thing, I think.

On the other hand... not telling him could be fine, too. If only because my mind cringes and squirms every time I think of how I'll bring it up to him or what I'll say. Worse, I can't even begin to imagine what *he'll* say.

Will he find it funny?

Will he brush it off and make a joke, like he normally does when I find myself in an uncomfortable situation regarding class?

Or will he be upset? Maybe he won't believe me that I didn't know it was him the first time I watched. Maybe if I don't tell him straight away on Monday, he'll think I was trying to hide it or something else that's less than honest.

"Drop it," Juniper suggests with a shrug. "You've got two more days to drop it, don't you? Take the loss and next semester, double down since it's that bad. You don't *have* to suffer, Blair," Juniper points out wryly. "I've never known you to be such a masochist."

Maybe I'm just a masochist. Her words bring to mind Oliver's chuckle from that day in class I'd questioned him about Professor Solomon's wrath. He'd looked up, as if waiting for a response, and I'd thought for sure our professor would end him then and there.

Of course, thinking of his smile, and the sultry tone of his playful banter during his streams does nothing to quell the way my insides squirm at the thought of coming clean with him.

Thanks a lot, Juniper.

Stirring my noodles faster, I rest my head on my hand and shrug. "I need the credits," I remind her, for what feels like the tenth time this week. "I don't want to be slammed next semester before I graduate."

"Then suffer."

The words make me snort, and I can't help but roll my eyes up at her. "Thanks, *bestie*," I say, and she swipes my near-empty bowl that I haven't taken a bite out of for a few minutes now.

"You want to keep the leftovers? They'll suck if we try to reheat them," she says, already heading for the trash.

"Nah, I don't think so." I tap my chopstick on the table that I hadn't lost to her clean-up, though I eye the dark brown drop of sauce that falls to the fake-wood with a sigh. Surreptitiously, and so she can see, I swipe my sleeve across the mess and toss my chopstick onto the napkin with hers before she dumps into the trash a second later. "You're going out with the band tomorrow, right?" I ask, referencing her small friend group that takes Sunday to find the weirdest, most off the wall places to hang out and do something out of the norm.

Like live poetry readings.

It's not that I judge it, or that I wouldn't want to go, exactly. Except I have gone, and fallen asleep, because appreciating the finer things in life, as Juniper likes to call them, is not for me. I'm boring, simple, and easily amused by reality tv.

"We're not a band."

"You could be. Can't you play the recorder?" I ask, being purposefully facetious when I know full well she's a very accomplished flutist and semi-proficient violinist. It's always seemed like a weird combo to me, but what do I know? Finer things in life, and all that.

She doesn't respond, but I don't exactly expect her to. I'm not being serious, and she likely has better things to do and think about. But I do want to know *when* she'll be gone. Normally on Sundays she leaves at three or so, and is never back before nine. Hopefully that's what will happen tomorrow, since I'd said I'd be streaming then.

"I'm leaving earlier than usual," Juniper replies apologetically. I try to look like I'm put out, even though I'm anything but, and nod along with her as she outlines her plans with the band that will put her out of the apartment for at least seven hours. And it'll give me more than enough to stream and wind down from it, since when I'd done this yesterday, I was so nervous that afterward I'd still been jittery when Juniper had gotten home and had to make some excuse about why.

All in all, I don't want to do that part of it again. Though my heart pounds nervously in my chest at the general idea of streaming again, after how things went yesterday. Not that it was bad. And I'd made more than I'd ever thought I would.

But it was, admittedly, slightly terrifying.

"Hmm?" I look up, realizing I've missed whatever Juniper has been saying for the last ten seconds or so.

She stares at me, dark eyes narrowed as she scrutinizes my face like she thinks something might be off with me. "I said I'll bring you dinner if you want. Since you usually eat late, anyway."

She's right about that, and I perk up, feeling a little better about things. "What are you bringing me?" I ask, shoving back from the table and swiping my phone from the surface.

"Whatever we end up having. But how hard is it to find chicken tenders and fries at a restaurant?" If anyone else were to remark on my limited palette and picky taste, I would've been upset. But then again, no one else knows.

Just Juniper, and she's not about to tell anyone.

I shake my head and go to my room, prepared to flop over on my bed and read for the next hour or so. If I don't skim through my photography book, I'll look through my new Roman Studies text. We've been assigned a couple of plays, two of which I've already read, and the section we're reading in our textbook is information I've looked at before.

Call me an overachiever, but I love reading about the things I study. Folklore is my favorite, to the point that, for my class that revolves around Eastern European folktales, I barely need to do any work this semester at all. I've read all of the stories already, and looked at some of the more popular discussions surrounding their meanings.

I'm sure if I was handed a pop quiz on *Baba Yaga*, which is what we're studying at the moment, I would be able to put down more information than even our professor knows. It's a shame I can't make a career off of being a folklorist or researching folktales, but I'm sure that I'll figure something out.

My phone lights up from the corner of my eye as I'm leafing through my photography book, and for a moment I'm able to ignore it until it lights up again.

This time I snag it, pulling the phone toward me and up to my face to read the message that's been sent from another, unknown number.

Hope you don't mind, but I got your number from our class roster.

The first message isn't signed, and the second message clarifies.

This is Oliver, by the way. Can I call? I'm going to call.

My heart pounds in my throat as I read it, but before I can reply back to him, my phone vibrates, causing me to drop it from my fingers to my bed. I stare at it, breath stuck in my lungs and lips parted, before realizing that letting it go to voicemail after he knows I've read the messages is worse than not answering at all.

Damn it.

I drop the book and pick up the phone like it's a hot potato, pressing it to my ear a second later with fingers that tremble. "Hello?" I ask, not knowing what exactly to say to him. "Oliver?"

"*Yeah, hey.*" He sounds as excited as the golden retriever puppy he brings to mind anytime I see or hear him. "*I'm sorry if I interrupted something. Are you busy?*"

I look down at my textbooks strewn across my bed. "No. Not really. Do you need me for something?"

"*Yeah, umm. You know how I tried to lend you my book yesterday?*" he asks, sounding a little ashamed of himself. I don't answer. Instead my mind fixates on the image of him, getting naked, with the fucking book visible on his stream.

Oliver is Letsplayjay and I still have no idea how to tell him I know.

"Yeah," I say finally, clearing my throat. "What's wrong?"

"*Did you take it with you, by chance?*" he asks guiltily. "*I just can't find it. I'm sure I laid it somewhere or something, or it's in a pile of stuff in my room. But I just wanted to call first to see if you took it home.*"

"No," I say, without thinking of my words. "It's on your

desk, isn't it?"

Shit. *Shit!*

I don't know why I've said it, and my heart races at the silence between us.

Shit. He's going to know something's up. I shouldn't know that it's there, that's for sure. And I shouldn't sound so certain.

"Sorry, I didn't mean it like that. I just meant that's where mine lives. Especially when I forgot it yesterday." I force a soft, breathy laugh into my voice that sounds like I'm choking on air. "Maybe you've left it there?"

He still doesn't respond for a few seconds, and when I'm ready to say something else to try to pull my foot out of my mouth, he suddenly announces, "*I found it! Holy shit, Blair. You're fucking psychic. It was right in front of my computer in some shit that fell yesterday.*"

The excited tone never leaves his voice, and I smile at nothing. "I'm not psychic," I promise, wondering when my heart will calm the fuck down. "It was just a hunch."

"*You're amazing,*" he praises, his voice warm and almost a purr. "*You don't know how much I appreciate you, Blair. Thanks for not dropping out of photography.*" There's something else there. Something strange and deeper than just an acquaintance being overly-friendly.

It's not unkind, like he'd seemed towards Juniper that one day. But it's still strange, and I can't put my finger on what it is.

"It's no problem. And I'm not amazing," I promise. "I'm just lucky, I guess."

"*You think so?*" Yet again there's something in the words that give me pause, but he's quick to add, "*What are you doing tonight? Did I catch you mid-party? Are you getting ready to go out or anything?*"

"Nah," I admit, settling back against my pillows. "I'm just reading. I like to read on Saturdays." And every other day of the week, but I don't really want to tell him that. If I can, I want Oliver to think I'm interesting.

Of course, maybe that's just because every second that I don't tell him I know that he does cam work, I feel worse and worse about myself. I bite my lip, still drumming my fingers on my top book with its shiny, hard cover.

"Just textbooks? Not something more interesting? You could come to my place if you wanted," Oliver offers. *"I can give you a photography crash course, and you wouldn't have to open that book ever again. Rook doesn't give me enough credit, but I know how to pass his class with ease."*

For about three seconds, the length of time it takes for me to suck in a breath and let it out, I can't help but think Oliver is flirting with me.

"Where do you live?" I ask, not because I plan on going over but because some part of me is curious about where he calls home.

When he recites an address to me, my first thought is that it's far. Like, thirty minutes by Uber far.

My second thought is that it's in a way nicer part of town than I have any business being in. I nearly choke on that information, but don't say anything about it. I find it *insane* that a college student, even a masters student, can live in Hollow Oaks, but maybe he comes from money or something. It's none of my business.

"Maybe sometime," I reply, trying not to give him a commitment one way or the other. I still can't decide how I feel about Oliver. There's something off about him, and I would rather figure out what it is before I let him in.

If I let him in. Hell, I don't even know how much he wants from me. He's so friendly, so could it just be that he wants to be my friend? I've met a lot of people like that in college. We get to know each other in a class, spend the semester as friends, and never talk to each other again unless we end up scheduled together again. It doesn't make me feel bad, or anything. It's just the way things go.

Maybe it's how things will go with Oliver as well.

"*By sometime, you mean—*" he breaks off suddenly, and a few seconds later he's talking again, but further away from the phone so I can't hear what he says. He chuckles, I think, and someone else says something in a much less kind voice before a gasp that sounds like Oliver meets my ears.

"*I have to go,*" he says with a laugh, a grinding, dark note in his voice.

"Are you okay?" I can't help but ask, and he pauses at the question.

"*Yeah. And it's nice of you to ask. I'm fine, Blair. Don't worry about me, wonder girl.*"

"Well, someone has to," I say, before my mind takes note of the nickname that's come out of his mouth. "Did you call me—"

"*See you on Monday,*" he cuts in, the other person in the background sounding more insistent. "*Have a good weekend, Blair.*" He hangs up, the line going dead in my ear as I sit there and try to figure out what in the world just happened.

What a strange conversation.

That's the thing that I can't stop thinking over and over, the last few minutes on a cycle through my brain. Oliver is... *weird*, that's for sure. For all his overly-friendly energy and attitude.

But maybe it's a good weird. My stomach curls at the thought and I bury my head in my hands, rem that along with not having told him that I know it's him streaming, I also can't deny that every time we talk, it's more obvious that I have a crush on Oliver Greer.

Damn it.

CHAPTER 8

Take it off.

We just want to see.

You're so **** pretty let me see your face

I tip my head to the side, heart hammering in my chest as I pretend to consider the words on the screen from my viewers. I'm up to seventeen today, and most of them have stayed. Especially once I took off my bra thanks to a nice donation from some random person with their name blocked, even if they never bothered to say anything in the chat.

My heart hammers in my chest, but I don't let the smile fall from my face as my fingers skim up over my tattoos, then eventually come to a stop against my bottom lip. "Sorry," I laugh, trying to channel Oliver when he refuses to take off his mask. "Hmm... Without it, I wouldn't have the courage to do this. And I've really started to like it..." I tease the edge of the half-mask, pushing it up slightly before letting it fall back into place.

"I don't think so. Not this time, and probably not ever."

Definitely not ever. That's a line I refuse to cross, thank you very much. "Sorry!" I say it like I mean it, because I sort of do. I hate refusing, when saying yes would probably get me more money today and in the long run. But it's still a hard no from me.

"Also, that's unfortunately the end of my stream." It's Sunday, meaning that Juniper could be back in thirty minutes or four hours. But I don't want to take the chance of it being thirty minutes just to try to make a little more money. "I'll be back on Friday, though. So I hope to see all of you then, too." I give them my sweetest, fakest smile I can muster and wave, then turn off the stream and sit back in my chair.

This time, I've made closer to one-eighty. I'm just under it, in fact, and I can't really scoff at that. Though, I'd love to be making thousands, or millions. I'd accept thousands. *Oliver* has made over a thousand. I saw that on his stream when I first watched. To me, that's insane.

That's real, adult money and I wouldn't have to worry about anything ever again. But I shouldn't be ungrateful for what I've gotten.

Even though it's starting to feel like I'm exactly that.

Without putting my bra back on, I grab my red tee off of the desk and pull it on, glad that it's oversized so I can wear it and not feel like I'm in a straight jacket meant to smother me. Before I can push away from my desk properly, however, the small *ding* of a private message catches my attention.

I pause, looking back with a frown, and see that the messenger tab of the camsite is lit up.

God, it's probably someone bitching about me not taking off my mask.

When I click to my inbox, however, I notice that it's not. Instead, the message is from one of my first fans. My lips twist into a tiny grin as I take my laptop over to my bed, not wanting to sit in my desk chair any longer while I read it. *Thrillingterror* has messaged me again, and even though he's someone without a profile picture and instead sports just the black box in place of an avatar, I don't really mind.

Though, the curiosity in me would love to know what he looks like.

I'm sorry I missed the first part of your show. His message is short and sweet, and I don't really understand why he's apologizing. Besides, he still tipped me quite a bit today.

That's absolutely fine, I reply, cringing when I sound more like *Blair,* the college student than *MaskEnvy,* the confident streamer. Not that I think I'm fooling anyone into thinking I'm confident in any capacity. Even on-stream, I've quickly realized that's just not my thing. I might be cute and shy while my fans offer 'suggestions,' but I don't think I'll ever be like Oliver.

Then again, Oliver is *perfect* when he streams. There's no way I even could be like him.

Is it? Did anyone say anything to you about doing things you aren't ready for, Envy? The way he uses part of my username like a pet name makes me shiver, and I bite my lip.

No, I say simply, then add. *But I appreciated you standing up for me last week. And that you came back.*

Another message goes off, this one from *rob784.*

Fuck Rob. I care a lot more about *Thrillingterror* than I ever could about *Rob.*

Don't mention it, love.

This time I nearly choke on air. He has no way of knowing that he's using my last name, but god does it feel good, anyway. A shot of arousal courses down my spine, heading straight to my center when I read the message again.

Sorry, was I too forward? The message comes through when all I can do is stare, and I shake my head even though I know he can't see.

No, no you're fine, I type back finally, leaning back against my headboard with my knees propped up so I can rest my laptop against my thighs. *I just wasn't expecting it.* Because it's my fucking name and all.

You didn't reply, so I figured you were either horrified, or you liked it. I wish I could hear him. Well, sort of. On the one hand, I want to hear his tone of voice in these messages instead of just reading them.

On the other, if I could hear him and he could hear me, he'd realize just how much of an act I put on when I stream. I should probably laugh this off and just tell him a polite thank you. I don't know anything about him, except that he gives me money and has probably provided about half of my income so far.

But instead, I find myself typing out the words *I liked it,* and hitting send before I can stop myself.

Are you busy? I missed part of your stream, but I'd love to talk to you for a little bit if you'd want to. The words give me pause. Talk to *me?*

Why? I ask simply, not willing to give him an answer just yet.

Because you're interesting. Do I need a better reason?

That barely feels like a reason at all. Everyone is interesting. There are a thousand other interesting girls streaming right now. I don't know why I say it. Self deprecation isn't a good color on me, but I can't help but say it, anyway. As if he somehow doesn't know I'm not the only girl streaming at this very moment. And I'm certainly nowhere near the most interesting.

That's subjectively not true, he replies, like he's correcting me. *I think you're interesting, not them. Why don't you think you're interesting, love?* Again, I feel a tingle travel down my spine when he says it. And I wonder if I'd feel the same if it wasn't my name.

But I won't take my mask off. I've only really talked and tried to go slow. I haven't shown you everything, even. There are other girls who do way more than me.

When he doesn't reply straight away, I figure I've turned him off. If anything, he's probably not looking for someone to tell him that she's not interesting. A good streamer would've flirted with him, made him more interested and more engaged with her stream.

I'm, quite obviously, not very good at this.

I didn't ask for that.

My heart jolts with surprise when he responds. I'd assumed he was long gone by now, but here he is, still talking to me.

I know how many other girls stream, love. They aren't that interesting to me. Does it bother you that I'm interested? Do you want me to leave you alone?

Every stranger danger lesson I've ever been taught is screaming a big, loud *yes* in my brain. I don't know him. He could be as unpleasant as rob784 if I don't keep talking to him. If I don't give him the answers he wants, he could turn mean and stop watching my stream.

So, even though I know I should politely excuse myself and say that I'm busy, when I reply, it isn't with the smart thing.

Not one bit.

I don't want you to leave me alone. I just don't want to disappoint you.

I bite my lip as I wait for his reply, but he's nice enough not to keep me waiting for very long.

I don't think you could, love, he says, and again I wish we were actually talking so I could hear his voice. *What are you doing? Am I keeping you from anything?*

No. I'm quick to type the word and send it, then I follow up with, *I'm just sitting on my bed talking to you.* As if that doesn't sound weirdly obsessive or desperate.

Or both.

Another message comes through from Rob and I frown, not caring enough to open it. Fuck Rob. He's not the important person in my inbox right now.

If you need to go, don't let me hold you up, all right? I didn't mean to keep you for this long anyway, but I enjoy talking to you.

What are you doing? I ask, turning his question back on him. *Am I keeping you from something?*

Not at all. Not one bit. I have all the time in the world for you. And I'm just sitting on my couch hating that I missed the first part of your stream.

Even if it wasn't the interesting part? I ask, pausing to listen for Juniper. I doubt she'll be home for a while, but still. There's no harm in being careful.

It's all interesting to me.

Why? Sure. It should be obvious. I doubt the answer is going to be anything other than 'because you're hot' or whatever, but I ask anyway. I want to know, at least, and my expectations are low enough that if he doesn't meet them, I'll be incredibly astounded.

Didn't I tell you already, love? Because I find you immensely interesting. I enjoy watching you, and hearing you talk. I'd rather you talk more about what you like instead of letting your viewers bully you into taking your clothes off sooner.

Ouch. The suggestion hurts, because he's right. Anytime I think I have control of my stream, that I won't give into anyone's demands of nudity, I prove myself wrong when the crowd mentality is *take it off*.

I'm getting better at it, though. At least, I like to think I am. And besides, I haven't done more than teased. I haven't done more than take my bra off yet.

That's good for me, right?

So talk to me, won't you? What do you like? What are you into? Do you like being watched?

The rapidfire questions give me whiplash, but I answer the first one, anyway.

I'm into art. Don't judge me, please. I want to do more, and I know it's not exactly a field where I'd be swimming in money, but I want to be an art historian. Maybe I'll teach on the side, or something. I like folklore way too much, and actually I'm kind of into photography right now.

Weirdly, that is. It's hard to be into it when Professor Solomon is such a terrifying jerk, but I get by.

He doesn't reply for a few moments, and I worry again that I've lost him.

Why photography?

Sucking in a breath, I frown. *It's an elective I'm taking right now and it's more interesting than I'd expected. I kind of want to work it into my senior project, though I doubt that's something I'll get help with... and I'm completely boring you right now. Sorry.* I'm dumb. I'm an idiot. No one gives two fucks what I like in terms of *college courses.*

You're not boring me, love.

You're being nice, but I'm sure I am. Anyway, you asked what I was into and if I like being watched? Honestly, I don't know about the second part. I kind of started this spontaneously, so I'm still figuring out how much I like it or if it will last. And umm... I send the message, thinking.

What *am* I into? I've had boyfriends, and I'm obviously not a virgin. But all the things I've wanted to try are things I've been too terrified to bring up to either of my boyfriends. They were way too conservative for that, or just not adventurous enough.

I'm into trying new things, I say finally. *Well, in theory. I haven't done a lot of things I'm interested in, actually.* There I go, being boring again.

What are those things?

I squirm on the bed, thighs pressed together. Am I really about to tell a complete stranger what I'm into?

For a moment, I consider lying to him. About saying something plain or kind of predictable. But a second later, I scoff. Why lie? What's the point, when he has no idea who I am or where I might live? He'll never find me, and he's never going to have a chance to act on what I say, obviously.

So why not be honest? It's kind of like a fantasy, in a sense. A way to test the waters and see how it feels to admit the things I'd like to try. Maybe if I do it with this anonymous stranger who will never see my face with the whole internet between us, it'll be easier when I do it for real.

A lot, I say, sending it before explaining more thoroughly. *I don't know a lot about most of what I'm into. But pet play, for sure. That's a big one.*

His response is quick, but I'm not surprised at this point. *Pet play? I bet you'd make a cute little puppy.*

I'd been thinking cat, but what can I say? I don't mind him thinking what he wants at this point. *And age play. A little? I don't know about that one, though. I don't know if I'd be able to act younger than I am.*

Go on. By my reckoning, he doesn't seem particularly interested in that one. But that's all right, because I certainly have more.

Don't judge me, I repeat, feeling a little nervous about admitting the last one.

I won't judge you, love.

Somehow, I feel like he means it. *I'm into CNC. you know*

what that is? Consensual Non-consent? It feels weird to admit it. To type it and send it in a message to someone across the internet. It's the one desire I keep locked up the most. After all, it's the most problematic one. The one people would question me for, since it's not *normal.*

He's quiet for longer than I expect, and my breath catches in my throat as my fingers itch to ask if he's still there. Has it weirded him out as well? *Are you still here?* I finally manage, hating that I'm worried about his reaction. As I stare at my words on the screen, about liking CNC, I wish I could take them back.

Of course I'm here, love. You just surprised me is all. What do you like about it? Do you want someone to break in and take you on your bed?

My breath hitches in my throat as he sends the message, but he doesn't stop there and I wouldn't know what to say if he had.

Or would you rather someone take you home? A poor, sick little puppy like you deserves to be taken care of. You want someone who knows what's best for you? Who makes you feel better than you think you could? Maybe you won't mind if they clip a collar and leash around that pretty throat and have you sit at their knees all day, hmm?

This isn't going where I'd thought it would, and I find myself unable to stop staring at the messages.

Are you still with me, love? the man asks and I jump to reply.

Yeah, I'm here. I'm here, but I'm fucking dumbfounded.

Is that what you want? Am I close, at least?

Yeah, I mean. I haven't done it, like I said. But that seems... good? Is good the right word here? It feels lame, honestly.

Want me to tell you what I like?

I want nothing more in the world, but I only suck in a breath, press my lips together, and respond with a quick, *yes.*

I want to show you what your fantasies would be like in real life. My boyfriend and I like the things you do, but so much more. I want to bring you home like the sweetest little puppy who needs a place to live and someone to take care of her. We could both take care of you, love. And I bet you'd love all the attention we'd give you.

My heart hammers in my chest, and my face feels hot. My thighs press together at his words, and I can't help but rake my teeth against my lower lip as I read them. *Holy shit*, he's a lot better at this than me.

Maybe I'll let my boyfriend fuck you in front of all your viewers so everyone knows who you belong to. You'll both be so popular. He likes being in front of the camera, too. I'll take pictures of you, so we can all remember how sexy you look on your knees while he's filling you up.

The mental image has me squirming, and my mind is blank except for the fantasies he creates there. *Holy shit* is all I can think, over and over in my head.

Holy *fucking* shit.

Are you still with me, love?

No. Not really. My brain has left and is currently orbiting the earth along with my consciousness as I fight the urge to bury my fingers between my thighs.

Yeah, I say finally, hating that it takes me a moment to say the simplest thing. *Sorry.*

Don't be. Do you like it when I talk to you like this?

Yes.

Do you want to touch yourself?

I hesitate until he asks again. *Maybe,* I say, hoping I sound flirty instead of needy and unsure.

Then why don't you, hmm? Touch yourself for me, love. My sweet, sick little puppy. I want you to tell me how wet you are for me.

For some reason, I follow his directions. My shirt is already up over my hips, so all I have to do is shift my laptop off onto the bed and slide my fingers under my panties. Am I really doing this? Am I seriously about to slide my fingers into my entrance just to tell him if I'm wet?

His message comes through while I'm staring blankly at my laptop, and I blink to read it.

I'm still waiting.

Shit. *Shit.* I take a deep breath, heart pounding, and part my thighs enough to slide my fingers into my body. With a shock, I realize I'm more turned on than I thought I'd be. Awkwardly with my other hand, I reply to him as I curl my fingers forward.

I am, I say, feeling stupid. *I mean, I am touching myself. And I'm wet. For you. For this.* God, I have to be the worst cyber-sex-haver on the face of this planet.

Good girl. Doing so good for me, love. Keep going. I bet you feel so good. I bet you're so fucking tight, aren't you? How many boyfriends have you had?

I don't even think about the answer. *Two,* I say, and hesitate. *But I only had sex with one of them.* Why does he need to know? It's stupid of me to think it's some flex.

But his response makes me tighten around my fingers, and I bite my lip.

That's almost nothing. I wouldn't have to train many bad habits out of you, would I? And I'd have such an easy time making you all mine. Ruining you for everyone except us.

The 'us' part is... interesting. Does he really have a boyfriend who'd be into this as well?

I want to make you suffer, but right now I'd rather you just work yourself up for me. Can you do that? Can you get yourself close for me?

Yeah, if I use my vibrator. I'm too impatient for just fingers, and I mean to tell him that, except the message comes out not quite as intended.

Can I use my vibrator?

Of course you can. Do you already have it? Will you slide it against that sweet little clit of yours for me? I love the panties you were wearing on your stream, and I bet you're still wearing them, aren't you?

Yeah, I say, moving to grab my vibrator from the drawer and then settling back down.

Take them off.

The message surprises me and, confused, I type out, *I thought you just said you liked them?*

I did. But I'd rather imagine you without them. When I bring you home, I won't let you wear anything. You wouldn't need to. I'd keep you warm and comfortable. Better that you're not wearing anything so I can touch you whenever I want.

I decide not to tell him I'm wearing a t-shirt I'd put on after the stream. It's not really any of his business.

Slide your vibrator against your clit for me. Don't worry about going slow. I bet you want to get off, don't you?

I do. He's not wrong, and I'm excited enough that, as I tease my clit with the small vibrator, I shudder and hold back a moan. Not that it would matter, since I'm alone. But this would be a bad time to learn that someone's kitchen is on the other side of my bedroom.

Work yourself up for me. I bet you look so sweet. Are you loud or quiet when you're fucked, love?

Quiet, I type back, my lips open as I fight not to pant. My thighs tremble and my knees fall open so I can give myself better access. The cold air on my clit is sharp, and I nearly shiver at the feel of it on my wet entrance. *Fuck.* This is way easier than it should be when talking to a stranger.

Not with us, you won't be. I bet we'll have you making the prettiest sounds. Do you want to come for me, love?

It's an easy answer, and easy to type with one hand. *Yes. Yes I do.*

I want you to. His answer is immediate, like he was waiting for it. *Come for me, my sick little puppy. Grit your teeth together so you don't make any noise. I bet you're so sweet when you come.*

I read that and my soul exits my body once more. I come, gasping softly before gritting my teeth together like he'd said. My thighs shake in earnest, toes curling, and I ride out the waves of my orgasm before pulling my vibrator away from my body and turning it off.

By the time I look back at my laptop, he's messaged me again.

I bet you're gorgeous when you're getting fucked. Since you're stunning the rest of the time as well. Did you have fun?

I did. I had a lot of fun, I admit, wiping my fingers off on my shirt for good measure before touching my keyboard. Making a mental note that I'll definitely need to disinfect it this weekend.

Play with me again sometime, won't you? I hate that I have to go so soon, but I wanted to make sure you got to have some fun. You deserve it. You earned it. Have a good week for me, love.

You too. And I mean it, I really did have fun talking to you.

I hit the send button right as the notification box lights up, drawing my attention. I click it, and my eyebrows jerk up in surprise.

Treat yourself to something that makes you happy this week.

The message, and the hundred bucks, are from *Thrillingterror*. But this time when I tell him thank you, he doesn't reply. I guess he really did have to go.

As I'm closing my laptop, I notice another message from r0b784 pop up, and roll my eyes. I don't have time for him right now, nor am I in the mood. He'll just have to get a reply some other time, when I feel like being nice.

For now, I'm going to text Juniper to not worry about bringing me food, and find the best pancakes in St. Augustine to see if they'll cover them in cherries and whipped cream so I can have the world's best dinner while watching the world's shittiest reality tv.

CHAPTER 9

I frown as I stare down at my ankle boots. They're well worn, and the shiny black material looks cracked and creased from every angle now. Of course I could replace them. They're knockoffs, for one. But they're also comfortable now that they're broken in, and I don't want to have to get rid of them. Not yet. Not when it's taken me this long to make them absolutely *perfect*. The heel on them adds a solid couple of inches to my height, and since they're chunky to match the aesthetic of the combat boots, it didn't take any practice to get good at walking in these.

In fact, I'm pretty sure that if I were going to be dropped into the middle of a zombie apocalypse, these are the shoes I'd pick to go in. Probably. At the very least, they'd be good to kick zombies with. Paired with them are my favorite black tights, a black skirt, and a dark red tee that's nearly the color of dried blood. Tucked into my skirt, it's still loose enough that I can run or twist to a spontaneous yoga pose at a moment's notice.

I feel fine. I feel comfortable, especially with my hair in a loose bun that's starting to collapse from the weight of my intelligence, surely. That, or the humidity. But that's not new. In fact, my bun has done remarkably well today, and my mascara has only run enough to make me look like I'm still in the first act of a Shakespearian tragedy, instead of the third.

But I don't *feel* fine. Not completely. I feel like there's something wrong. Something off. Like if I just turn my head far enough or fast enough, I'll see someone tickling me with the tip of a pen or something else that's just as far-fetched.

Stupidly, I give into my intuition, turning to look across the campus grounds at the people lounging in the grass, or in hammocks, or sitting at tables with cups of coffee. There's no one here even bothering to look at me, let alone charging across the grass with a knife raised like they're going to end my life.

But I still just feel so on edge.

So... not quite right.

"Are you going in, Love?" The drawling, dry tone has me wincing, and I turn to see Professor Solomon standing near me, obviously wanting to enter the part of the campus center where the coffee shop is housed.

"Sorry," I mumble, sidestepping the doors. "I didn't mean to be in your way."

He shrugs and opens the door, then... doesn't move.

I throw him a quick glance, confusion in every line of my body, only to be met with a dramatic and loud sigh. "You were going in, weren't you? Before you decided to stare into the abyss?" He raises a brow, his light brown eyes sharp in the warm sun. With the afternoon light sinking into his hair, I see that it's lighter than it appears to be in his classroom, with flecks of auburn and not a hint of grey. I wonder if he dyes it.

"What?" I ask, even though I've heard him just fine. Thankfully, the coffee shop is empty at this time of day, save the students studying at the tables, so we're not really creating a scene or holding anyone up.

"Forgive me if I'm wrong... but don't you have class in twenty-five minutes? With a professor who would never allow you to bring coffee into his room?" His eyes glitter and I fight the urge to wince away from his look and his disdain.

I don't know what I've done for him to dislike me so much, but it's clear that the feeling hasn't lessened since the first day of the year.

"I just need some caffeine," I mutter, like I have any room to argue. "It'll be gone before your class, professor."

"Not if you don't order it, Love." God, the way he says my last name still does the worst things to me. I'm happy he can't know my thoughts, and I don't give him any outward signs that it's the one thing I enjoy about him.

Other than staring at him in class. He is exceptionally pretty to look at, after all. When I glance back across the campus grounds, the feeling of something being wrong has evaporated. Though I don't know if it's that or that all of my feelings have scuttled under the proverbial carpet to hide from Professor Solomon's glare.

Either way, I feel a lot better about getting coffee now. I walk through the door he's holding, mumbling a thank you, only to be met with a sound of distaste that I want to pull my hair out in response to. I haven't done anything to him, but he acts like I'm the most disappointing creature to exist since the dodo, and twice as stupid.

"Sorry," I say once more, throwing a probably unfriendly glance back over my shoulder at my professor. I wouldn't dare act disrespectful towards him, but I certainly don't have to like him.

"For what?" he asks, his voice quiet as I stand in front of the counter. With the baristas busy, all I have to focus on is the way I can feel his eyes burning on the back of my neck. God, I hope I remembered to scrub there last night. It would be embarrassing if he's staring at some almost invisible speck of dirt I'd missed.

"For inconveniencing you," I say, and fix a smile on my face as the short, brown-haired and round-faced barista comes over to take my order. "Could I get an iced caramel macchiato, please?" I ask, my hands gripping the granite of the counter.

"Sure hon." Her hand hovers over the stack of cups and she asks, "What size for you?"

I should say small. After all, he's right. His class starts in less than twenty-five minutes, and I'll have to throw it away if I don't finish it all. But I cast a quick look up and over my shoulder, finding that Professor Solomon is looking at me with boredom etched in every fiber of his being. I smile, turn back to her and say, "Extra large, please."

Even over the sound of her shaking the cup free, I swear I hear him *snort* behind me. Deftly and politely, I step out of the way once I've paid, content to go wait at the end of the counter for my too large drink that I wouldn't even get if I had all the time in the world to drink it.

But fuck it, and fuck him. Because I really don't need his *permission* to get a drink. Nor does he know what I can do in twenty minutes... or in this case, how fast I can drink coffee. It's probably a weird flex, and absolutely means nothing, but I can't bring it in myself to let it go. Especially when they hand me the huge cup of caramel, cream, and espresso and I nearly want to *die* at the size.

I couldn't drink this in a year.

Professor Solomon gets his iced black coffee a second later, and toasts me dramatically. "Just remember, Love," he says, in a too-sweet, too-friendly voice, "no drinks in my classroom." and with that, he brushes past, his sunglasses dropping back

AJ MERLIN

into place from the nest of his hair, and breezes out the door while I wonder if I could use my drink as a weight to do strength training with.

By the time I make it to the arts building and the hallway outside of his classroom, I've only managed to drink a third of my macchiato. My teeth ache at the sweetness, and I lament at the fact that I'm going to have to throw it away. Even worse, I think as I pass by Professor Solomon's office and see him at his desk with his mostly empty coffee, he'll probably hear me do it and know that I failed.

His eyes don't even flick up as I walk past, and I'm so busy staring into his office like he's going to jump out of it that when I walk into a larger, taller body that smells of spicy-sweet cologne, I gasp and nearly spill my drink all over them.

"Whoa, whoa—" Smartly, Oliver's hand comes up to cup my drink, fingers brushing mine to keep it from spilling. "You're okay, Blair. It's just me." I turn to look at his dazzling smile, and for just a moment my heart dips when I think that I *really* need to tell him that I know he's *letsplayjay*.

Right? A good friend would let him know. A good friend wouldn't wish she could still swoon over his streams before doing her own.

A good friend wouldn't have nearly spilled coffee all down his black tee.

"Sorry," I murmur, frowning up at him. "I was just distracted."

"He's not a gargoyle, unfortunately," Oliver points out, and I swear his voice raises in volume like he wants Professor Solomon to hear. "Just because you stare at him doesn't mean he won't move. I hate to break it to you, Blair. But you're never safe."

"Thanks," I mutter, and step back to disentangle myself from Oliver. He beckons me over to the couch he's occupying,

82

dropping onto it and taking up over half. I don't mind, though I have to remind myself that I can't sit with my legs curled up under me like normal. No, instead I have to sit like a proper lady who isn't interested in flashing half the art department.

"That's a lot of coffee," he points out, glancing up at the clock above us. "Are you going to be able to drink that in ten minutes?"

"Thirteen, if I leave it to the last second to go in," I say, feeling defeat creep in from every angle. "I was hoping to make a point... I saw him in the coffee shop and he was all—" I lower my voice then say, in a nasal tone, "*Remember I don't allow drinks in my class, Blair. Don't forget, Blair.*" I roll my eyes, feeling like they're going to rocket off into orbit if I keep doing it at the mention of Professor Solomon. "So I turned my small into an extra large, hoping I could drink it all and throw it into the trash can in front of him to make a point. But I definitely overestimated myself." Only now does it occur to me I should've dumped some out either in the grass or in a sink.

Now it would be too obvious. He's too observant to not know.

"Want some help?" The offer shocks me, as does Oliver flopping over onto my side of the sofa, head almost on my shoulder.

"You like caramel macchiatos?" I ask, not really finding a reason to say no. I doubt he has foot-and-mouth disease or mono, after all. "And you really think you can drink this that fast?"

"Absolutely." He gazes up at me with soft, bright green eyes and grins. "Then you can slam dunk it into the trash can while he watches if we succeed."

"Just don't get sick or something," I snort, feeling like the responsible one as I relax and hold the straw up to his mouth.

I realize belatedly I should've just given him the damn cup.

Especially when his eyebrows climb towards his bangs and he stares at me in slight surprise. Before I can apologize or take it back, however, he reaches up to curl his fingers around the plastic cup and my fingers. He pulls my hand higher until his lips close around the straw and he lazily drags the liquid up through the straw and into hollowed cheeks.

It's both the stupidest thing I've ever seen and one of the hottest. Oliver himself is fucking gorgeous, and when he's acting like this, I can't help but feel like it's a turn on to some weird part of me. Well, not as weird as the part of me that loved talking to *Thrillingterror* over the weekend, so there's that.

"You look... well you certainly know how to suck," I tease, feeling more at ease with him than I expect to. His lips turn up in a grin, and he lets the straw fall out of his mouth.

"I would say I'm trying to flirt with you, but I don't think my *sucking game* is of much interest to you," he snickers.

"Yeah, probably not." I take another sip of my drink, positive I can taste Oliver on the straw. Mixed with coffee, it's a damn good flavor.

"Did you have a good weekend?" he hums, taking the cup back when I offer it. Thanks to him, we have less than half of the contents left, and I let out a breath and moan at the prospect of drinking the rest.

"There's so fucking much," I nearly sob, then add, "It was okay. I didn't do much. I just read a lot and ate ramen. And pancakes. I had such fucking good pancakes from Goldman's Diner."

"That's pretty nice. My roommate got shitty and kept telling me I needed to study instead of going off and doing what I wanted."

"Did you listen to him?" I ask, more curious than anything.

"Some, I guess. He gets scary when he's mad. You want

more?" I hesitate, then take another drink just as Professor Solomon's office door closes and I jump, choking on my coffee.

Oliver snatches it from my fingers, a hand on my back as I cough and my eyes stream. There's sure as hell no way to be subtle about it now, and when I have myself under control and Oliver is sipping our shared drink once more, I glance up to see Professor Solomon's eternally disapproving gaze squarely on us.

"Five minutes," he says, then breezes into the room without a look behind him.

Oliver sighs, and I groan, throwing my head back against the couch.

Or what I thought was going to be the couch. In reality, it turns out to be Oliver's arm I'm leaning against, and I can *feel* the heat from his body as he curls around me, his cologne the perfect mix of spicy and sweet.

"Sorry," he murmurs softly. "Though you could still do the thing. He doesn't know you didn't get this for us to share. He barely knows anything, after all. Maybe you really like me."

"Maybe I do," I agree with a loud sigh and try to sound as flippant as him. "Maybe I'm the kind of girl who buys coffee for the guys she really likes."

"Maybe you are. And maybe I'm the kind of guy who shows off his sucking game with girls he wants to impress."

I open my eyes to meet his, a nervous smile on my face. "Or maybe we're just drinking so much coffee we're going to throw up in his class," I say, trying to sound funny and sounding almost nervous instead.

Oliver doesn't pull away. Not quite, even when he puts the cup down and moves to lean closer to me again. He could kiss me, I realize. He's close enough that if I just leaned forward a few inches into his amused face, I could press my lips to his soft, full mouth.

God, I shouldn't want to do it so badly, and I curl my hands in my lap at the way my heart pitter-patters in my chest.

What *is* it about him that gets me going like this?

"I like the first option better," he says finally, dragging me gently to my feet. "Now..." Oliver picks up the cup and, holding my eyes, drains the rest of my coffee to leave a sip for me, which I gratefully take before shaking the empty cup. "Go in there and *slam dunk* this into his trash can. Right in front of him."

"That's kind of dramatic. Maybe too dramatic," I say, a little unsure at the prospect of pissing him off that much. Oliver chuckles and shakes his head.

"Nah, it'll be fine. Prove a point. Prove your *dominance.* Show Rook you aren't afraid of him and you'll get whatever size coffee you want."

Even if it has me running to the bathroom for the next six hours, I suppose. I just hope it's worth it. When we get to the room, I hesitate just inside the door, until Professor Solomon expectantly looks up at us, unamused.

Though I don't slam dunk the cup into the trash, I rattle it enough to prove that it's empty before dropping it into the plastic can. Though I nearly miss, and it hits the sides of the plastic bin on its way down, causing Oliver to frown in sympathy.

Professor Solomon just *looks* at me, disdain oozing from his pores. "Close the door before you sit, Love," he says, a sigh in his voice. "Since you waited until the very last minute to come in here."

He looks away and down, and even though I realize this was all for nothing as I gently close the door and sit, I can't help the small spark of satisfaction as I sit beside Oliver and pillow my chin on my hands as our professor gets up and starts his lecture.

Who knows? Maybe I'll take advice from Oliver on my next stage of passive aggressive disrespect and start calling him *Rook* when he can barely hear and certainly can't do anything.

I blink, thinking through that, and press my lips together so I don't grimace. Well, I won't be going that far, I don't think. But a girl can dream, can't she?

CHAPTER 10

I t's so hard to look like I'm not uncomfortable. It's hard to look relaxed when I'm not wearing anything at all, except for my mask, and more than anything I wish my heart would stop hammering in my chest when I do this.

God, when does this get easier? If I could sacrifice the leftovers in my fridge to an unseen god for an answer to that question, I would in an instant.

"Sorry," I laugh, trying to sound pleasant, amicable, and flirtatious. I succeed, I think. At least, my viewer count isn't going anywhere, so that's saying something. With it being Friday, I had expected the count to be low. But instead, it's higher than it has been before. I've caught and held about forty viewers for this whole time, and once I'm pretty sure that number had gone up into the low fifties.

"But I'm about to end the stream." I sit back on my chair, one knee up and toes curled over the edge of my desk chair. A viewer, who is surprisingly *not* rob784, begs me again to touch myself.

But I really don't want to. Not when I want to go drink

coffee and eat the mint chip ice cream that's screaming my name from the freezer.

"Next time, okay?" I ask, lips curled into a sweet smile. Or, so I hope. "Catch me before I'm about to head off..." I trail off as four different men flood the chat, begging me to stay longer and saying they'll make it worth my time.

At least, until a tip of eighty fucking dollars comes through from one of my now-favorite people on this earth. *Malevolent-Mask* messages right after sending the money, causing my smile to grow into something more genuine.

Now that I'm top tipper, I get to ask you for something, right? I blink at the message, hesitant. I can't turn down his request with a tip like that, can I?

"What did you have in mind, new friend?" I ask, hooking my arm over the back of the chair.

End your stream and go buy yourself a really great fuckin' meal. They don't deserve you.

My eyebrows shoot up at the request, and my fingers stop tapping on the wood of my chair as I blink once, then again. "Well, you all know the rules." I laugh, dropping my knee so I can lean closer to my laptop. "Highest tipper wins, and that is definitely the highest of the day. Besides, it really is time for me to go, and I don't have a lot of free time outside of what I spend with all of you." I bite my lip, hoping I look cute or shy or whatever gets these guys off, instead of like some species of beaver.

Some of the men wish me a good weekend, while a few others make remarks about me not doing what they wanted, but I ignore those. There's nothing else I can do; because I refuse to entertain some of them since they are just... not very nice. Hitting the button to turn off my camera, I grab my trusty red tee and pull it on over my head, along with my pajama shorts that barely cover more than my ass. As usual, Juniper won't be home for a while. I have the apartment to myself and

I can decompress from this new, interesting way to make money.

The notification for my inbox lights up as I carry my laptop to the bed. My heart twists, butterflies take flight in my stomach, and I can't help but hope it's *ThrillingTerror*. Or *MalevolentMask,* but he's never messaged me after the first time.

Sitting down, however, I sigh as I see that the message isn't from either of them.

It's from Rob.

Fuck Rob.

But I also can't just leave it there. I can't alienate one of my few fans, no matter how annoying he is, when he diligently returns stream after stream to watch me do very little. I'm boring, no matter what *ThrillingTerror* says. If I wasn't, then I'd have more viewers. Not just the few that trickle in while I stream. Sure, forty-two was a lot. But I doubt it'll happen again.

Is your semester going well, MaskedEnvy? The message makes me shudder as I read it, and I hate that he knows I'm in college.

Hell, I barely remember talking about it on stream. For the most part, I like to keep my life under wraps with these people. I don't need them figuring out who I really am. But I'm also pretty certain that half of my appeal is the fact that I'm a college student.

I can't ignore it, so I politely type back that I am and I hope his evening goes well before clicking out of the message and ignoring when it lights up again.

Sure, I can't totally ignore him. But I shouldn't need to encourage him too much, either. If he wants to keep watching, great. I'm pretty sure he's never tipped me, so I'm not *that* attached to him staying.

My eyes flick down the notifications, and I delete the stupid spam messages about me being gorgeous and someone wanting to meet up with me. I don't want to meet up with any of these men... with one or two exceptions.

And somehow, as I clean out my inbox, both exceptions suddenly appear, sending messages within a few seconds of each other.

I open *MalevolentMask*'s message first, letting out a breath as I read it.

You're always so good when you stream, you know? But you don't have to be so nervous. I promise no one is ever thinking bad about you, okay? How could they, when you're you? There's a string of emojis after it that make me snort, and I take a moment before typing back my reply.

How can I not be? Have you seen some of the things they want me to do? I'm willing to get myself off on stream with a vibrator, but not with fucking vegetables. Also, I really appreciate what you did. It kind of feels like I rely on a few of you to help me end my stream sometimes.

His reply is almost instant.

Yeah, the vegetable thing is weird. But I'm pretty sure I saw someone saying they wanted to see you with a tail. You know, the kind that doesn't clip on. Don't hate me, but do you know how hot that would be on you? Pretty sure you could just get on your knees and wiggle for an hour and people would throw money at you. And hey, it's no problem. You're just too nice to tell them to fuck off, so I've got you.

I snort at the message, shaking my head. *Sure buddy,* I say, and take a moment before I add on to it. *I don't know about that. I doubt my ass is that enticing. Plus, I've seen some of those. They look like they're painful if you're stupid about, uh, attaching them. And I'm kind of stupid.*

He's quiet for a few seconds, but before I can do more than open another tab to read the messages from *ThrillingTerror*, he replies.

Well, I could help you with that. Emotionally. Uh, moral support, I mean. However you want. I'm not being creepy, I swear.

It doesn't really *feel* creepy. It makes me snicker as I open the other message, and one makes my toes curl against the sheets.

You did so well today, love. But you should learn to stick to your boundaries a little better.

I frown at it as I read it again, tucking my legs up under me. It feels almost like a reprimand, and I don't really know how to reply. I'm bristling at the words; I can feel it, and I type the word *sorry* before sending it off.

No one gets to condemn my actions or tell me I'm not good enough when I'm finally doing something for myself. Even if I am kind of bad at it. Sure, if he'd said something a little more supportive, like my other message I'd gotten, I would've been a lot more okay with it.

I flip back to my other messages, and finally respond, *You're not creepy. But I still don't know about the whole tail thing.*

They're not that bad. I have some experience. Not my thing personally. Not on me, you know? But fuck, would I still love to see you with one.

It still just feels weird to consider. Would it hurt? Being inexperienced with anything other than boring sex, I have to imagine it would hurt. And at the very least, I'd need to practice a few times *off* camera before doing it on. I'd probably put it in before, truth be told. I wouldn't want to embarrass myself on camera.

I'm scared it would hurt, I admit finally. *Like, that's the only thing that really comes to mind when I think about it. Other than that it would be pretty cute, like you said. Maybe a fluffy cat tail?*

I send the message and hop back into the other chat, wondering if I've scared off *ThrillingTerror* with my shitty attitude. If I have, then I'll sure as fuck regret it in the morning.

Love. I cringe as I read the message in Professor Solomon's shitty tone. That's inappropriate, and I try to bleach my brain of the thought. I definitely shouldn't be thinking of *him* while talking to someone who got me off a few days ago. Inappropriate doesn't begin to cover it. Especially since if I'm already imagining his voice, who knows how long it'll be before I see his face in my mind to go along with it?

No, I definitely need brain bleach.

I blink, forcing myself to read the rest of his message, even though *Love* gets a line of its own.

You don't need to get an attitude with me. I just don't like seeing you get flustered. You think those men don't know they can work you up to push you past your intentions? They've been doing that much longer than you've been live streaming, I promise you that.

I read the message twice then, because I don't know what else to say, I ask, *How do you know I was getting an attitude? Maybe I was really just sorry.*

And with that, I flip back over to my other chat. Mask is talking again, extolling the virtues of tail butt plugs. But his next message sticks out, making me blink in surprise.

I think you'd make a better puppy than you would a cat. We'll get you a cute wolf tail. A purple one, don't you think? I bet you'd look so good in purple. Matching fluffy ears and the cutest leash. You'll be such a good puppy.

Do I really give off *canine* energy, instead of a cat? Well, I guess it's his fantasy, not mine, but he's the second one to say it.

Maybe, I say, feeling weirdly guarded about the situation. Maybe it's just that I feel like this is going down the same route of the conversation I'd had a few nights ago.

Or maybe it's because I have a headache.

You know, I like other things too.

After sending the message, I flip back over to my other

chat, and try not to read the words in Professor Solomon's voice. If I fail, at least there's no one around to know except me, which is definitely bad enough.

I'm not an idiot. I can tell that you don't like the advice. You don't have to take it. I blink and look away before I finish, knowing where this is going. I'm sure it will be followed with a declaration of him taking his attention, and his tips, elsewhere. Good job, Blair. There goes your pancake money.

When I turn and refocus on the screen, rereading the message, it takes me a moment to realize I'm wrong.

You don't have to take it. I don't mind helping you when you need it. And I always make time for your stream. You'll be alright one way or another, but I just don't want you to get taken advantage of, since I don't know what other men are sending you in their dms.

What the ever loving fuck? He sounds so... sincere. Like he actually gives two shits about my well-being, or about how I might feel after one of my shows. It sinks into me, like water against my skin, and I frown. I don't know what to say, frankly, but 'thank you' doesn't feel like enough.

It has to do, though. At least initially. *Thank you,* I tell him, and then add. *But why do you care so much? I'm not trying to be mean or obtuse. I just don't get why you do.*

I can't find it in me to flip back to the conversation with Mask while I wait. Instead, I sit there, eyes fixed on the screen, until another message lights up my screen.

I told you, didn't I? You're just so interesting and I can barely ever take my eyes off of you. I'd like to get to know you, though I don't want to scare you off. And I want to do more than tip you a few dollars here and there.

What does that even mean? For certain, he isn't tipping me *a few dollars.* He's almost half of my income, with Mask being a portion of the rest.

You give me too much already, I say, feeling suddenly modest. Maybe this is a chance at gaining a sugar daddy, and here I am blowing it. *It's not just a few dollars that you're giving me. It's really nice of you, for one. And it's more than I ever could've asked for.*

Not wanting to neglect Mask, however, I flip back over to that conversation to see that he's asked me what else I'm into.

CNC I reply without hesitation this time. I don't have to give myself the whole mental song and dance about them being strangers. They're never going to see me. They'll never meet me or get the chance to act on my fantasies, or theirs. *Do you know what that is?*

Do I fucking know what that is? His response is quick. *Of course I do. Holy fuck, Envy. That's so hot. That's what you should start leading with when you stream. You could say you're into it and become a millionaire. Especially if you're already naked. Fuck. I'm so serious. Do you know what you look like? Do you know how hot you are?*

The string of praise is unexpected enough that I switch conversations once more, to the one with a slightly more serious tone.

It's not all that, love. Not at all. I'd rather buy you something outright, if you'd let me. Let me send you something just for you. Just because I want to.

Send me something? Hell fucking no. While the idea of getting gifts is... tempting, there's no way that I'll tell someone where I live. Not even the city.

No. I'm sorry, I say. *I don't want anyone to know that much about me. Are you mad?*

You'd have to do a lot more than be cautious with me to upset me, baby girl. This new nickname is enough of a switch that I feel like I have whiplash. *You're so good for being careful and protecting yourself. Let me show you what I want to get you, and I'll send you the money for it. How about that?*

I can't help my response, and I switch inboxes after asking, *What if I don't get what you want?*

Mask is just as sweet and overly excited as he had been a few seconds ago. Another paragraph of praise waits for me, and I can't help my little grin.

Though at the next message, I sigh with disappointment and flop over onto my side.

Sorry, I have to go. I don't want to go. All I want is to talk to you for the rest of the weekend, but my roommate says it's my turn to fix dinner. Have a good night, okay? And if you ever want to just, like, talk or something, you can totally message me. Anytime.

I hope you have a good weekend too, I say, waiting for signs of another message before turning back to my active conversation with Terror.

You won't do that.

I have to reread my prior message to remember what I'd said to him, and I blink in surprise at how... *sure* he sounds.

I won't? I ask, unable to help it.

No, love you won't. I know you won't. Can I send you a link? Show you what I want to get you, then I'll send you the money?

Should I do this? I go over all the ways he could know it's me, but I can't find any that are a genuine concern. If he's just sending me the money over this site, then it's just like a tip, isn't it? He doesn't know where I am at all.

Okay, I say finally, and I have to wait for a few tense moments until he comes back with two links that take me away from the site in different tabs.

Almost unexpectedly, neither of them is a tail. I say as much to him and get a response asking if I'm okay with what he wants to get me.

Taking another look, I blink in surprise at the pictures.

Neither of them are sex toys, to my absolute shock. One is a black oversized hoodie with a purple dog on it. One sleeve is lined with lilac hearts, and the model it's shown on wears the hoodie like a dress.

It's definitely something I'd wear.

The other is a camera. I bite my lip, unable to figure out how to take this one. It's a lot better than the one I'd bought for class, and a lot more expensive.

Why? I ask finally into the chat. *Are you sure you sent me the right links?*

Because you're a cute little puppy, first of all. That part should've been obvious in my brain, I guess. I'm probably stupid for not making the immediate connection, but it's still a surprise that he wants to get me a *hoodie* and not, like, a tail and ears.

And because you told me you like photography. You're taking it as an elective, right? You seemed excited about it the last time we spoke.

That's rather observant of him, actually. I don't know how to take that, and so I say instead, *Yeah, but it's too expensive. I can't accept that.*

It's not expensive for me. It's honestly pocket change, Terror dismisses. *I wouldn't spend money on you if I didn't have money to spend. Do you not want them?*

No, I want them, I promise, and a moment after I send it, I see that I've gotten way more money as a tip than I'd need to cover the purchases and shipping. *You sent me too much. I wish I could send some back to you. I could've calculated shipping and told you what I needed.* Is that guilt stirring in my stomach? Maybe. But then again, it could also just be excitement at the amount of money in my account. There's enough left over to get pancakes again.

I didn't send you too much. It's fine, love. It's perfectly fine. Will you order them for me, please?

I don't respond until I do so, and in a few quick movements I screenshot the order confirmation and crop out all of my information except for the part that shows that I did, in fact, buy what he wanted me to.

Thank you. You're such a good girl.

God, it does wicked things to me when he says things like that. But all I can think to say, again, is *thank you.*

You're welcome. I have to go 'attend' to my boyfriend for a little while, but I hope I'll see you on Sunday. Get yourself something nice tonight? Coffee, if you like it.

I fucking love coffee.

I will. I'll get a giant caramel macchiato and think of you the whole time, I joke. *Thank you, again. I know it's kind of a lame response, but I really appreciate this. Thank you so much.*

Good night, love. The finality has me certain he's not going to reply anymore, and I close my laptop then sit back with a sigh.

This is wild, frankly. I don't understand what either of them sees in me. How can I, when they're the only two who see anything at all past someone to beg to take off her mask, take off more clothes, and just do *more* in front of the camera?

And yet, both Mask and Terror don't treat me like that at all, for all of Mask's enthusiasm about me being into CNC and wanting to see me in a tail.

"Coffee," I tell my ceiling, pushing the other stuff from my brain. "You're going to order coffee and a croissant. And you're going to stop worrying about your sexy strangers for now." Though is it really worrying when I wish I had cause to talk to them more often? Or that I wish that somehow, maybe, they were close enough for me to meet at least once?

Never, I tell myself, shutting down that thought instantly. *They could be crazy. They could be serial killing cannibals.*

Or worse, a soft, unfriendly part of my mind adds. *They could hate you in person, couldn't they?* And that, I think, is the scariest part of all.

CHAPTER 11

I should've said no.

The thought rings clearly in my brain as my old, worn combat boots hit the sidewalk. I look up at the frat house, able to pick it out from the other houses with ease. It isn't difficult, after all. The aura of stale, cheap beer and girls who are prepared to lower their standards for the night radiates off of it like steam; and I can't believe I've let Juniper bring me back to this house in particular.

"You okay?" She comes closer to me, looking incredibly attractive in a short black dress that barely covers the top of her thighs. She wears boots similar to mine, but without the cracks and creases, and her purse is slung over her shoulder.

I grimace. "Tell you what. I'll compliment you all night so you don't have to swagger around here looking for it. All night, and we'll watch whatever you want for a week. All I ask is that we go home."

"No," Juniper replies, smiling sweetly while shutting down the plea I make every time we do this. "If you didn't want to come, you could've stayed home. It's not like I *dragged* you here against your will. Hell, you're the woman who told me she had a new outfit she wanted to wear almost before I finished saying what I wanted to do."

The sad part is, she's right. I tend to forget how much I dislike frat or sports house parties until the last minute, and this is it. The eleventh hour. The penultimate moment where this outing tips into compulsory unless I want to get an Uber and go home.

Not that I couldn't. I have more than enough money, thanks to my new fans, and I could absolutely call a car to take me home. Though, since I spent almost an hour getting ready and came all the way here, it feels like a waste to do so this early.

"An hour," Jun promises, smoothing her lacy dress that zips up the back from ass to neck. "An hour, and I'll be over it. Marcus is here, and I would really like to see him. Is that okay with you?" She's not really asking, but I lift my chin imperiously anyway before answering.

"Fine. I suppose. But I will be counting the minutes," I sniff, crossing my arms over my chest. If I'm honest, I'm excited to get to wear this somewhere, since the skirt had only come in the mail earlier this morning. It's dark purple plaid and brushes the top of my knees or just about. Only, one side of it is completely open, like someone forgot to sew it together, and under it you can see the attached black shorts that hug my thighs. A belt sits at my waist, and I've skipped the tights today so my legs are bare under the skirt-shorts combo. I hadn't been sure what to wear with it, and had eventually settled on just a black, cropped tee that's already ridden further up under my boobs than I would've liked.

But hey, at least my tattoos are visible and look great. Without a hoodie or tights, they're all on display, and I've never loved them more than I do now that I have my snake and flower arm and hand tattoo.

"Sure. Why don't you set a phone alarm so you can be sure to catch me *right* at sixty minutes. Time starts at the door, I presume?" She sets off at an easy pace, locking the car behind her as I take a few longer strides to catch up. Even with our boots on, we're almost the same height. She's an inch taller than me, maybe, but it barely makes any difference unless someone is really looking.

She takes the lead up the sidewalk and we automatically go round to the back of the house, where the large deck looks out into the yard and in-ground pool. Sure enough, other students have jumped in. With clothes or in their underwear. I'd never have the balls to do it, but I can't help but do a quick survey of those actually in the water before hopping up on the deck with Juniper.

Well, at least it isn't the hockey house. My fingers graze along my tattoos as we go in, with Juniper flashing a grin instead of a twenty to get us in the house. It works. It always has, and I follow behind her as the scent of weed and, predictably, stale beer slams into my face like a wayward traffic cone.

It takes only a few minutes for my boredom to set in. Though as I watch, Juniper comes alive at the chance to socialize with people she barely knows. She's a born socialite, and it isn't a coincidence that her major is in marketing, where she'll do a lot of face-to-face interactions in her work.

She's made for it.

Not me, though. A few people compliment my tattoos, though the thrumming of the bass and the loudness of the house make me regret coming here all the more. I leave Juniper's side and she barely spares me a glance. It's been a long time since we refused to let go of each other at these things. As seniors, one would hope we're old enough not to get into trouble.

My steps take me through the house, and I glance into rooms I haven't seen in over a year. Not that I expect them to have changed. They haven't, and the same pictures line the walls. The same badly built bar in the large living room stands against the wall, looking like it's going to fall over if one more person leans against it while they're served warm beer.

I watch and finally make my way over. Beer is beer, no matter how much it sucks, and I trade a five for a plastic cup filled with the stuff.

"What is it?" I yell, leaning over the bar to the frat boy standing behind it who's pouring another one.

"No idea!" he replies just as loudly, beaming. Of course he doesn't have any idea. Why would he? I roll my eyes but thank him anyway, extracting myself from the crowd and walking toward the front end of the house, which has always been the quietest.

Is it to keep a semblance of quiet? I've never known if it's a rule to keep your loudness to the back of this house, but it feels like that might be the case. But I'm not loud, and no one stops me as I sit down at the bottom of a staircase that looks at the front door. If anyone's upstairs, I can't hear them. But then again, I can't hear much over the sound of the music and the way my heart pounds in my ears in response.

It's not that I hate people, or something so dramatic as that. As a freshman, I'd loved coming to parties like this. I'd had a bigger friend group then, as I'd wanted to fit in with the people that came from places much more exciting than I had. I'd tried weed, and drank all kinds of alcohol, and it wasn't until I'd ended up on someone's yard with vomit all over my face and shirt that I'd realized I was trying to fit in with people that weren't what I wanted in life.

Though even since then, I haven't discovered what those people are. Except for Jun, of course. She's been the one constant since I'd started college. Maybe she'll be the one constant after it, too. At least until she lands her dream marketing job and leaves me.

I frown at the empty cup of beer in my hand, and realize it's my third as I tip it over to watch the amber drops run down the plastic inside of it. My head swims a little, though not enough to set off the blaring warning signs of being drunk. Tipsy? Barely. This is a pathetic attempt at it, at best, and I'm sure it'll wear off in the next hour or so. Well before the time Juniper actually *wants* to go home.

Pushing to my feet again, I move just as someone comes around the corner. A yelp of surprise fills the air as I collide into them, and belatedly my brain recognizes the spicy-sweet scent of Oliver's cologne.

"Whoa, I'm sorry. Are you..." he trails off when I look up at him, feeling as if my feet are glued to the floor. "Blair?" His lips curl into a delighted smile, and his hands rest on my hips without moving.

"What are you doing here?" I ask directly, hoping I don't slur my words or anything else so embarrassing in front of him. His hands are warm where they brush my exposed skin, and I find that I can't look away from him.

"This is a party," he reminds me, the half-smile still curling his lips upward. "I think it's obvious what I'm doing here."

I want to ask if he isn't a little old to be here, until I remember that this is a frat house and some of them are probably a little older too, thanks to our college offering multiple masters programs. Surely some of them stay, right? Or, well, there could also be members that just stick around, or started late, or just *don't graduate.* Who am I to judge why Oliver's here?

"Oh." Is all I can think to say, when staring at his face is a much better use of my time.

His eyes search mine and I can *feel* his hands slide millimeters higher on my skin, causing a small shiver to go through me. "You're drunk," he accuses, eyeing the cup in my hands even as I shake my head.

"I'm barely tipsy," I correct, but it does seem that I might be a little more than *barely* with the way my head swims. At least I'm not staggering or falling over yet.

"I believe you." Oliver reaches out and extracts the plastic cup from my hands, only to set it down on the stairs before straightening once more. "Let's go outside? It's kind of gross in here, and you could probably use the fresh air." I don't argue with him as he pushes open the front door and leads me out onto the porch. There's no one here, and the only movement I see comes from two girls in the shadow of a large tree in the yard who aren't as hidden as they think they are. When I glance their way, however, they seem to realize it and, with a giggle, duck further into cover before continuing whatever they were doing.

Oliver eases down onto a porch step and looks up at me expectantly. Not needing any convincing, I follow with a less graceful movement that still ends up with my ass planted on the concrete beside him, so it's still a win for me. He chuckles, and before I can say anything, throws an arm over my shoulders. "I didn't think you came to places like this," he admits. "You seem too classy for college parties."

"I only come to them when Juniper wants to go," I admit, not stopping myself from leaning into his warmth. The air is warm in St. Augustine, and muggy with the promise of rain by morning. But Oliver's warmth isn't overwhelming. In fact, it's perfect. But what else do I expect of him, when he's—

I close my eyes hard, hating the guilt that floods me. I still haven't told him, and when I straighten, he turns and looks at me with raised brows.

"Sorry," I murmur, meeting his eyes in the darkness illuminated by streetlights and the porch light behind us. "I am a little drunk."

"Don't apologize. Are you all right?" Tenderly, he pushes my hair back behind my ear, his eyes never leaving mine. "Do you want to leave? I can drive you home—"

"No," I say quickly, hating the thought of leaving Oliver. We've never done anything outside of stolen minutes before Professor Solomon's class, and it's great to not have *him* hovering like the world's most toxic helicopter.

The thought of Solomon in a helicopter and glaring down at us swims into my brain, causing me to giggle. My hand darts up, and I cover my face before I can embarrass myself further. But Oliver tilts his head and asks, "What are you laughing at, wonder girl?"

Wonder girl. I know he's called me that before, but I have no idea why.

"I was just thinking that this is the first time we're together without our dear professor glaring at us or threatening us with the aura of his presence," I point out. "And it's nice."

His grin widens as he leans back on one hand, his other arm still around me. His hand readjusts, knuckles brushing against my tee as I take in a breath to try to get a hold of myself. It isn't just the beer that's making me like this, and that's the problem. For three weeks, I've tried to ignore my attraction to Oliver and his voracious, overly friendly attitude that's so different from what I normally want in a friend.

But the beer makes it easier to stare at him and wish he were mine. "Why do you call me wonder girl?" I ask after a few moments, breaking the silence before he can.

"Why?" He raises his brows like he's surprised I've asked.

"Maybe it's because you're *wonder*ful, Blair." But there's a teasing, taunting edge in his voice that makes me almost certain it isn't that. Before I can say as much, however, he goes on with wicked humor, "Or maybe because it's a wonder you haven't earned Rook's wrath by now. A wonder that you didn't leave after that first day. A wonder that you sucked down that much coffee and nearly *missed* the trash can during your slam dunk."

I grimace at the memory, hating how he'd looked at me with sympathy and his gorgeous green eyes. God, I love his eyes. "That's a weird reason," I mutter, but he just chuckles and pulls me tighter to him.

"Maybe to you. But I like it. Are you sure you want to stay, Blair? You really don't seem like you're having a good time."

"What makes you say that?" With Oliver, I'm having a great fucking time.

"I found you on a staircase on the quiet side of the house, completely avoiding anyone else that's here during a frat party. Tipsy, but probably a little closer to *drunk*," Oliver points out skeptically. "I don't drink, and I'm sure Juniper wouldn't mind if I took you home. Especially if that's what *you* want." His other hand comes up to smooth back my hair again, and I barely realize that he's still asking if I want to leave.

I'm too busy trying not to swoon for him. Still, I can't help but lean into his touch, and when I do, his eyes narrow, darkening.

Shit.

Shit.

Awareness slams into me, and I sit back, eyes widening. "I'm sorry. I don't mean to make you uncomfortable, and I know you're just being friendly—"

"Blair." His voice is rough, and lower than I've ever heard it before. "Let's get something straight. If I were just trying to be nice…" He leans closer to me, until he's just as close as he was yesterday when he'd been helping me get rid of my coffee. "I would've taken you back to Juniper." His voice is almost a purr when he says it, and he's so close that I can feel his breath on my lips.

"Yeah?" I breathe, wide eyes not leaving his. "Then what are you doing, Oliver?"

"Trying to decide if you're too drunk to be kissed."

Anticipation courses through me, and I reach out to grip his shirt. "I've suddenly never been so sober in my life," I lie, drawing a soft chuckle from him.

"That's just not true. And we both know it." He doesn't move away, and it's torture having him this close to me with him teasing me about the thing I want so badly in this moment. "I'm not going to do something you might regret later, wonder girl. I'd never put you in that position."

"You're not," I assure him. "Oliver, I'm pretty sure I've been in love with you for a week—" I break off, hating the way I'd phrased that. "I mean... that I've been interested in-in being more than friends, if that's something you want. But I'm not very good at—"

"And here I was thinking you fell for me yesterday when I showed you my sucking game," he cuts me off smoothly, sweetly, and a grin pulls at his lips. "Do you promise, Blair, that you want this with or without the beer?"

"Yes," I promise him, all my thoughts are just blurs zipping around between my ears. "Oliver, I *swear*—"

I don't get the chance to finish whatever it is I'm *swearing* to him. He closes the distance between our mouths, catching me up in a hard kiss. His arm tightens, pulling me against him as his mouth coaxes mine open slowly. He's patient, and sweet, though I can feel the intensity burning under his skin as he holds me in an iron grip and explores my mouth at a suddenly frenzied pace.

And then the guilt sets in.

I'm *lying* to him. I haven't told him that I know he's a camboy. I haven't told him I'm *finalistgirl*.

I'm lying to him, even if it's just a lie by omission. But it's not alright, in my mind, and every moment he kisses me and I haven't told him is another moment I feel like dying.

"Wait," I whisper against him, repeating the word when he nips my lip instead of complying. When I say it once more, he jerks back, eyes searching mine as they widen with concern. His arm slips free, and he moves to pull away from me, as if he doesn't want to touch me at all.

"What?" he asks, concern etched in his face. "What's wrong, Blair? Did I hurt you? *Fuck,* I shouldn't be kissing you after you've been drinking—"

"That's not it," I promise, too nervous to reach out and touch him. "I need to tell you something. I...I've been lying to you, and it's not okay." I lick my lips anxiously, not looking at him. Will he be upset? Will he be angry with me for not telling him sooner?

Will he walk away and not want to be my *anything* anymore?

"What's wrong?" Oliver urges, leaning in close again. "Blair, what have you been lying about? You look like I'm about to kill you or something."

"No, I—" He leans in again but my hand flies up to press against his chest. "If I don't tell you this, then I'll always worry you hate me, Oliver."

"Okay?" he sounds bemused more than anything.

I take a deep breath, try to will myself to sobriety and say slowly, so I know I'm not mixing up my words, "I know you're a streamer. And I know you're *letsplayjay,* because I've watched you before. I'm sorry."

He doesn't reply at first. Oliver just watches me, and it's

not until I look up into his searching gaze that his smirk curves up over his lips again. "I know." He chuckles, shocking me to my core. "I know you know... *finalistgirl*."

How in the world could he know that? But if it's not a big deal and he's okay with it, then I'm fine. Everything's fine, since he doesn't seem to be mad, and I can get back to being—

"Or would you rather me call you *maskenvy?*"

CHAPTER 12

My heart nearly stops, and it feels like every beat of it is forced and unnatural. Time slows as I look up at him, my foggy brain trying to work through what he's just said. First of all, he knows I'm *finalistgirl*. That's bad enough, but not really terrible in the grand scheme of things. It could be cute, actually, if we were in some rom-com situation and about to fall in love on screen. No, that isn't the problem here.

The problem is that he knows I'm a streamer. He knows that I'm *maskenvy* and that means—

"You watch me stream?" I breathe, sure my face is as red as it has ever been. "How do you know it's me?"

"I do," he admits readily, and reaches out to stroke a finger over the ink on my arm. "No offense, Blair. But these are incredibly unique. There was no way I wouldn't know it's you. And you're so fucking adorable, wonder girl. How could I not watch?"

He's seen me naked.

Oliver, who has been sitting beside me in class for three

weeks acting like he's auditioning for the position of ride-or-die best friend, has seen me *naked*. Of course, I've seen him naked too, but that isn't the point.

I bury my face in my hands, still able to hear his huffed chuckle over my groan. "You've seen me naked," I lament. "You've literally seen me at my worst and I've only known you for three weeks. God, I'm such a loser."

"At your worst?" Genuine confusion flits through his tone. "Uh, Blair, you're gorgeous. Do I need to repeat that? And you're good at what you do. Not to mention, you've seen me naked, too. Though I've noticed you don't watch me anymore..." His voice turns teasing as he leans in close and tugs me against him so he can whisper in my ear. "Is it because you're being polite? Preserving my modesty out of some weird sense of chivalry?"

"It felt rude," I admit, face still burning scarlet. "You're my friend, and you didn't know. Well, I thought you didn't know. I just thought we were crossing the line of *friendship*, quite frankly."

"That's nice of you. You're much more considerate than me, since I make sure to watch your streams every fucking time." He pauses thoughtfully, then adds, "I can't believe you thought I'd be upset that you watch my streams. But I'm curious how you found out." His hand loops around my shoulders again, urging my face out of my hands and closer to his.

"Your photography book," I admit. "It's pretty unique, Oliver. It fell in front of your camera the day before you called me asking if I had it." Enlightenment lights up his eyes before fading back into interest. "Then I realized I knew your voice, and the rest is obvious. Anyway, I guess I should apologize, since I kind of copied your mask-thing."

"Don't apologize," he dismisses, shaking his head. "Who cares if you stole it? I don't *own* masks. What I'd rather know is..." He leans so close that our lips brush before asking, "Did you learn anything from me? Take any notes while you watched me get off? I would've put on a better show if I knew it was you the first time. I only found out once I started watching you, and then you never came back." He kisses me lightly, blowing all of my potential responses out of my brain.

Finally, when he pulls away, I ask, "How did you know I'm *finalistgirl* too?" He never heard my voice or spoke one-on-one to me, exactly. There's no way for him to—

He taps my nose almost like a sweet reprimand and says, "Because, wonder girl, you used the same site email for both accounts."

"You *looked*?" I ask, brows shooting upward. "Why would you ever think to look?"

He doesn't answer. His eyes dance as I watch him, and he just fucking *stares* at me. "Have you ever said anything in my stream? Do you just watch, or—?"

A laugh pulls from Oliver's throat as he looks at me, a little incredulous, like I'm missing something obvious. "Do I just *watch*? Come on, Blair. *Come on.*" His words are teasing, goading. Like he enjoys seeing my face stained red in embarrassment. But who in the world would be into something like that in a situation like this?

Am I missing something?

"Not only am I your second highest tipper..."

Oh God.

"Unless you lied to me, I'm now very aware of the things you're into."

Oh, fuck.

I don't know what to say. Part of me wants to say it's not me, that he has the wrong blonde, masked streamer with a snake and flowers tattooed on her arm. Part of me wants to say I was lying to make him more into me. To make him tip more.

But those would be lies, and I don't want to lie to Oliver.

"Oops," I say finally, still watching his face. "This feels... really awkward now."

"Why?" His question feels genuine, and his face melts into a perplexed expression.

"That's kind of embarrassing. I've known you for three weeks. As a friend." I kind of wish he would've told me before this that he knew.

"So? You're still my friend. Though I don't know how to be much more obvious that I want you as more than that. But if you don't, that's totally okay. I'll stop watching your stream if it makes you more comfortable. I'll—"

"No." The word is out and I can't stuff it back in. Especially not at the delight that grows on Oliver's face, and the way his eyes darken. "No. Umm." I suck in a breath and let it out slowly. "I like you. Really, I mean that. I don't know you that well, but I know that I'd like to know you as more than a friend, too." I hate that my mind is jammed with memories of his body, his cock, and the way he sounds when he touches himself. Having suddenly allowed myself to think of him that way, now I can't stop.

"Do I get to still watch you stream?" he murmurs against my ear. "Better question; does this mean you'll start watching me again?"

"Do you want me to?"

"Of course I do. And I want all your honest feedback. In detail. I'll give you mine, if you want. Though I doubt I'll be that helpful, since everything you do is *perfect*."

"You're being dramatic. I suck at streaming," I say crisply, not pulling away.

"If you say so." He turns his face suddenly, pressing his mouth against my neck. Before I can do more than take a sharp breath, my stomach clenching in anticipation, he bites down lightly and drags his hands up my hips, bringing my shirt up with them. My breath becomes a gasp, ending in some sort of yelp that has him chuckling as he pulls away.

"You sound like a sweet little puppy," he teases, reminding me of our conversation online before I knew it was him. "Do it again for me, Blair. I bet you make the cutest little sounds while you're flustered, and I want to hear all of them." He kisses me before I can reply, holding me tighter against him until I'm all but in his lap. I lean into him without complaint, closing my eyes as he coaxes my mouth open once again.

That is, until I hear someone clear their throat, and the sound of someone's boot tapping on the porch. I jerk backward, able to hear Oliver's soft, irritated sigh, and look up into Juniper's face.

She looks... unamused, to say the least. Her eyes flit from my face to Oliver's, and her brow furrows in unease. "Are you okay, Blair?" she asks finally, not taking her eyes off of Oliver.

"I'm totally okay," I promise as Oliver pulls away just enough to smile lazily at Juniper. The friendliness oozes out of him like water, and takes my body heat with it, somehow. For a moment, it's as if I'm looking at a completely different person.

"Have you been drinking?" she goes on carefully, still sizing up Oliver like she's prepared to duel him to the death for my honor.

"Just a little. But not that much, and I'm not drunk, Juniper." I sigh, raking my fingers through my hair. But Juniper doesn't look at me. Her brows rise by increments as she stares down Oliver, expression exasperated as if she's telling *him* he should've known better.

"I wasn't going to go any further, Juniper," he promises, getting to his feet with a chuckle. It's not like the ones he has for me. There's no sweetness, and very little friendliness in the sound. Is he mad she interrupted, or does he just not like her?

"I know she's tipsy, all right? I'm the one who found her all alone, after all."

The words are an obvious jab toward my best friend and she looks away, frowning. "I thought we'd go home," she says finally. "It's been an hour, and I know you don't love these things. Come on, Blair." She brushes past me, going down the stairs and pausing on the sidewalk to look at us when I don't move.

I do try, though. Only for Oliver to hold my arm lightly as he drags my attention back to him. I can hear Juniper's exasperation, but my eyes are on Oliver alone. "I'll see you later, okay?" he purrs, leaning in to kiss me again. "Tomorrow, maybe?" His eyes dance at that, because we both know *why* he'll see me tomorrow. The thought sends shivers through me, and I nod.

"Tomorrow," I promise, and brush my lips against his one more time before pulling away from him and following Juniper down the sidewalk.

"It's nice to see you again, Juniper," he calls, not moving from the porch. I don't turn to look at him, but Jun does, and her expression isn't entirely friendly.

"Same," she replies flatly, and walks ahead of me away from the frat house. I do turn, finally, and I'm surprised to find that instead of having gone back in, Oliver is still standing on the porch.

And he's staring at me.

He watches me as I walk away, and finally the privacy fence is what breaks my sight of him, instead of him having gone anywhere at all.

It's also then that Juniper lets out an exasperated sigh. "What were you doing?" she asks as we walk back to her car. "With *Oliver*?"

"Uh, kissing him?" I answer dryly. "Pretty sure you saw it, too."

"He shouldn't have kissed *you*. You're drunk."

"Tipsy."

"*Drunk*."

I shake my head slowly, feeling mostly in control of my actions and not like I'm about to walk into the street. "Buzzed, I'll give you. But nothing else. I like him, Jun. I've liked him for longer than tonight."

"Blair..." Juniper frowns and looks at the keys in her hand, like she's forgotten what they're for. "Can't you pick anyone else? Someone who isn't Oliver Greer?"

The words surprise me, and I look at her in shock. "Why not Oliver? You said you knew him, that you tutored with him and didn't act like there was anything wrong with him." The conversation is killing my buzz, but maybe that's a good thing.

"Well, I wasn't entirely honest. I don't know, he's just." She turns and looks behind us, like he might be listening. "I just think he's not who he's pretending to be. Especially with you. I've seen him mean before, okay? I don't want him hurting you."

"Well I can assure you with every fiber in my being that he has not hurt me," I say, then add, "And actually, I'd be kind of into it in a rough-during-sexy-time way."

She makes a noise of disbelief and maybe irritation. But before I can go on, my steps slow and I come to a stop at the back of her car.

There it is again. The feeling of being watched, of being trailed or like someone is breathing against the back of my neck. I turn, unable to stop myself, and scan the street and both sides of it, only to find nothing and no one. Am I imagining this?

"Are you coming?" Juniper asks, getting into the driver's side of her car and turning the key in the ignition.

I don't reply. Not while I'm still standing frozen, searching the darkness for anything out of place. My eyes rest on a large tree that casts a multitude of spindly shadows, thanks to the light on the house behind it. For a moment, I feel like I can just see someone standing against it, in the darkest shadows of the trunk.

But when I blink, the edges of a figure are gone and it's just me, my mostly-clear vision, and the St. Augustine night. I'm alone, and as I look around once more, the feeling of unease seems to fade a little bit until, finally, it feels like nothing was wrong at all.

Maybe I am drunk. With that thought and a sigh released from parted lips, I open the passenger door and slide into her car, ready for the verbal take down I'm going to get for being so irresponsible and letting Oliver seduce me when I'm drunk. Not that it'll matter, because she *is* wrong about this. I've liked Oliver for longer than tonight, and it's not like he's been waiting around to take advantage of my moment or weakness, or something equally as unbelievable.

Not that she'll believe me.

CHAPTER 13

When my eyes lock with Oliver's and I see him on what I'm starting to call *our* couch, I feel a flush of embarrassment that I'm sure shows on my face. It's weird to know that he *knows*. To have him tip me and send me messages during and after my stream. Last night there were a few times I'd felt almost like I wanted to throw on my t-shirt and end the stream.

But I hadn't. Still, the thought makes me squirm even as I sit down beside him and let him throw an arm over my shoulders.

"Are you okay?" he asks, voice soft and considerate.

"I'm kind of embarrassed," I admit, looking up at him with slightly-wide eyes. "Sorry."

"About what?" The confusion in his voice feels genuine, and yet again I wonder how it's so easy for him to flip on a dime when he's talking to my roommate instead of me. "About...?" he trails off, his brows rising as his smile lessens like he's worried he's done something to upset me.

"I just. I don't know. You've seen *everything* of me. You

know way more than my boyfriends ever did," I admit quietly. "I feel like you'll think less of me, or I should be more upset that you watch me like other guys."

"Don't be." His words are firm, and sweet, and he presses his nose against my cheek. "Jeez, wonder girl. Have a little faith in me. I do the same thing you do, so who would I be to judge? I don't, in case you're confused. I *like* watching you. I like seeing other guys want you so fucking bad they're willing to upend their life's savings for you."

"I don't think anyone is upending their savings for me," I snort. "Apart from you and that other guy, *Thrillingterror*, people barely tip me more than five dollars or so."

He's quieter than I expect while he thinks about it, and instead of answering, he kisses my cheek and draws a surprised laugh from my lips. "Were you okay on Saturday night? I didn't get a chance to really talk to you about it yesterday. Was Juniper mad at you?"

"Nah, but she's pretty mad at you," I retort lightly. "Maybe you should watch your back when you tutor with her. She might stab you with a pencil."

"I don't think she would," he promises absently. "But I've been worried you were more drunk than you said, and more than I thought you were. I would've felt incredibly bad if I'd taken advantage of you, or that you regretted kissing me."

How could I ever regret anything about him? I stare up into the older boy's face, unable to hide the smile curling over my features. "I wasn't very drunk," I assure him. "You didn't take advantage of me in any way, all right?"

Before he can respond, I pause. My lips are parted enough that I'm sure I look like a fish gasping for water, but when a shudder goes through me in response to the hair at the back of my neck prickling, I can't say anything. Instead I turn, half nervous and half accusatory, until my eyes find Professor Solomon's.

Of course he's the source of my misgivings and my anxieties. He always is. Sucking in a breath, I meet his harsh, dark gaze and hold it, like I'm not afraid of him failing me or anything else. Though, I do suddenly wonder what he'll think of the new camera I'm bringing to class today. Not that we normally need to bring them *to* class. More than anything, I've been wanting to show it to Oliver.

Professor Solomon might not even notice it, truth be told.

He blinks, looking like he's fighting the urge to roll his eyes, and strides toward his classroom like he's walking down a runway. I hate him, obviously, but it would be impossible not to appreciate his gorgeous *everything*.

I even hear Oliver give a little sigh, and I turn to look at him only to see him watching our professor as well. "It's a shame he's so pretty," Oliver says without trying to keep his voice as quiet as I feel he should. Though, if he's heard, Professor Solomon doesn't even look over. "No one that mean should be allowed to be so gorgeous."

Snorting, I get to my feet. Professor Solomon's arrival into the classroom always means that it's time to go in, since he barely gets there more than five minutes before class starts. I don't go too close, however, as he unlocks the door and fumbles with his keys for a moment. It's strange to see him nearly drop them, since I had thought only mere mortals did such things.

As if hearing me, Professor Solomon turns to look at me as the door opens, his expression anything but friendly. I still hold his gaze, feeling better with Oliver at my back, and relax slightly when our professor turns his glare on him instead.

And then he's gone, slamming his bag onto his desk, and it's easier to breathe without the stain of his disdain in the air.

I walk over to sit down at my spot at the U-shaped set up, Oliver beside me and scooting the chair closer than it really needs to be.

"I got a new camera," I admit, setting my backpack down gently onto the floor. "I wish I knew more about it, but I think it's a nice one?"

"Yeah?" Oliver looks up with interest clear on his face. "Can I—"

"You could show me instead of him." Professor Solomon's voice makes me jump, and I nearly knock my chair backward at the words. I hadn't been quiet enough, and when I glance up at the clock I'm surprised to see that it's closer to ten minutes before class. No one else will be here until it's almost time to start. Professor Solomon is just that good at keeping them away. "Since I'm your professor and all. And, for the time being, a bit better than he is at all of this." He strides across the room like he owns it, looking down at me expectantly.

"Okay," I murmur, wishing I had some bit of the backbone I'd shown when I'd been in the coffee shop with him. I fish around in my backpack until I can pull out the expensive case that came with it, and set the whole thing on my desk seconds before our professor leans forward to hold onto the case with one hand and open the zipper with the other.

He smells so good. The thought runs rampant in my brain before I can stomp it down, and when I do it's only because he's letting out a sigh I can almost feel against my cheek. His deft hands pull the camera free, examining it before taking off the lens cap to look it over more thoroughly.

"And here I thought you weren't very interested in photography," he murmurs, dark eyes flicking to mine under long, thick lashes that would make any girl jealous. This close, it's so easy to admire the strong line of his jaw, and the way his full mouth accentuates his face perfectly. *Fuck.* Oliver is right. No one this mean should be so pretty. "Where'd you get this?"

That's not what I was expecting him to say, and no matter how hard I wrack my brain, I can't remember the name of the website *Thrillingterror* had me order this from. *Fuck.* Biting my lip, I realize that a lie is going to be obvious, though I'm not about to tell him the truth.

"Someone who means a lot to me got it for me," I say, edging around the truth. *Thrillingterror* does mean quite a bit to me, just not in the way I'm implying. "They knew how interested I was in doing more with this class and sent it to me on Friday."

He stops and looks at me, like he doesn't believe me, before putting the camera back in the bag and zipping it closed again. "It's nice," he repeats. "It's a definite step above the one that you had to get for this class, and I definitely suggest you use this instead. You know how to use this one, right Oliver?" he asks, almost seeming bored.

Oliver snorts. "Yeah, Rook. I think I do." There's a joke in his tone that I don't quite understand, and our professor's eyes flick to his, disapproval filling his expression.

"What did you call me?"

Oliver sits back, grimacing. "Sorry, *sorry.* Professor Solomon—"

"If you want to keep auditing this class, Mr. Greer, I think you should remember that I am still the one teaching it."

To my surprise, Oliver looks... embarrassed. He shifts in his seat, looking away from our professor like he can't quite hold his gaze, and nods again. "Sorry," he says, looking like he means it more than I expect he does.

Professor Solomon snorts, and walks back to his desk when another student strolls in with their eyes on their phone to collapse in their seat near the back. I wait for him to go, and when he's safely seated at his desk and hopefully distracted, I lean close to the still-tense Oliver. "Are you all right?" I ask, a little confused. "He wouldn't really kick you out of here, would he?"

"Hmm?" Oliver blinks like he's just realized I'm talking to him, and his eyes narrow. "No, I don't think so. I'm just usually a lot better at not calling him that to his face." Slowly the grin returns to his features, and he shakes his head as if to clear it. "Don't worry about me, wonder girl. He's more bark than bite." But his voice is softer when he says it, like even he's not too sure about *Rook's* level of irritation with him. His hand wanders up to the back of my chair, and then to my shoulder, and before I can really register the brush of his fingers against the bare skin of my arm, he hugs me to him for a moment before letting go and sitting at a more proper distance from me.

Like he's afraid our professor is going to get on him for that too.

I watch him during class, half-worried about my usually unshakable friend. Though... is he my friend, when he's seen me stream and I've seen him do the same? Is he just my friend, when I spent part of Saturday night kissing him and desperately want to do it again?

When Professor Solomon announces that we're free to go, and to remember to pick our partners for our first project, I hesitate.

Will Oliver be allowed to be my partner? He's not exactly a student, obviously. Not in this class at least. But without him, there are an uneven number of students in the class. *With* him, everyone would have a partner.

"Be right back," I murmur, catching Oliver's surprised look as I get to my feet and walk toward Professor Solomon's desk. Even before I get there I hear him sigh, like he's dreading my arrival, and he looks over at me with his eyes on my middle first, at the line where my denim shorts rise to under my hoodie.

"Can I help you, Love?" he asks, and I can't help flashing back to how *Thrillingterror* calls me that as well. This isn't the time to compare the two, and a small frown creases my lips at the sound of my name from his mouth.

This isn't the time, I chastise myself silently, lips pressed together as I stare him down like I can will him to my way of thinking. "I want Oliver as my partner for this," I say, not asking. Maybe If I'm not as terrified, or I don't act so frightened by him at least, he won't say no.

Slowly his gaze drifts up to mine, and a frown curls his lips downward. "Okay," he says blandly, the one word flooding me with partial relief.

"So it's okay? Even though he's not really a student in the class?" I can feel Oliver at my back, his hand at my waist for a moment, until Professor Solomon fixes him with an irritated look and he drops it.

"Yes, Love," he sighs. "That's what I figured you would do anyway. Though, I suppose I appreciate you asking me permission." Is he... amused? Satisfied? Then again, he might just be disgusted, as he usually is at seeing me.

"Cool. All right." I hover, uncertain, my hands balling into fists at my sides.

My professor glances down at them, then back up at my face. "Did you want something else?"

"No. Nope," I promise, still holding his gaze.

"Then let me be the first to assure you that you can go." He turns away from me again, looking back at his phone as I beat a hasty retreat to my table. I scoop up my backpack, Oliver beside me, and I don't stop until we're close to our couch.

"You didn't think he'd let you be my partner?" Oliver asks,

AJ MERLIN

stepping close and pushing me into the small alcove between the wall and couch.

"Hey, he's still got to walk by," I hiss, a hand on his chest even as butterflies take flight in my body. He makes me nervous, though not in a bad way. At least... I hope it's not in a bad way.

Though, when I stop to think about it, and really examine things, my nerves feel different than just a crush. I feel—

Oliver sweeps in with a low snicker, pressing his lips to mine. He coaxes mine open, standing closer as he works his mouth down to the mark he's left on my neck, and over his shoulder I see Professor Solomon pass without a look toward us, until he gets to the door of his office. Only then does he stop and turn, as if we've made some sound to alert him, and his eyes land directly on mine.

His gaze is unreadable, though I swear I see his eyes narrow just slightly. He hovers, standing there, when suddenly Oliver draws a gasp from me by biting down against my skin. Professor Solomon's brows rise slightly; his mouth presses into a line as he watches me. Watches *Oliver* lick and nip at my skin while holding me against the wall.

I should stop him. Obviously we're about to get into trouble, right? Professor Solomon is going to get us some kind of academic reprimand for inappropriate behavior in the near-empty arts building. And yet he just stands there, watching me, while Oliver's hands slide up my sides as if somehow he, too, knows that we're being watched. Heat climbs into my cheeks, surely staining my face brightly enough for him to see. Butterflies flutter against my ribs, their wings seeming to hammer against them as my fingers curl in Oliver's hair.

I should stop him.

He looks toward the open doors of the visual arts department, blinking a few times as his lips turn down into a frown.

126

Before I can say anything, even if I could say something, our professor disappears into his office and my hand grips Oliver's hair tightly just as I see someone round the corner.

It's Juniper.

She takes one look at my face, but she doesn't just stand there and watch. She grimaces, a look of disappointment on her face as she makes sure to shake her backpack to get our attention, as if she didn't have mine already. "I got out of class early," Jun says briskly. "I thought we'd go home together."

Oliver sighs, resting his jaw against mine. His eyes flutter closed, and for *just* a moment I see something that makes me nervous. He's upset. Not at me, that much is clear. But when his eyes open, he's looking back as well as he can without moving, and all of that frustration and dislike are directed at my roommate.

"O-okay," I say, reaching out to grip his shirt. I've known for a little while now that he doesn't like Jun, and that the feeling is mutual. But I've never seen him look at anyone like this, let alone my roommate.

It melts off of him a second later, however, and Oliver straightens with a light laugh as he runs his hands through his hair. "I'm sorry," he apologizes, flashing her a bright smile. "I'm really sorry, Jun."

"Juniper," she corrects automatically, her dark stare fixed on his. "I don't know why you're sorry." She tilts her head when she says it, like a question, even though it wasn't phrased like one. With her thin lips pressed together and her eyes narrowed, it's obvious to anyone in a ten mile radius that she's not happy.

"Juniper..." I sigh, stepping around him even when his hand tightens on my arm like he doesn't want to let me go. "It's fine. We got carried away, but like I told you the other night, it's really fine." She doesn't look like she believes me, and Oliver sighs again.

"It's okay," he says, in a voice that tells me it's *not* okay that some girl four years younger than him is trying to boss him around. "I need to go talk to Professor Solomon about something, anyway." He flashes me a quick smile and leans in to kiss me on the cheek, his gaze fixed on Jun the entire time. "See you later today?" he asks quietly, and I give him a nod, hoping Jun hadn't heard.

"Bye, Juniper," he says, much too sharply, as he pushes past her to stride across the room. His shoulders are set, back straight, and by the time he's closed our professor's door behind him, it's obvious how irritated he is.

But Juniper only rolls her eyes and folds her arms over her chest. "You're getting a lecture," she promises, as I fall into step with her towards the parking lot.

"You came here to make a scene," I point out, some bit of frustration churning in my chest and pushing out the anxiety at Oliver's reactions. I glance up through the small window of the office door, but I'm unable to see more than Oliver's back as he sits down in a chair. "There's nothing wrong with me liking him, Jun. Nothing wrong at all."

"Yeah?" she asks quietly, reaching out and gripping my hand when we're safely outside. "Then why did he look so upset?"

She'd noticed it too. I shake my head though, frowning. "He looked upset because you're treating him like a child. He's an adult, and so am I. He likes me, and I really like him."

She searches my gaze, her shoulders falling. "Can you please just be safe?" she asks, squeezing my hand supportively. "I don't want to upset you, and I don't want to ruin something for you. But Blair..." she trails off, looking back at the door we'd just come out of.

"What?" I ask, somehow wanting her to say something that would confirm the way I feel about his reaction today.

"I don't know. I guess just be careful. Don't let him hurt you, or I'll have to kill him." She grins, breaking the tension, and I reach out to hug my best friend around her shoulders.

"God." I sigh burying my face against her shoulder. "Our professor fucking *saw us*, Jun. He saw us making out in the hallway right before you came up."

"Fuck." She laughs, gripping my arms as the rest of the tension leaves her. "You must have been so embarrassed."

"...Yeah," I agree, belatedly realizing that I hadn't felt any embarrassment at all. "Yeah, I was really embarrassed. I'm surprised he didn't try to suspend me, or kick me out of college or something."

IT ISN'T UNTIL LATER, when I'm sitting in bed on the phone with Oliver after his stream, that a news header flashes up on my laptop. With the show on silent while I'm having a conversation, it takes me a moment to read the words that pop up on screen.

College student found dead on Wicket University grounds.

"Oliver, hey. Hold on a second," I interrupt, dragging my laptop into my lap. "This is wild. I don't know..." I trail off, turning up the volume as the special report kicks in.

"*What's wrong?*" Oliver asks, concern etched in his voice. "*Are you okay?*"

"Yeah, it's just... some girl was found dead at the university," I murmur, my hand tightening on my phone. "This is insane."

"*What?*" He's just as shocked as I am. "*Do you know her?*"

"No. Well, I don't know; I don't even know who it is. They just said they think it was suicide or something. That's so fucking sad." The report only shows a stretcher being rolled up to an ambulance, a sheet covering all of the body except the top of her head. Her hair is shiny black, the same as Juniper's, and I shake my head again. "That's so sad."

"*That's... awful,*" Oliver echoes. "*Wow, I really can't believe it.*"

"Neither can I," I murmur, shaking my head again and feeling more on edge than I had been before. "I wonder who she was."

"*So do I,*" Oliver says, a sigh on his lips. "*I still can't believe it. On Wicket property? That's awful.*"

"I'm going to go," I say after a few more seconds of watching the news for any other information. "Not because I'm upset, or anything like that. I need to eat, I'm literally starving."

"*I understand,*" Oliver promises with a soft, sweet chuckle. "*Go eat dinner. I'll see you later this week, wonder girl.*"

I hang up with a sigh, staring at my phone, and realize I still need to address the fact that, since he knows who I am outside of my stream, he really doesn't need to send me exorbitant amounts of money anymore.

Next time, I promise myself, falling onto my side as I close my laptop lid. *I'll tell him next time.*

CHAPTER 14

No matter how much I stare at my art history book and try to read the chapter we've been assigned, I can't stop thinking of the girl whose hair reminded me of Juniper. It's a stupid comparison, since a lot of girls have glossy black hair like hers. But for some reason, the thought just won't leave my head, even though it's been two days and Juniper is most definitely fine.

I sigh and open my laptop, navigating to the supplemental reading about late Egyptian art detailing the women in history. My favorite of Egypt's women, of course, has always been Hatshepsut. As Egypt's only female pharaoh, she should be everyone's favorite, in my unasked-for opinion. If not because her reign heralded in a time of prosperity for Egypt, then for the fact that history has tried so hard to erase her without success.

Actually, if I could ever bring someone from history back for a day, or even just for a coffee date, it would be her.

I sit back, sipping my chai, and stare at the laptop as I scroll through the articles we were given to look through, should we have the time and interest. I, of course, have both. Even though I'd chosen a Roman studies minor, it was mostly because Wickett doesn't offer an *Egyptian* minor. Otherwise, I would've been enrolled in a heartbeat. And all that means is that anytime I get to study or look at things pertaining to Egyptian history and art, I'm all over it with frenzied aggression.

Unfortunately, it also means that even though I'd love to find something that distracts me, these articles are ones I've already read. Professor Carmine isn't in the habit of re-assigning work from one class to another, but last year when I'd expressed interest in this, she'd given me work from the advanced class to sate me for the time being.

This, apparently, was that work. Even the reading in the textbook looks familiar, except the last time I'd seen it had been in a stapled together packet of pages with faded text in some spot thanks to a shitty, half-working printer.

I go through it anyway, crossing and uncrossing my legs at the table in the library café. This isn't my favorite place to study, but with no study rooms open and the library louder than usual, being closer to coffee was the best option I could think of.

Sighing, I look up from my work just in time to see Oliver breeze through the doorway of the library. He doesn't look my way, and for all intents and purposes he looks... bored. Especially when he drops a reference book on the return counter, gives a distracted smile, and says something to the desk worker, who takes it from him with a genuine smile on her pretty face.

I'm not jealous, because that would be stupid. There's nothing to be jealous about, since her smiles don't garner more attention from him and we're not, exactly, dating.

My hand hesitates over my phone as I watch him, and I wonder if he wants to be left alone today. Would he welcome a text message from me, telling him I can see him? Or would he find it more bothersome than anything and only come over here because he feels like he *should*?

It occurs to me that there's only one way to find out. I tap my phone to unlock it, then go to the conversation I'm sharing with him to type, and instantly send the words, *I see you.*

Only after, do I realize I sound like a stalker, and I grit my teeth together in regret. That was kind of dumb, but oh well. Might as well not say anything else, since I'm good at making things worse.

Oliver stops talking to the girl and reaches into his pocket to dig out his phone. He glances at it, and even from here I see the bemusement on his face as he reads the message. But he doesn't reply. Smartly, he looks around him until finally turning to look into the attached café through the open glass doors that lead from one building directly to the other.

If I'd thought for a moment he wouldn't be happy, I had been wrong. Delight catches and holds, and he walks toward me without even bothering to tell the girl goodbye. Not that she seems to mind, since she falls into conversation with a professor who's holding a stack of papers.

"Blair," he greets, coming to stand beside me so he can lean down and kiss the top of my head. Warmth blooms in my chest, and I look up at him with a smile of my own. "You're studying," he says, eyeing what I'm working on thoughtfully. "Are you leaving soon?"

"I don't know. But I guess I could," I admit, shrugging. "All of this is material I read last year, so I don't really need to go through it thoroughly once more."

His gaze flicks to mine in surprise, and he says, "I need a book for one of my criminal justice classes, then I'm free. Do you want to wait for me? We can leave afterward.then go get dinner, if you want?"

"I'd love that," I admit, closing up my book. "I have no life, and nowhere to be tonight."

"Give me just a minute, okay?" He jogs away before I can reply, and I'm left with my coffee and laptop in the café, waiting for him. Absently, I throw everything in my backpack and drag my phone closer. In the search bar I type *St. Augustine, FL* and tap the news tab, wondering if I'll see anything coming up about the girl who'd killed herself a few days ago.

Body of student found on Wickett University grounds shows signs of violence.

My heart sinks at the statement, and I scroll down to see if the article will even say *where* she was found, or who she was. Unfortunately, it does neither, and by the time I've read all I can about her, Oliver is back and panting with his backpack slung over one shoulder.

"What are you looking at?" he asks, with interest rather than suspicion. I show him the article and he frowns, his own eyes flicking over the words. "Violence? Holy *shit*," he murmurs. "What does that even mean?"

"Do you think it could be something worse? Like... murder?" I ask, my own voice just as quiet. Every class I've been in since the episode has buzzed with the conversation of the dead girl, though so far, I haven't heard guesses on who it really is. Rumors abound, of course, but nothing to be taken seriously.

"I don't know," he admits, shrugging slightly. "It's fucked up. I know this stuff happens but..." He shakes his head. "Surely, if they thought she was murdered, we'd be on curfew or something."

"Well, not if the killer was really good at making it look like a suicide," I mutter, getting to my feet. When I look up, I see Oliver looking at me with a strange, almost stricken look on his face. "What?" I ask, feeling the cold start of nerves working their way up my fingers. "I just meant—"

"It's a scary thought," he says finally. "That's all. I mean, I hadn't considered that, and it's horrifying." My shoulders relax when I realize he isn't horrified by *me*, which is good enough.

"Where do you want to go?" I ask, following him to the parking lot.

"Did you drive?" he asks instead, and I shake my head.

"I don't really drive," I admit. "I can; and I do when I'm at home. But since Jun has a car and we go almost everywhere together, it seems a little redundant. And she likes it more than me."

The look on his face isn't quite as friendly as it could be when he says, "That's gotta be inconvenient to rely on her for your transportation."

"Ubers and buses exist. So does walking. This is St. Augustine, not some small town in Kentucky."

He grins wryly, shaking his head again. "Coffee or dinner? It's a little late for lunch." A *little*, he says, when the sun is about to sink below the horizon.

Before I can answer, Oliver fishes keys out of his pocket and hits the unlock button, causing the lights of the car beside me to light up and making me jump. "This is your car?" I ask, awestruck. At best, I'd driven a twenty-fifteen sedan.

But this has to be this year's model of a black Mustang with white striped details.

"Yeah," he chuckles, opening the driver's side door. "If you're really good, I'll let you drive it sometime."

I get in beside him, already shaking my head. "And risk wrecking it? No way, Oliver. You'd *own* me if something like that happened." Though it does make sense now how he's okay dropping so much money in my stream... which is still something we need to discuss *now*. "Dinner," I say after a moment. "If you're okay with—"

"I'm okay with anything," he interrupts. "Anything you want to do, just tell me. Except skydiving. I don't like the idea of it, and I don't love heights."

"Okay, well, I doubt we're going to dinner while skydiving," I point out, buckling my seatbelt with my backpack on my lap. He turns the key in the ignition, the car purring to life. I grin and look at him, saying teasingly, "I'm moving in with you so *you* can be my primary mode of transportation. This car is nice."

"Don't say that, wonder girl," Oliver chuckles, shoving the car into gear and pulling out of his parking spot as the moon roof slides open. "You wouldn't like my roommate. He's a snob, and it would be what you'd expect."

"Why not?"

He flashes me another grin. "Because I've heard I'm a shitty roommate." I doubt he ever could be, though I guess it's possible. Messy, maybe? Or maybe he throws loud parties on the weekend.

"You live in Hollow Oaks, right?" I ask, recalling that he'd told me that a while ago.

"I do."

"Is it as nice as the real estate pictures make it look like?"

He thinks about that for a moment, then replies with, "Yeah, actually. I didn't think it would be when I moved in, but I have to admit, it's really fucking nice. Lots of space so I don't have to hear my neighbors, no matter how loud they get, and lots of room for hobbies in my house."

"Do you own it?"

"Nah, my roommate does. Where do you want to go for dinner, Blair?"

He turns to look at me, his foot on the brake and a lazy

smile splayed across his lips as I think back to the matter at hand.

"Have you been to the Mexican grill near where I live?" I ask slowly, wondering what he'd think of cheap Mexican food. "Or there's a diner that serves the best pancakes on this earth near my apartment, too."

"Yeah? Will every food place you suggest be near your apartment, Blair?" he teases, playfulness in every word.

My face burns at the implication, and I close my eyes hard. "I didn't mean it like that," I promise, hands clenching in my backpack. "I only meant—"

"I'll eat breakfast for dinner with you, wonder girl. You don't even have to ask."

It's dark by the time we're done eating, and my mouth hurts from smiling and laughing at Oliver's sense of humor. He pushes the door open for me, having insisted on doing that and paying for our meal, and walks beside me down the sidewalk toward his car.

But I've put off the tipping for long enough, and I suck in a breath to ruin the mood. Thankfully, even though he obviously hears the loud intake of air, Oliver lets me speak. "You don't have to tip me when I stream, Oliver," I tell him, hating the way I sound almost whiny.

"Of course I don't," Oliver agrees, lightly wrapping two of his fingers around two of mine. Juniper's warnings loom in my brain; the most recent being that I'm letting this move too fast with a boy I know too little about.

And maybe she's right, but there's something about Oliver that I can't let go of. I like him; more than I reasonably should, and unless I'm misreading a lot of things, he feels the same about me.

"But I like doing it. And it's not putting me out at all, Blair." He slows to a stop beside his car, smiling sweetly at me in the dirty light cast from the street lamps above us. If this were a movie, it would give him a sweet halo, a romantic glow, even. But instead, it mottles his face in light and shadow, giving him an almost macabre grin instead of the smile he's wearing for me. Even his eyes, his gorgeous green eyes that are brighter than most I've seen, read sinister in the waning light. And for some reason, it makes me pause and just *look* at him.

You really barely know him, Blair, Juniper's voice echoes in my head. *What if he wants this for all the wrong reasons? What if there's something you don't know about him that will hurt you in the long run?*

I stomp down on my thoughts when Oliver starts talking. "If you really want me to, if it makes you uncomfortable, I'll stop."

"I just don't want to feel like you're paying me. I like you," I admit. "You don't have to pretend to be just some guy, because I like you with or without the money you send."

"Then I'll stop," he offers, not making any kind of big deal about it. I thought he'd be a little miffed, or tell me it was an insult to his manhood. "I'll just have to buy you dinner more, instead."

My mouth twitches with a smile. "That's not what I meant."

"Sure it isn't," Oliver teases, striding quickly to the other side of the car as I get in the passenger seat, directions to my apartment on my lips that he follows to perfection. At last he ends up in our parking lot, in the guest spot, and I hate how little I want to leave him.

"Do you..." Juniper's horrified look fills my head. I know what she'd think of this, but she'll be at class for another two hours. Such is the life of a marketing major. "Do you want to come in?"

Oliver doesn't answer immediately. He traces the back of

my hand that rests on my lap, obviously thinking about the question. "Is your roommate here?" he asks finally, not looking up when I shake my head.

"No," I say, when it's obvious he hadn't seen the movement. "She won't be home for at least two hours."

"Do you *want* me to come up?" He finally looks up at me, and the sarcastic words about playing Trivial Pursuit or Uno die in my throat.

"Yeah," I murmur, more softly than I'd intended. "I do; but only if you want to."

His grin is wicked, eyes bright as he gets out of the car and I follow. He waits for me to take the lead, following close at my heels and riding the elevator silently, save for his soft humming and the way he taps the toe of one shoe on the floor.

Am I really letting him come into my apartment?

Am I really doing this?

There's nothing wrong with it. Nothing wrong with any of this, even though my heart flutters in my chest like I'm taking some huge risk. He's not dangerous. Or mean. He's just *Oliver*. Who I'm falling hard and fast for, sure, but at worst this doesn't work out and I have some regrets.

At best, it does, and the possibilities of that are both terrifying and exciting.

I step off the elevator on my floor, my keys in hand as I walk to the end of the hallway. My awareness prickles, and I feel almost as if my neighbors are watching me as I casually unlock the door to my apartment and bow him dramatically with a grin on my face that matches the one on his.

At least, it would if mine wasn't half made of nerves.

"Nice," he appreciates, walking through the foyer and into the kitchen as I lock the door behind me. My keys are hung on the wall before I follow him, trailing behind as he walks around the apartment to see as much of it as he can.

"Juniper's room?" he assumes, jabbing his thumb toward her door.

I nod, heart flipping in my chest like a fish out of water as I push my door open with one shoulder. It's not like it's impressive, or fun, or something interesting.

It's just my room.

Oliver waltzes inside and flips on the bedside lamp like he owns all of it. He walks to the window, looking all around the view, and at my desk where I stream from. His eyes flick to mine when he does, but I all but ignore him as I take off my shoes and lay my laptop on my desk, and place my backpack in the chair.

"It's a lot less cool than your room," I admit, remembering his better computer chair and the dark color of his walls.

"It's fine, Blair," he chuckles, walking to my bookshelf and running a finger over the few titles I have there. "I wasn't expecting some super secret place that told me all of your pitch black secrets."

"I don't think I have any," I admit after a moment's thought. I flop down on the side of my bed while he explores, legs curled up under me so I can watch him as he looks for specks of dust or something else I can't figure out.

"Really?" he asks, coming to sit on the bed beside me. "Not even one?" He doesn't hesitate, and after how much we talked at dinner, I'm not sure I should've expected him to.

Whatever I *was* expecting, it isn't this. It isn't the way he leans forward to catch my lips with his, or the way his hand smooths down my jaw to my throat, where it stays. "Hi," I whisper, when he pulls away just slightly, eyes searching mine. "I wasn't expecting that."

"And that makes it better every time." His eyes dance in the dim light from my bedside table, his other hand coming up to grip my thigh. "We don't have to do anything," he promises, voice soft. "I love your company as much as I love everything else about you. Do you want to just hang out?"

Love is a strong word, though I suppose it does make a point. I know Oliver doesn't *love* me in the true meaning of the word, after all. How could he, when he's only known me for a few weeks?

"No, I'm fine with this," I breathe, then back up to try again, saying quickly, "I mean... I'm more than okay with this. I love you kissing me. And I love kissing *you*. You're—"

He cuts me off with a chuckle, and another soft kiss. "Just remember that you can always tell me to stop, and I will. I would never go further than you want, Blair. I'd never hurt you like that." Strong words, for someone who hasn't known me long enough to know what *too far* might be.

My head spins when he pushes me back onto the bed and takes a moment to kneel between my parted thighs.

Suddenly, it feels like today was a bad day for a skirt—or a really good day, I suppose—as it falls to my hips with the help of his hands on my thighs. He rakes his hands upward, dragging my shirt up from my waist and stopping when it's at the same level as my bra.

Oliver stares at me as my heart races; then leans forward to come down on his hands pressed to either side of my face on the bed.

"You're gorgeous," he says, voice rough. "But I've always known that." He lifts one hand to move it back to my stomach, splaying his fingers against my pale skin before curling them in the waistband of my skirt. My breath catches in my throat, but after a moment, he releases the waistband and instead moves his hand upward, palming my breasts through my bra before wrapping his long fingers lightly around my throat. "You look so good with my hand here," he tells me, sending a thrill of fear-tinged excitement down my spine and straight to my center.

"You didn't tell me you were into choking," I murmur, not knowing what else *to* say.

His smile is apologetic, but he doesn't move his fingers. "Sorry. I got caught up in thinking about you as my sweet, *sweet* little puppy. I like breath play." He gives a soft squeeze of his fingers that sends another jolt through me. "But I would never hurt you, wonder girl. I know how to make it feel so good, but you'll never be in any danger of real damage."

"That's kind of terrifying," I admit, locking eyes with him. Am I really going to let Oliver *choke* me?

He chuckles, his fingers releasing at once so he can brush my bangs back from my face. "I know. We'll work up to it. I won't force you to accept all my kinks, or show you them all at once. I'm not very patient, but I will be for you." He kisses me once more, the same soul-sucking kiss that he's so good at.

When he pulls away, I can't help the words that flow from my mouth, though I definitely should have kept them inside. "What if I want you to?"

"What if you want me to what, wonder girl?"

"Choke me."

His eyes widen, pupils dark against the whites of his eyes as he studies my face. "We're skipping a lot of steps, I think," he says at last. Though I feel the way his hand curls up and over my shoulder, like he wants to so badly he can barely stop himself.

"I've never let anyone choke me," I admit, watching as he moves from between my thighs to the space beside me on the bed.

"What *have* you let someone do to you?" he asks conversationally, while his hand finds the bottom of my tee and lifts it up over my bra. His fingers tease the thin material under it, curving along the wire, and when he meets my eyes, I hesitate. "We don't have to," he reminds me, skimming his fingers back down my body. "I want whatever you're comfortable with, and that's all."

"Liar," I accuse smartly, and he rolls his eyes up to look at me in a way that's just so suddenly reminiscent of our professor that it nearly makes my heart stop.

"Don't be mean to me," Oliver chuckles, sitting up to brace himself on his elbow. He drags my bra up and over my head, with only a little assistance from me, and then locks eyes with me again as his fingers tease at the dips of my collarbones. "And answer my question."

"I've... had missionary sex a couple times," I say finally. "With the same guy."

His fingers pause, but he only shrugs and asks, "Was it simply the most fulfilling thing you've ever done in your life?"

I can't help but snort, fixing him with a dry look that has him grinning once more. "What do you think?"

"I think a girl like you deserves to be *fucked* until she can't stand," he answers smoothly, searching my face for a reaction. I'm sure he gets it. The shock is so quick, that by the time it's dissolved into a pleasurable shudder, it's been plainly written across my face for him. His fingers move, teasing one nipple until I can't help but press my thighs together at the excitement coursing through me.

"I'll never get over kissing you," he adds, his hand coming up to gently grip my throat once more. "Has anyone told you that your mouth is just perfect, Blair?" he leans down, but just before he kisses me, adds, "I can't wait to feel your lips wrapped around my cock."

My gasp at the words is swallowed by his mouth, his hand wandering down my body once more as he teases my other nipple into the same stiffness as the first. His kiss is hard, nearly bruising, teeth nipping at my lip whenever his tongue isn't exploring every space available to him like it's his.

When his hand finds my thighs, he gently taps my leg, a clear signal for me to relax. My hand finds his hair instead, and he waits patiently until I have the courage to let my thighs fall open once more, shivering under his hand.

"So sweet," he purrs against my mouth, wasting no time before his fingers dip under my skirt and panties. "You're always so sweet for me, Blair. Bet you're just as sweet down here." He slides a finger into me slowly, savoring my shiver and the way I chase his mouth for the taste of him. "Greedy," he purrs, delighted, before kissing me again and adding a second finger.

He's so slow, so *relaxed* while he fingers me that it's almost a surprise when I realize that I'm close. His thumb brushing my clit becomes more insistent as I whine against his lips, and when I am finally allowed to breathe again, I can't help but stutter, "I'm going to come, Oliver."

"I know," he replies, a soft laugh on his lips. "I can feel how much you want to. Is this okay? Can I make you come for me?"

"Is that even a question?"

"It is, if I'm asking it."

"Yeah, Oliver. Please make me come."

He groans hoarsely at my words, adding another finger that he languidly pushes in and out of my body. "Come for me, Blair," he growls against my lips, nipping at them more harshly than he has all night. "Come on my fingers. I can feel how wet your sweet little cunt is. Show me how you look when you come. I want to fucking hear the sounds you make."

My hand twists in his shirt, eyes locked with his as his hand moves faster, fingers driving into me and scissoring against my inner walls. His thumb on my clit is suddenly more intense, and I cry out sharply as my orgasm hits me hard, like a pillow full of bricks. My toes curl against the sheets, back arching as he continues to finger my pussy with his eyes fixed on my face.

"Good girl. Good *fucking* girl, Blair. Just like that. Just a little more."

"I can't."

"Yes, you can; I bet you can. I bet you can come again for me."

I shake my head against his chest, my body tense and thighs shaking. I'm too sensitive as my body rides out the aftershocks of my orgasm, and he finally kisses the side of my face and pulls his fingers free, wiping them on his shirt. "You're so hot when you're coming," he tells me, kissing me again instead of letting me reply. "Well, you're sexy as hell all the time. But you're really something else like this." He reaches out, fingers teasing my nipples again.

"Do you want me to—"

"I want *everything* from you," he assures me quickly, as if he's afraid my feelings are hurt. "But I'm also afraid your roommate might be home soon... and if she sees me with my hand in your hair while you're choking on my cock, she'll probably shoot me." He grins when he says it, like it's the biggest joke in the world to him.

Unfortunately, he's right. I shrug on my red tee that's under my pillows, pulling off my skirt as I sit up. The shirt is long enough to cover me anyway, and by the way Oliver reaches out to run his hands up his thighs before standing, I have a feeling he appreciates this more, anyway.

"You don't have to go," I tell him, striding to the window to look down at the street. "I mean, we could always..."

The words die in my throat, and all I can do is stare as I look down at the man standing on the opposite sidewalk.

Is he watching me?

I can't see his face. I can't see anything other than the silhouette of him with his hands in his pockets and the way his face is upturned to look *straight* at my window. Almost instinctively, my arms come up over my chest, and Oliver is on his feet a moment later, arms at my shoulders.

"What's wrong?" he asks, looking down and around. "Blair? Are you okay?"

"I think... he's watching me. He's looking up here—look at him." I gesture toward the man, and Oliver's eyes finally land on his.

"Do you think so?" he murmurs, glancing back at me and pressing a kiss to my cheek. "Why? Who in the world would be watching you?"

"I don't know," I mumble, eyes not leaving the dark shape. "Oliver, I-I know it sounds dumb, but I've been feeling like this for a week or so. Like someone's watching me, or following me. What if they are? What if it's not in my head?"

"I think it's just some weirdo, to be honest," Oliver admits, obviously trying to soothe my fear. "But look, I was going to head out anyway. Why don't I go check for you, okay? I'll see who he is, if he's still there, and I'll chase him off if he's some fucking creep."

"What if it's one of the guys from my stream?"

He's quiet for a moment, considering, then he shakes his head. "No way. You don't give out any private information. There's really no way it's someone like that. You're okay, wonder girl. You're fine. I've got you, I promise." He touches my cheek and I lean into it, eyes still fixed on the shape on the sidewalk.

"Don't get hurt," I murmur, heart rising nervously in my throat. I can't take my eyes off of him, because I know somehow that he'll disappear the moment I do. "Maybe you shouldn't—"

"It'll be fine," he says again, more firmly. "Good night, Blair. I'll text you from my car after I check on this. It's okay, I promise." He kisses my cheek again, and I turn my head just enough so that I can keep my stalker in view while kissing Oliver back. I reach out to touch his arm as he leaves, and his grin is nearly infectious as he turns before leaving the room.

How do you know it's him? my brain whispers softly. *Maybe it's just some guy. You don't even know if he's looking at you.*

Because it's someone, the other, terrified part of me says. *Someone is following me. Someone is watching me... I know it.*

I watch until Oliver jogs across the street, the light no longer illuminating him once he gets to the other side. He talks to the man for a few seconds, finally clapping the other on the shoulder before both of them turn and walk in different directions.

Within a few seconds, the stranger is gone. They turn the corner and vanish from my sight, just as Oliver calls me, and I run to my bedside table to grab my phone.

"Just a homeless guy," Oliver assures me, his voice sounding tinny as he gets into his car. *"He saw lights, was all. And he's waiting for a friend of his or something. He said he'd be more careful, okay?*

"You're... sure?" Disappointment and relief flood my body, and my hand clenches the phone more tightly.

"Yeah, Blair. I'm sure. Nothing's going to hurt you. Just have a good night, okay? Everything's okay."

"I'm probably exaggerating," I agree, after a moment's pause. "You're right, Oliver. I'm sorry."

"Don't be."

"You're headed home then?" I wander back to my bed and sit down, still feeling like I'm not really alone.

"Yep." I hear the purr of his car, and sigh.

"Have a good night, okay?"

"*Right back at you, wonder girl.*"

But I doubt I will. Not when every breath I take makes my lungs want to close up, and certainly not when I wander back to my window and look down to see the shadow of someone at the end of the street, leaning against another building with their face upturned in my direction.

Oliver's wrong about this. Someone is watching me. Following me, maybe. And until I figure out who it is, I doubt I'll have a 'good night' again.

CHAPTER 15

I t's not that I don't trust Oliver, or that I think he would lie to me. Quite the opposite, actually.

It's just that I don't think he's right this time.

My fingers drum against the table, eyes fixed on my iPad as I go through some information for Art History I've looked over at least eight times. By this time through the information, it's nothing I don't already know. It's just me, being me, and not wanting to feel like I've missed something.

And besides, the coffee shop a few minutes away from my apartment is a great place to do work. Especially at five in the morning when it's still dark outside and I simply cannot sleep. Even Juniper isn't up, and since it's Saturday, it's not like I have class.

I just have my loud, unpleasant thoughts to deal with that tell me something is most definitely wrong and that somehow, Oliver is, too.

I chew on my lip as I read, or skim, really, and I don't look up when the door opens again to admit more customers to the shop. It's early, sure, but apparently not early enough for the coffee-addicted to consider staying home.

Finally, I glance up, looking out the window to the street beyond. It's going to rain today, that much is for certain. Already it looks like mist is falling outside, and the sky is so absent of stars or the moon that I can only imagine the storm clouds covering it now.

Will it rain all day?

Taking a drink of my coffee, I turn to another chapter in the book I'm reading, looking for something that I can't recite from start to finish. My book is worn and tagged. Small, bright colored sticky notes are stuck to random pages in a way that looks almost unintentional. Some are marked with a pen with a letter or a dot, but most aren't. Most are just things I'd found interesting or that I knew I'd need for classwork.

Hesitantly, I flip to one, finally glancing up at the woman now leaving the coffee shop. She meets my eyes with a polite smile, brushing sleek black hair back over her shoulder with her small white purse in the same hand, making it awkward. Her eyes are dark, like Jun's, and I notice only a few similarities before looking back down at my book while she pushes her way out of the coffee shop's doors.

While she might look a little like Jun, and be similar to our age, I don't know her. Yet, I can't get the newly-released picture of the dead girl out of my head, stomach churning at the memory of seeing it on my laptop.

Because she looked like Juniper, too. Not that I'd brought it up to my roommate and best friend, because I have no idea how to approach the subject of her looking like the woman who was murdered on campus.

And besides, by this point, I'm sure she's seen it too.

Sighing, I sit back in my chair, one foot drawn up so I can hook my heel on the edge of the seat, and lean back to stare up at the lazily spinning fan above my head. I don't need to be here, studying. It was mostly an excuse to leave the apartment when I'd started to feel claustrophobic and closed in.

Unfortunately, just as it had back home, the memory of a few nights ago and the man standing outside my window drags me back into its depths. Had I been exaggerating? Had I just been worked up over *Oliver* and seen things that weren't there? It isn't a crime to stand across the street from my apartment, even if it seemed like whoever was there had been staring up at me.

"That's dumb, Blair," I sigh softly, and rake my fingers through my hair. I'm being weird for nothing, and I don't know *why*.

Is it because of the way I've been feeling lately? Whether or not the man from outside my apartment had been watching me, I can't deny how I've been feeling or the sense that someone is right behind me, just out of sight, and that they want something from me.

I just can't figure out what, or why, or *who*, even.

Professor Solomon's face flickers through my head, making me cringe. I can't forget the sight of his face, his eyes, the way he'd just stared at me while Oliver kissed my throat.

Why hadn't he looked away?

Better question for myself, I suppose, is why hadn't I stopped Oliver? It isn't like I wanted our professor to see, since there's definitely a chance that it could come back to bite me in the ass with some kind of disciplinary action. Or perhaps he'll just dislike me more in class tomorrow, though I'm not sure if that's really possible.

Either way, I should go home. The rain really is starting to pick up outside, and I don't want to get caught in some torrential downpour that'll sweep me away and out to sea.

It only takes me a minute to stuff my books back into my

backpack, and drain the rest of my cup so I can chuck it on the way out the door. It's not cold enough for a jacket, exactly, but that doesn't stop me from wearing the cute, light-weight hoodie with the puppy on the front that *Thrillingterror* sent me over a pair of denim shorts. I wave at the baristas, who wishes me a good day, and push my way out the door, staring down both sides of the sidewalk and seeing almost no one.

But really, had I expected anything else at this time on a Saturday?

It isn't until I turn for my apartment in earnest that my steps slow, coming to a stop, and I look across the street where I need to go.

Is that him again? A figure covered in dark, loose-fitting clothes is leaning against a building I'll have to pass. With his hands in his pockets and his head bowed, there's no chance of me seeing anything about him. None at all, and somehow that makes it worse.

It's probably nothing.

It's probably no one that'll hurt me.

It's probably *fine*, but the more I try to walk that way, the more my body protests. Finally, I give up; rerouting my steps in my head and remembering I can go down a couple of blocks, over, and up to get to my apartment from the opposite side. It'll take about ten minutes longer, but it'll be worth it to not have to deal or worry about this person jumping out at me to confirm all of my deepest, darkest fears.

Even when logic says he won't do that, and that I'm making a big deal out of nothing. But for this morning, logic can eat a dick. I'm choosing comfort instead.

I take long strides down the block, crossing at the opposite street from where I need to, and travel another block quickly. This isn't a difficult way to go, either. There's still no one around, and I can walk as slow or as fast as I want. Which, this morning, means that my long strides eat up the distance between here and—

I stumble, nearly falling over the purse someone has so obviously thrown into my path as an obstacle. Rapidly I look down at it, confused, and see a small white purse with a delicate chain attached wrapped around my sneaker.

"What the heck?" I mumble, wondering if I'm about to be on one of those candid reality shows that have to do with finding a thousand dollars in the street. If so, I'm about to disappoint all the viewers by not donating it to charity.

Slowly, I unwind the chain and pick up the now-dirty purse. It sports my footprint on one side and grime on the other, but I open it anyway to see if I can figure out who it belongs to, since the surrounding streets are as dead as can be.

I fish around, finally finding a tiny pocket with a few cards placed into it. I grab all of them, hooking the chain over my arm as I do and bringing the cards up to my face so I can read them in the dingy light from the lamp above me. As I do, I try not to notice the way the rain soaks into my hoodie, or drips down my legs uncomfortably.

The first is a credit card, with the name MIKAYLA HAYES typed on it in raised, shiny letters. I run my fingers over the words, committing the name to memory, before moving onto another credit card that sports the same identification, but this time against a background of a black, fluffed up puppy. Moving that one as well, I finally find something that resembles an ID, though when I glance at the state, I see that Mikayla Hayes isn't from St. Augustine, or even Florida at all. It seems she's a resident of Indiana.

I blink once, then again rapidly as I try to make out the picture. Finally, at my wits' end, I fish for my phone and yank it out of my pocket, turning the light on to illuminate the picture on the card.

I know her. The thought rings loudly in my head as I look at the woman who I'd *just* seen in the coffee shop not fifteen minutes ago. Black, glossy hair frames a pale, round face and bangs hang just over dark eyes.

This was the purse she'd been holding at the coffee shop, now that I'm thinking about it. I stuff the cards back into it and look around, confused. If this is her purse, where in the world is she? All I see are a couple of people across the street who haven't even noticed me, and none of them are her.

Turning again, I take a few steps in the direction I'd been heading before. With her purse still clasped in my fingers, I'm not sure what in the world I'm doing, but I wish she'd just pop out of the woodwork and take it off my hands. She has to be looking for it, right? Surely she can't go anywhere without her credit cards and ID.

My eyes fall on the cup a few seconds before my foot hits it, and I roll it around with the toe of my shoe until I can see the logo from the coffee shop I'd just been at. Ice is spattered on the sidewalk, and the lid lies a few feet away from the cup itself, like it was kicked or popped off spectacularly.

Is she okay?

I walk over to the lid, leaning down enough that I could pick it up if I want, but instead, just stand there and stare at it.

Surely something hadn't *happened* to her, right? It's only been fifteen minutes since she was at the coffee shop. Had she fallen? I straighten and look at the fronts of the shops to my right, as if I've somehow missed an adult human leaning or sitting against one.

I haven't.

But my gaze does find the opening to a darker side street that cuts between the buildings, and I can't help but be transfixed, now that I've seen it. Is she down there? Hurt, or maybe with some sort of medical problem?

And am I really going to walk down what's basically a dark alley, before the sun has risen? Taking a deep breath, I clutch the purse more tightly. If something has happened to her, or she's hurt, shouldn't I help?

Well, not according to my brain, which is screaming at me to go the other way, call the cops, or just forget this ever happened. But I don't listen, because obviously I'm not having a hard enough time with my life right now and need a little extra spice.

I don't hesitate once I've decided. I quickly walk down the alleyway, strides long and confident, though I don't feel anything of the sort. My eyes search the shadows, and when darkness swallows up the street, I fish out my phone once more and turn my light back on to see my surroundings.

Instantly, I wish I hadn't. I wish I'd stayed away, that I'd done anything but this. The purse falls from my fingers and I stare at the woman, at Mikayla Hayes, leaning against one side of the alleyway with her eyes open wide, unseeing, and her throat cut so deeply, the wound still gapes and drips with blood that's almost black in the light from my phone.

Things move quickly once I've somehow called the cops, and in my head it's almost like a slideshow playing in front of my eyes, instead of real time. They show up and drag me away, asking me questions I barely hear over the white static in my brain. All I can do is stare at them, mumbling responses to their questions, as I'm backed up and told to *stay*.

Stay, they tell me, as the crime scene tape is unfurled and hooked around the buildings leading into the street.

Stay, I think; with my feet planted on the sidewalk, feeling like they'll never move again.

Stay.

I'm not a dog, but all I can do is stand here, stare at them, and watch the ambulance with its blaring sirens come right up onto the sidewalk with the back doors open wide like arms to receive the dead lady.

It takes me until then to realize I'm no longer the only person here. Someone tries to talk to me, to ask what happened, but I only shake my head like I have no idea. The cops had said to *stay*, so I'll stay. But I won't tell anyone else that I was the one who found her.

I was the one who got here first, and—

"Love." The sharp use of my name drags me out of my thoughts and I jerk around just as a hand comes to rest on my shoulder. My movement forces it off, just as my eyes find the deep caramel gaze of my least favorite professor.

"Professor Solomon?" I mumble through numb lips, confused as to how he's materialized behind me. "What are you doing here?"

He doesn't answer, but then again, he's also transfixed on the body being loaded into the ambulance. "Are you all right?" he asks, eyes finding mine again as his attention falls completely on me.

"Y-yeah," I lie, sure my face is as white and clammy as my hands are. "I'm fine, I—"

"You don't look fine. Did you know her?" Is there expectation in his voice? Resignation? Does he hesitate when he asks, like I think he does? Or am I simply just imagining that he's giving me any signs of having a personality at all?

"Why?" I ask stupidly, not really understanding why I've done it. His eyes narrow, and he shoves his hands in his pockets.

"Because you look like you knew her," he says at last. "You seem really shaken up by this, Blair."

Blair. Has he ever used my name before? I wasn't sure he was capable, until right now. But his words drag the hairs on the back of my neck up and at attention, and I don't answer him right away.

"No," I say at last. "I didn't know her." But something's wrong here. Warning bells are sounding in my head as I look at him, and that feeling of unease hits me in the gut once more. The same one that I've been feeling for weeks.

He shouldn't be here. This feels like something more than coincidence, and I side step around him as a flicker of irritation crosses his features.

He isn't concerned for me, I realize. He wants to know *what* I know, and who she is to me.

"I have to go home," I murmur, my heart in my throat. A frown touches his lips, but he shrugs and shoves his hands in his pockets.

"Just don't get arrested if the cops are still trying to talk to you," he advises in a bored, dry tone. But I know better. I've seen that this isn't nothing to him.

"I can take care of myself," I promise, taking a step back, then another. He only looks at me once, the disinterest fading in his eyes as I retreat from him like a frightened deer. Something in his look changes, for only a second. Anticipation, or excitement, maybe? It's gone too fast for me to tell, and he only shrugs again, as if he could care very little.

Without another word, I flee from him, and I stop by one of the officers to make sure they don't need anything else from me before I head back to my apartment, long strides eating up the distance between him and my locked doors.

CHAPTER 16

I t's not until Juniper texts me and reminds me she won't be back until Monday afternoon, that I realize how alone I am. I remember she'd told me last night, before I'd gone to sleep, that she was leaving around two in the morning to get on her flight home, but I hadn't even thought about it until now.

I *need* her, and her grandfather had the audacity to die and drag her home for a funeral. Well, then again... I hesitate, folding my arms as I stand in my room and just hover. Maybe it's better she isn't here. It's impossible to not draw connections between the two women who looked a lot like my roommate. From their hair, to their eye shape, to their complexion and face shape... *all* of them had similarities to her.

So maybe it's not safe, as long as Jack the Ripper of Juniper-lookalikes is running around. But if she's not here, then I need another option. My nerves thrum and pulse just under my skin, and my heart seems to race in my chest as I recall the look on Professor Solomon's face.

Maybe I'm going crazy. It's a strong possibility, with the

week I've had, and maybe I'm just throwing blame wherever it seems to fit, even without a reasonable excuse to do so. There's every chance that he was just *there*, or that he really does live around here.

So why am I jumping to him being some gory, seasoned serial killer hiding out in St. Augustine, Florida? After all, what serial killer ends up *here*, when there have to be less conspicuous places to go? Like Canada. And would he really be a photography professor?

I'm being stupid.

But that interpretation doesn't hit right, and I still can't shake the way my professor looked at me, or his questions. As if it mattered if I knew her. If he'd killed her, would he have cared? If she were my friend, would my least favorite professor have some kind of regret for what he'd done?

Well, in the month that he's known me, he hasn't exactly shown any kind of fondness toward me, so I doubt it. Though, I can't help flashing back to Oliver kissing me in the hallway, my professor's eyes on mine. And it doesn't help one bit.

Sitting down, I try to figure out what I'm going to do. I have nothing *to* do, for the most part. No homework, no stream, no laundry. I'd planned to just take it easy today and maybe call Oliver, but now I'm not so sure.

Now, all I want to do is stare at the table and run the past hour's events through my head over and over again. Look for some kind of connection or explanation that I can use to chase away the fear and apprehension I feel.

That lasts all of twenty minutes, max, before I drag myself to the sofa and collapse onto it with a groan. My hand finds the remote automatically, and I turn on one of my least favorite talk shows before burying my face in the rough, embroidered pillows that are arranged just so on the sofa.

I'd prefer one of my own, and a better blanket than the

quilt I drag onto myself, but well... It is what it is, and now that I'm here, I don't feel like moving. Not even when my phone digs into my hip and I worry it's going to leave a bruise. My mind drifts, thankfully, until finally I'm dozing with the noise of the talk show and dramatic family reunions filtering through my brain, lending itself to the strangest dreams I've ever had.

My phone wakes me, ringing a muffled noise from my pocket as I turn over to lie on my stomach. The sound gets louder as I do, and I reach back, half asleep still, to drag it out of my pocket and up to my ear without bothering to look at who's calling. For all I know, it's a call to talk about my imaginary car's extended warranty.

"H'llo?" I mumble, still fuzzy as sleep clings to me like a better, softer blanket than the one draped over my legs.

"*Blair?*" Oliver sounds happy, as always, but a little concerned as well. It doesn't do much to wake me up more than I already am, and I just hum my agreement at my name. "*Are you okay?*"

"No," I admit, curling onto my side to face the back of the couch. "I've had a pretty shitty day, actually. What time is it?"

I don't get a chance to look at my phone before he says, quickly, "*It's almost six.*"

At night? Had I really slept for almost ten hours? Glancing at my phone screen, I see he's right. It's nearly six at night, and I haven't eaten all day.

Not that I really feel hungry, truth be told, but I roll off the couch and stumble into the kitchen, anyway. There are a few granola bars in the cabinet, and I snag a chocolate chip one to rip open while I talk. "I had an awful morning," I admit, sitting down at the table and rubbing my eyes. With him on speaker, I have both hands free, and I can still hear his soft sigh.

"*Are you okay?*"

160

"I guess. Maybe? I don't know." I hesitate, half-wishing that I could tell him about my suspicions.

But... can't I? I *like* Oliver. I trust him, even though I've known him for just over a month. But it's still so new, and I already think he's convinced I'm paranoid due to the man outside my apartment last time.

But if I can't tell Oliver, who can I tell? I need help. I need someone to understand my thoughts, or at least disagree with my suspicions. Can't Oliver do that? Besides, out of anyone, he knows Professor Solomon best. Surely, he'd be the right person for the job.

"I found a body this morning," I continue, tearing off a corner of the granola bar.

"Holy shit, Blair." He lets out a whistle, sounding half-horrified, and half-impressed. *"Who?"*

"Actually, I don't know. Some woman I saw at the coffee shop before I left. I was walking home, and I saw her purse on the ground. I thought maybe she'd dropped it and was looking for it and..." My brain so helpfully flashes back to the way her throat had gaped open like a second, smiling mouth and my stomach clenches in refusal as I swallow the stone-dry granola bar piece. It nearly makes me gag and scratches my throat the whole way down like it's covered in thorns.

I cough once, then again, and stand up so quickly the chair rocks back and nearly falls before I right it and grab a bottle of water out of the fridge to wash down the pain.

"Are you there? Are you okay?" The concern outweighs the curiosity in his voice as I sit back down, head in my hands.

"I'm fine," I say, voice only a little hoarse. "I choked on a granola bar."

"How'd she die? Was it...?" he trails off, not saying the last word, but I know what he's asking. *Was it murder?*

"Well, I doubt you spontaneously or accidentally slit your

own throat." I snort weakly, eyes closing hard against the mental image. "So, yeah. I'm going to go with murder, Oliver."

He's quiet for a moment. Then another, until it's been at least thirty seconds since either of us has said anything.

"*I'm sorry,*" he says finally, letting out another soft breath.

"Why are you sorry?" I mutter, fingers raking through my hair as I chase away the last dredges of sleep. "It's not like you killed her and left her for me to find."

"*I know,*" he agrees. "*But I can still be sorry, can't I? It's shit that your weekend is off to such a bad start.*" He pauses, and I hear something rustle, along with the soft, hushed voice of another person. "*Where's Juniper? Does she know yet?*"

"No," I deny, shaking my head even though he can't see it. "She's not here. She won't be back until Monday, and that's at the earliest."

"*Oh?*" He seems surprised, almost nervous, maybe? "*Are you alone, Blair?*"

I snort. "Yep. Alone with my granola bar." I finish it off with a flourish, though the theatrics are for me alone.

"*Why don't we do something? I don't like you being alone right now. I can take you to dinner, or—*"

"I want to tell you something, actually," I interrupt, though I hadn't really meant to.

"*Anything.*" He says it so sincerely, like he won't call me crazy for this next part.

"Professor Solomon was there, at the scene of the murder. He talked to me. I don't know, he was just..." I trail off, trying to think of a word that doesn't make me sound nuts. "I just don't know, Oliver. He was strange. It was weird, and just... It made me uncomfortable." I shrug my shoulders like I can protect myself from the anxiety creeping up on me.

"*Our photography professor was there?*" Oliver asks, voice sharper than I expect.

"Yeah. I know; tell me I'm overreacting. Tell me it's dumb."

"Tell you what's dumb?"

"That I'm half-sure he's stalking me. That I think he has something to do with the murders, or that he's planning to end my life. He saw you kissing me the other day, and he just fucking *stood there.* I don't know. It's just starting to freak me out. It has to be a coincidence, though, right? That he was there?"

"He watched me kiss you?" Oliver's voice is unreadable.

I huff, rolling my eyes behind closed lids. "That's not the important part of the conversation. I just need you to tell me I'm overreacting."

"But you don't think you are, do you, Blair?" Oliver's voice is slow and careful, like he's worried about frightening me. *"You think there's something to this. Will it even help if I say I think you have nothing to worry about?"*

I think about the words, scouring my brain for the depths of my feelings about Professor Solomon. It hits me all at once that I know what the answer is, and I close my eyes hard. "No," I admit, fingers pressed against the wood of the table. "No, I don't think so."

He's quiet again for half a second, and I strain to hear anything at all. *Nothing.* As if he's muted himself on the other end, or my connection has gone dead.

Then, all of a sudden, he's back with a sigh, the first part of it sounding sudden, as if he really had been muted. *"Good,"* he says, voice soft. *"Because I don't think you're wrong this time."*

My heart thunders in my chest, threatening to close off my airway. "What?" I whisper, staring down at the fake wood grain of our table. "What did you say?"

"I've had certain... thoughts about our professor for a while. And lately, with you? He's never been this mean. I think you might be right. And I'm scared for you, Blair. I'm terrified that if you are

right, then he's going to do something. Does he know where you live?" His voice picks up, words becoming faster, like the possibility of them has him nervous too.

My own body feeds off of it, receiving his fear and embracing it. I can barely breathe as I start to tell him no, only to stop suddenly. "I don't know," I admit in a whisper. "Fuck, *I don't know.*" What if he does know? What if he's always known, or maybe I told him today by coming straight here after finding the body?

Fuck.

"Okay, hey. It's okay. You're still okay." He sounds hurried, and I can hear the sounds of footsteps and a chair being pushed back from the table. *"Let me come get you, all right?"*

"Why?" I ask stupidly, getting up as well, like he'll be at my door in the next minute. "What are we—"

"We'll come back to my house. It's safe here. You'll be safe here."

"What about your roommate?"

"He just left a few minutes ago, and he'll be gone until Monday. You'll be safe here, Blair. With me." He makes a noise like he's frustrated, and I hear the jingle of keys from his end. *"I'm coming to get you. We'll come back here and figure everything out."*

"Promise?" I ask, leaning against the counters as a rush of relief fills me. "You really don't think I'm crazy?"

"No," Oliver's voice is resolute and firm. *"Never, Blair. I know you, and I know you're not crazy. Just let me come get you, and I'll help you figure this out. Okay?"*

"Okay," I agree, and tell him a quick goodbye as he hangs up and I'm left to wait until he gets here, every moment more agonizing than the last when he promises the safety and understanding I won't find in my empty, dark apartment today.

If only Juniper were here. But as it is, I guess I should count my lucky stars that I have Oliver.

Thirty minutes later, I'm bounding down the stairs of my apartment building, taking them two at a time in my haste to get to Oliver. He's exactly where he'd said he'd be, in his black Mustang that's right outside my building. The rain is coming down harder now, and by the time I'm in his car, my blonde hair is wet enough that I'll be feeling water seep into my scalp for a good five minutes, at least.

Oliver smiles, concern etched on his features, and doesn't move the car as he asks, "Do you have everything you need?"

"If you mean my phone, my fear, and my hoodie, then yeah," I assure him, showing him my phone. When I open my eyes, I see his eyes are fixed on my hoodie, however, and he gives me a quick nod.

"It'll be okay," he promises, and swiftly pulls away from the curb. The radio is on low, and I close my eyes to listen to the drifting sounds of a news channel, interspersed with music breaking in from another channel now and then.

Is this really what Oliver listens to? Or is he just too distracted right now because of me?

"I'm sorry," I say, jarring him out of his thoughts. Truthfully, this is the quietest I've ever seen him, outside of the penalty of death from Professor Solomon during his lectures. But it's hard to think anything of it when I'm not one for conversation right now, either.

"Why?" Oliver asks, surprised. He reaches out and lays a hand on my bare thigh, gripping it lightly with his fingers splayed across my bare skin. "You don't need to apologize, Blair."

Shivering under his fingers, I don't open my eyes, or move my head from the headrest behind me. "I'm just..." I suck in a breath, then let it out in a rush. "I didn't want to get you involved in my problems."

"I like you too much for you to keep me out of them," Oliver chuckles softly, trying to sound normal. "But seriously, it's okay. I'd rather help you than have you do something that gets you hurt."

The wording is strange, but it's probably just my brain making things seem off. I frown as he drives, watching the streets and businesses pass by outside the window as the sun sinks below the horizon. Closely packed buildings start to space out, and the facades look cleaner, fancier, and just all around nicer as we approach his neighborhood.

"You really don't think I'm crazy?" I ask, as he turns into the *Hollow Oaks* housing development. Large, pristine houses rise above us, trees decorating the yards with beautifully manicured bushes interspersed around large porches. I could never afford to live here in my life, and I still can't imagine how *Oliver* can.

"No," Oliver promises, pulling into a driveway at the end of the street. Woods bracket the far side of the yard, giving the house only one neighbor that's separated by trees and a privacy fence. "I just think the fact that both of these women look like Juniper is really messing with your head. Understandably so, I mean..." He gives me a look and gets out of the car, closing the door hard and walking around the front of it to come to my side.

He's right. That they look like Juniper *is* blowing my mind a little. I open my door and when Oliver reaches out to lace my fingers with his, I take them while my brain spins a mile a minute. His house is nice, I think, looking around the well-manicured yard with its pristinely kept trees that shelter the entrance almost completely.

But I can't appreciate it fully, and not just because of my lingering suspicions. He leads me up the step to the covered porch and shoves a key in the door, hand almost trembling. Is he worried too?

The lock turns, then he pulls me inside, and I finally realize what's been bothering me. When Oliver tries to lead me past the entryway, already closing the door behind me, I lock my knees and stand still, eyes narrowing.

He looks back, brows climbing toward his bangs in surprise. "Come on," he urges, gently pulling on my hand. "I figured we'd go to the kitchen to talk. I have food, and you look hungry."

"No," I say, my grip loosening on his until he's the only one holding on. His eyes narrow, and I can see him trying to calculate what's bothering me. "Oliver." I blink, my heart hammering in my chest as my stomach twists into knots. "When did I tell you that both girls looked like Juniper?"

I'm expecting an answer. I'm expecting a denial, or for him to tell me that I told him in the car and I just don't remember. It's possible, after all. I could've said it without realizing.

But he just looks at me, and a soft chuckle drifts towards us from further down the hallway, just as Professor Solomon rounds the corner to lean against the wall, arms crossed over his chest as his eyes glitter in the bright light of the house.

"I told you that you'd mess it up before you got back here, Oliver," he says, though his eyes are fixed on mine. "Didn't I?"

CHAPTER 17

T ime seems to slow and comes to a stop as I look at Professor Solomon standing barely ten feet away. He looks at me, boredom etched in every line of his body, and leans more fully against the wall. Dressed in a black tee and snug jeans, he looks just a touch more casual than he does when I see him in class.

"I didn't fuck it up," Oliver murmurs, obviously not frozen like I am. He throws a reckless grin in our professor's direction, then looks back at me, his fingers still gripping mine tightly. "Don't make this into more than it has to be, okay?" he asks sweetly, patiently even. His eyes, fevered and excited, say something different.

Does he *want* me to freak out?

"Let go of me," I whisper, pulling steadily back as I set my heels against the carpet.

"No," he replies, and takes a step toward me. "No, wonder girl. Not this time." He pauses, eyes searching mine as both of us seem to take a breath. "Don't," he whispers, a warning, but it's too late and I have no intention of listening to anything he says ever again.

I jerk backward with all my might, gasping as my hand rips free of his. Whirling, I scrabble for the doorknob, only to realize when Oliver's arms wrap around my waist that I never should've turned my back to him.

Screaming, I manage to open the door, his jerk on my waist only helping to pull it open. It comes with me, then slips free from my hands when he turns enough to slam his foot against it so the door crashes forward on its hinges and shakes the house.

I scream and writhe, and do everything I can to get out of his hold as he hoists me higher in his arms. My hands find one of his arms, and I dig my nails harshly into his skin, expecting him to loosen his grip, or at least yell at me for how much it hurts.

Instead, he *laughs*. Oliver fucking giggles as he carries me down the hallway, legs flailing as I kick out and try to grab anything I can. One of my shoes catches an end table, and Oliver doesn't even stop as it crashes to the floor, a lamp shattering and an obvious lost cause. My hand shoots out, catching onto a doorframe, and it finally forces Oliver to stop unless he wants to break my arm.

It should give me a few precious moments to think, except that Professor Solomon is there, gently unhooking my fingers. "You're going to hurt her," he admonishes, eyes narrowing at Oliver as he easily dodges a kick from me.

"She's going to hurt *me*," Oliver protests, once more the target of my heel against his kneecap that makes him grunt. My now-free hand goes up and back, and I find his hair and *pull*. "For fuck's *sake*, Blair!" he snaps, finally staggering into a larger room and spinning around enough that I realize we're in the kitchen. "I'm not *hurting you!*"

"Let go of me!" I scream, unable to do more than this. He bumps into the counter, and I throw my shoes onto it for some kind of leverage, but when Oliver pulls back, all I've managed to do is knock a bowl of bananas to the floor and shatter it.

"Find somewhere to *sit*, Oliver," our professor sighs, following after us and kicking the shards of porcelain to the side. "Unless you're going to throw her into the dirty dishes next." It's even more frightening that he's this calm, because that feels *wrong*. If he's this calm, it can't mean good things for me, can it?

"I didn't think she'd fight so much," Oliver snaps, finally shaking free of my grip. He sets me down enough to readjust, this time pinning both my arms even as I go deadweight to try to make him fall. It doesn't succeed, of course. Nothing seems to be going well for me today, and I sob in fear and defeat as he hauls me backward and sits down hard on a kitchen chair pulled away from the table with me in his lap.

I scream again, wordlessly, letting out the panic I feel and hoping that someone, anyone, can hear me. "Let go!" I cry, barely noting the tears streaming down my face as I turn my face to Oliver's. "Please!"

"Please?" He raises a brow as another chair is dragged over. "I might need stitches from your claws, and that's the best you've got?" In response I kick him, and he lets out a chuff of surprise and, somehow, amusement. "Don't make me—"

"Stop." Professor Solomon's hands are suddenly on my bare thighs, just above my knees, and before I can do more than pull back my leg to kick, he slips his fingers under them, scooting closer, and holds me there so I can't do anything that would hurt him.

Even when I try to kick backward at Oliver, I can barely move more than a few inches. It's just enough for the professor's fingers to dig into my skin, and for him to frown at my efforts. He opens his mouth again, but I cut him off with another, hoarser scream, and I can't miss the way his smile turns a bit dark.

"All right, all right, little puppy. Howl it all out." Which I do, screaming for help again and again as both of them hold me there, unable to move. "No one can hear you, Love," he informs me, when I gasp for more air to do it again. "But come on. You have more in you, I can feel it. Howl again, puppy, there you *go*." He enunciates the last word as I scream again, but it's starting to feel pointless, since no one has come to bang on the windows and the cops aren't speeding down the road.

Not only that, but it doesn't seem to bother either of them at all.

I tremble, gasping for breath as my heart pounds, and try again to writhe against Oliver's lap, trying as hard as I can to free myself from them.

"Are you done now?" Professor Solomon asks, letting go of one of my knees. "Kick me, and you're getting tied up," he adds, when my leg tenses to do just that. "I don't want to tie you up, Love. I don't want to upset you more."

"Too late," I gasp hoarsely, wrenching backward against Oliver's shoulder as he reaches forward with long, graceful fingers toward my face. He smiles, but it's not like I can go anywhere, and within a few moments, he's wiping the stray tears from my cheeks in a surprisingly gentle motion. "Just let go of me," I beg, trying to look back at Oliver and failing. His grip has loosened enough to no longer be painful, though he holds me firmly enough that I doubt I can go anywhere. "I-I won't tell anyone anything. I'll leave, and you'll never see me again, and—"

"Oh, baby girl, no," he chides, cupping my jaw in his hands.

I fight the urge to bite him, though I barely manage not to try. Instead, I bare my teeth at him, and I can see in his face that he knows what I want. "You're confused. And besides... you don't know anything *to* tell anyone. But don't worry. We'll change that for you—"

"I don't want to—"

"But we do," Oliver purrs against my ear. I tense up again, prepared to run, and he adjusts his grip so that my arms are comfortably pinned under one of his, and he can reach the other up to lightly grip my throat.

"Oliver." Our professor's voice is a warning.

"She let me do it before," Oliver argues sweetly, though his touch on my neck makes my breathing pick up and I draw my knees back to kick anything I can.

"Not right now." He knocks Oliver's hand to the side, his hands coming back to my knees to hold them gently in warning. "He won't hurt you, Love," he soothes, rubbing circles against my skin. "Just relax. You're not being hurt."

"Why?" I ask, my voice high and panicked. "Because you want to play some sick fucking game before you kill me?" I cringe at my own words, but I don't want to go out sobbing and simpering.

"No one's going to kill you," our professor promises. "No one's going to hurt you. Not Oliver, and not me." He reaches up to smooth his hands over the hoodie I wear, and murmurs, "I knew you'd like this."

"You knew I'd—" It clicks in a way that makes me sick. "You're *Thrillingterror*. So, you bought me the fucking camera and..." I can't finish, but he doesn't need me to. A smile spreads across his lips, only to fade a second later. "Let me go."

"No. We weren't going to do it this way," Oliver admits, his fingers plucking at my sleeve. "It was just going to be me for a while. I thought maybe after the semester, I could get you used to the idea, you know?"

"The idea of *what?* You being a murderer?"

He snorts and shakes his head. "Of *us.*"

Us.

Us?

"I don't..." I trail off again, eyes locking onto Professor Solomon's. "You," I accuse, like I don't need any other part of the argument to be said aloud.

"Oliver's so sweet," he agrees readily. "And you were practically in love with him when you first met. Even before you took what you saw from his stream and copied it for yourself. I only watched you because he asked me to help. He said he didn't want you getting bullied, and he knew I'd step in. But then?" He shrugs. "And don't lie. You liked me before you knew it was me."

"Don't worry," I assure him. "I don't like either of you anymore." I can't help but writhe once more, but I don't get far with their hands on me. Especially when I don't kick out at Professor Solomon, and I see in his eyes the confidence that I won't do it.

"I didn't mean for you to get so close today," Oliver explains sweetly, his lips brushing my ear and making me shudder. "I didn't know you were up, let alone at that coffee shop. It was five am, Blair," he laughs disdainfully. "What were you even *doing?*"

"You killed her," I breathe out, closing my eyes hard. "I thought it was *you.*" I let the words go, aiming them at my professor, who shook his head.

"No, Love. Not me. It isn't me who's lost a bit of control these past couple of weeks." He pins Oliver with a glare, and I can feel the younger man shiver behind me.

But that just makes it even worse. If *Oliver* was killing them and if *Oliver* knew that they looked like Juniper, then the answer to *why* is obvious.

"You want to hurt her," I accuse, fingers tightening on Oliver's wrist. "You want to kill *Juniper*. Why? She's never done anything to you. Jun's my best friend. She's my *only* friend, Oliver. Why would you—"

"Because she just. Won't. *Stop*," he goes on, desperation and frustration tinging his voice. "She keeps trying to pull you away from me. She thinks I'll *hurt* you. Even when you aren't around. Even when it's just me and her, and I'm trying so *fucking* hard—" He breaks off and turns, burying his face into the side of my throat so sharply that I can't pull away from his bared teeth.

"I want to kill her," he admits against my skin in a tone almost mournful enough that I think, for a moment, he's asking for absolution. "I want to *hurt* her, Blair, that's true. But I won't stop at that. I'll take her apart and teach her that she never should've stepped between us."

"No—"

"But I won't, because it would hurt you. I would *never* hurt you." His teeth scrape against my throat, and wildly I wonder if he'll bite down hard enough to draw blood. "So I kill them instead. They remind me of her, so I replace her with *them*. Because I don't want to hurt *you*."

"That's... You're insane," I whisper, unable to look at either of them and closing my eyes instead.

"I didn't think you'd be there. I wanted to be closer, so I could pretend... Just pretend it was her, especially with the way she looked and the way she fucking smiled—" he exhales against my throat. "Really, I'm doing it for *you*."

"Don't say that, Oliver—"

"I'm doing it so I don't hurt *you*, Blair, I—"

But I don't let him finish. I'm afraid of what he'll say, of what's going to come out of his mouth. So I scream, and lash out, kicking out at Professor Solomon hard enough that he has to catch himself on the table in order not to fall backward. The momentum allows me to slam Oliver back as well; the chair toppling with our combined weight and cracking against the floor. I don't know if it splinters. I don't stick around long enough to find out as I dizzily scramble to my feet and look around, trying to find the way out.

Except that isn't going to happen. Professor Solomon rushes to his feet and darts toward the hallway, blocking it with a warning clear on his face.

Shit. I don't know what to do. My head pounds, and my chest feels tight as I pant for air. Is this hyperventilating? Every time I try to drag in oxygen, my lungs refuse most of it and my chest *burns* as I frantically look for a way out.

"Be careful." My professor's eyes are on mine, but he isn't talking to me. "Don't scare her. She's panicking, Oliver—" I don't stick around to hear the rest of it. I dart off toward the back of the kitchen, realizing belatedly that it leads to a half-flight of slick wooden stairs that I scramble up.

Near the top, something catches my ankle and I scream, throwing myself forward so hard that I rip free, and my feet hit the landing above.

But I'm going too fast, and I'm too uncontrolled. Panic has my vision reduced to a pinpoint, and I can barely see anything except the door at the end of the hall. I just need distance and space. I need a wall between us, so I use my momentum to lunge forward, ripping free of Oliver's hand on my hoodie.

It's just enough, however. Just enough to pull me off course and cause my feet to tangle up with one another. I meet his worried gaze with wide, panicked eyes as I fall backward, hands flailing and floundering for anything to catch myself on.

A sharp pain in the back of my head lets me know that I

haven't succeeded, and the floor finds me sooner than I could've righted myself. I gasp once, as blackness floods my vision, and smothers my consciousness until even Oliver's panicked face has faded from view and I'm alone in a sea of blackness.

"You're an idiot." The words echo and reverberate like a worn out violin inside my head. As does the sigh that accompanies them.

"I didn't mean to! How was I supposed to know that she'd do that? It was crazy, Rook. How the *fuck* did she even kick you like that?" He laughs in spite of himself, and I can't help the groan that leaves me, though most of it is muffled by the soft, fluffy pillow under my face.

"You're all right." Gentle fingers touch my face, stroking down my cheek, and the ice pack on the back of my head is pressed a little more firmly against my skin.

"No, I'm not," I mumble, too afraid to open my eyes. "Not if I'm still in your fucking house."

Professor Solomon chuckles, still smoothing my hair under his fingers. "I think you might be concussed, Love."

"Don't call me that." The request is unreasonable, at best. It's my last name, after all. But I can't stand the way he says it like it's a nickname, or like a pet name.

"All right, baby girl." That's worse. "Whatever you want." He has to know I'm still upset, and I shudder when he runs a hand down my arm. "Can you sit up for me?"

"No."

"Blair—" Oliver breaks off suddenly and hisses a soft curse. "I didn't mean to hurt you—"

"You're killing people that remind you of my *best friend*." Hysteria is flooding back to me, and it makes my head throb. I groan, dragging one hand up as if to touch my head, but Professor Solomon catches my fingers in his.

"No, don't do that," he murmurs. "Not yet. You're all right."

"You're going to kill me." Fear twines through my words, and I finally open my eyes to see that he's much closer than he has any right to be. This close, I can see the fullness of his parted lips, and the way his eyes are such a prettier shade of brown than I've ever seen before.

"Never," he promises in such a sweet voice that I almost believe him. "Oh, Blair." I cringe away from his fingers that stroke my lips, but he doesn't seem to give a damn. "There are a lot of things I want to do to you, but none of them are meant to hurt you. I hate that it's reached this point, but now, at least, I can explain a few things to you."

"I don't want to hear them." He presses his thumb against my lip and my eyes narrow. "I'll bite you," I promise, showing him my teeth.

As if to encourage me to do so, he slides his thumb across my lips and pushes past my teeth until he can press against my tongue. I set my teeth against it, eyes still on his, and *bite.*

But he just... doesn't care. He doesn't move or pull back. In fact, he just fucking *chuckles* and slips a finger under my jaw to hold my face like this, so I'm unable to look away from him unless I close my eyes. Does he not feel the pain from my teeth?

"Oliver fucked up," he tells me emphatically, every word enunciated. "He's not what you think he is." I try to move my lips, to say something, only to realize that in this position, with him able to hold my jaw, I can't say a damn thing. His smile widens when I suck in a nervous, shocked breath at the realization. "He can't always help himself. Though, I'm working on that. He won't get caught from this, I promise. And he's not going to kill your friend. Though perhaps, if you give two shits about the women in this city who look anything like her, you'll tell her to back off, okay?"

He says it so sweetly, like the kindest suggestion, but it's not that. Not by a long shot.

"You're going to have to stay here for a few hours, as much as you obviously don't want to. I'm afraid you might have a concussion, and I just want to watch you to make sure you're okay."

When I shake my head, he only smiles empathetically and goes on, "Like I said before, this wasn't how things were supposed to go. It was supposed to be him, then me once you were more open to the idea. And maybe, at some point, we'd let you in on the rest of it. But not until you liked us much more than you do right now. But that's all right, isn't it?"

I bite down so hard that my jaws ache, but he still doesn't even flinch. He doesn't even seem to *notice*, quite frankly. Finally he releases me, and forcefully helps me to sit up, though even through that he remains so gentle and steadies me as I lean back against the sofa with nausea rising through my body.

"There you go," he praises, like I've done something worth celebrating. "How's your head?"

"It doesn't hurt enough for me not to walk on out of here," I promise hoarsely, glancing down at the hand I'd bitten. He notices, and shows me that, apart from a red mark on his thumb that looks like it's bruising, he's absolutely fine.

"Your roommate isn't here," he reminds me, as Oliver sits down gingerly to my right. I flinch away, but he grabs me gently, his face still etched with worry. "You're not going home tonight."

"I'd rather go to a hospital."

"You don't need a hospital, Blair," Professor Solomon

snorts, getting to his feet. "You just have a bump on your head."

"Then let me go, Professor—" I break off when I say it, hating that I still want to call him *Professor*.

He notices, though, and the smile twitches into place on his lips. "It's Rook," he informs me gently. "Outside of class and school, it's Rook. Don't be like him when he acts like he's getting away with it during class. He's just trying to get punished."

"What?" I murmur, looking at Oliver who grins apologetically. "So you're..." It clicks in my brain and I close my eyes again, thumping back against the plush sofa with a wince. "You were totally just fucking with me this whole time."

"*Blair*." Oliver sounds shocked, and a little bit hurt. "What do you mean?"

"You're with *him*, not *me*."

"Oh, wonder girl, no." He draws my hand into his lap, though I can't help turning to dig my nails into his skin defiantly. But just like Rook, he doesn't bother to even do me the courtesy of flinching. "Well, yes, I suppose. I love him. He keeps me out of jail, and he's been my everything for years... until you came along."

I open my eyes, feeling just as nervous now as I had a minute ago. "But—"

"But just because he's my everything, doesn't mean you can't be too."

"You don't even know me," I point out. "Not really, and I certainly don't know you. You can't say shit like that."

Rook walks away, as if bored with the conversation, and comes back while Oliver is explaining the fact that he can absolutely love more than one person at a time.

"Here." My professor cuts him off and holds out a can of ginger ale for me.

I swallow hard and gaze up at him, eyes narrowed. "Drop dead."

He grins. "Well, I can always *make* you drink it. It's not poisoned, Love." He sits down on my other side, giving me the impression that I'm caged in with absolutely nowhere to go. As I watch, Rook opens the can and takes a drink, as if to show me that it is not, in fact, going to melt my organs from the inside out.

That's what I'd thought, at least. He sets the can down and swiftly leans forward, kissing me hard and gripping my jaw so I can't go anywhere. I shriek in surprise, my arms suddenly gripped from behind as Rook opens his mouth and lets the ginger ale drip into my mouth, from his tongue to mine.

I don't have a choice. I swallow, nearly choking, but he doesn't *stop*.

He kisses me, barely letting me choke the ginger ale down, and his other hand comes to my waist to press against the bare skin of my side under my hoodie. Or rather, the hoodie *he* got for me that I'm still wearing.

"Do I need to do it again?" he growls threateningly, tongue tracing my lips to find any traces of ginger ale. I shake my head as much as he'll allow, dragging air into my lungs as I stare at him.

It hits me, then, for the first time. He isn't like Oliver at all.

He's so much worse.

"Then open your mouth." I wish I could beg for him to go back when he was letting me drink it on my own. I wish I hadn't told him to drop dead. Especially when he lifts the can to my lips and pours just enough into my mouth for me to swallow. But the can is replaced with his mouth a second later as he presses his tongue against mine to make sure I'd done as he'd said.

"I can-I can do it myself," I whisper, eyes wide as I stare

into his face. I find myself pulling away from him, even though that means going closer to Oliver. But frankly, right now, Oliver feels like the lesser of two evils to me.

"Sweet Blair," Oliver purrs in my ear. "There you go; I'll be your safe haven." The words make me shudder, and I realize I haven't been as subtle as I'd intended. His arm wraps around my waist, pulling me flush with the front of his body as Rook closes the distance between us once more.

"Please—" I choke out, feeling my heart thrumming in time with the pain in my head. "I won't tell. I don't know what you *want* from me."

"You don't?" Rook tilts his head to the side and holds the can out for me to take. I do, fingers trembling, and take a small drink of it that I hope is sufficient for him. Of course it isn't, though, and he touches his fingers to the can in a clear message to drink more.

"Love, we just want *you*."

The words make me choke, and my eyes stream as I nearly cough ginger ale all over his nice t-shirt. But he doesn't seem to mind. Instead, he pulls me closer to him, so that I'm held between them in a living, breathing cage. He rubs my back, taking the can from me in the same motion, and murmurs in my ear that everything is fine.

Even though it isn't.

"Are you going to let me go? For real?" I ask, when he sits back again and I'm no longer hacking up a lung. "Tonight?"

"As soon as I know you're okay," Rook promises. "Like I said, I want you to stay here until I know you aren't concussed."

"What if I tell someone?" I don't mean to say it. I don't mean to say a fucking word other than 'okay' or something else just as innocent, but I can't put the words back in once they're out.

But Rook just... shrugs. Behind me, Oliver chuckles against my hair. "Then you tell someone. Maybe a cop comes looking at our door, and they don't find a damn thing. Maybe they do an investigation, and they find nothing. Just like they've found nothing every single time Oliver has laid a body at my feet before. Do you think this is the first time I've cleaned up one of his spree victims, Love?"

"Are you not a killer, then?" I ask, hating the curiosity I feel at his words. "Is it just Oliver?"

"No," Rook promises, shaking his head. "I'm just better at controlling myself. And I don't have a lot of time to have my own fun when he's out killing lookalikes of your roommate for his own needs. If you go to the police, it's likely no one believes you. No one looks at us twice. Neither of us gets caught, and you look like the girl who cried wolf."

There's no threat there, and I shiver at the touch of his fingers on my jaw.

"What if I don't want *you*?" God, I should really learn to keep my mouth shut. "Either of you?" I don't, obviously. How could I?

"Then prove it," Oliver growls in my ear. When I start to speak, he cuts me off with a finger against my lips. "Prove it when you aren't so worked up, and we haven't scared you so badly. *Prove it* when it counts, not when your fight-or-flight instincts are taking over."

"I won't feel any differently in the morning," I reply, eyes on Rook's. "Or the next day or whenever."

"Then prove it," he agrees with a shrug. "Prove you want nothing to do with us, sweet little puppy, and we'll leave you alone."

It can't be that easy, I think. Even when they watch me drink the rest of the ginger ale and leave me alone on the sofa, only coming in to check on me once in a while to make sure I'm not dead, I know nothing can be this easy.

Not even when I'm in an Uber on the way home, with Rook having paid for it himself and the driver promising to get me home safely, do I think for *one moment* that all I have to do is *prove* I don't want anything to do with them so that they'll leave me alone.

Because if so, this will be the easiest thing I've ever done, and I won't even have to try.

CHAPTER 18

By the time the door opens and I can hear Juniper shrugging off her jacket in the entryway, I've thought of twelve different ways to tell her about Rook and Oliver. I've come up with seven plans as well, and at least two of them involve moving to Bora Bora. Another includes reinventing myself in the Arctic Circle, and since I like the cold, it seems like a good option. Maybe I'll become a sled dog trainer up there.

I've considered all the ways I'm going to tell her. That I'm even considering springing it on her when she opens the door into the kitchen, but when she does...I just sit there and smile. "Welcome back," I say, in response to the clear confusion on her face. Normally I'd be asleep by this time, though, to be honest, I've slept most of the day, including during the time I normally stream.

But I can't stream when I know who's watching.

"Are you okay?" Juniper asks, sliding into her seat at the kitchen table. I sigh and look down at the fake wood grain, rubbing my finger along it while she watches.

"I had a hard weekend," I admit, and relay the story of finding the body in the alleyway. I don't mention that it looked like her, because that would lead to more confessions that I'm suddenly too afraid to tell her.

Even when I think I will, when the words are on my tongue and the look on her face is both concerned and curious... I can't do it. I can't tell her about Rook and Oliver, and for a second I'm sure it's because I'm terrified of what they'll do to her.

It has to be that, right? Just like the reason I haven't gone to the cops is because I'm scared that if I do, they'll do something awful to *me*.

"That's fucked up," Jun murmurs, tapping her nails on the table. "Has there been any word about who the killer might be?" She frowns, glancing at her phone when the screen lights up.

Yeah, I almost want to say, as I just frown at her. *I know exactly who they are, and you were right to be worried about Oliver.* I *could* tell her. After all, she's smarter than I ever give her credit for and would know what to do, hopefully without getting us killed or run out of town. Though, my Arctic Circle plan still looks good in my mind.

"I haven't heard anything," I lie instead, shrugging. "Who knows? Maybe it's some weirdo just going around frenzy killing."

"Maybe it's a serial killer?" Juniper suggests instead, her voice casual. I look up at her, finding that her eyes are on mine, and concern softens her gaze. "Are you really okay?" she asks gently, reaching across the table to poke my hand with one long nail. "You just look... I don't know, off."

"I have a headache," I admit, and it isn't exactly a lie. Not when the knot on the back of my head still throbs with pain, and I still get a little woozy when I stand up or lay on it wrong.

But what else can I say? If I show her, and I tell her, then things won't be in my control anymore.

Besides, it feels *wrong* to tell her. It feels... I don't really know, I guess. I just want to push it out of my brain instead of letting it show on my face, because somehow, it doesn't feel like Juniper's business.

It's *mine*, and that I'm so territorial over the business of Oliver and Rook makes me nervous in a way that I don't quite understand.

"I'm going to go to bed," I say finally, getting to my feet with a loud exhale. "I wanted to wait up to make sure you got home okay." That's a lie; I'd stayed up because I was sure that I'd tell her, and I was *so sure* that I wanted her to give me her opinion or maybe go kick Oliver's ass. But now that the time is here, and passed at this point, I just *can't*.

"I'm going to bed, too," Juniper groans, sitting back in her chair. "I'm fucking *exhausted*. Have I told you I hate flying?"

"About six times," I assure her, grinning as I stretch my arms over my head and stand on my tiptoes. "In the past month. If you hate flying so much, stop doing it. Take a bus, or a balloon." It's hard to talk so casually, like I'm not bothered, but if it keeps everything normal enough around here, then I'm damn well going to try.

"A balloon," Juniper agrees, getting up as well. "Yeah, that's what I'm going to do. A *balloon*. Good night, Blair." She nudges my arm as she walks by and I throw her a smile, waiting for her door to close before I make my way into my own room.

It occurs to me that I'm not quite sure what I'm doing. I was lying about wanting to go to bed, though I know that I should. I have classes tomorrow, unless I'm going to just not go. It's not like this is high school, and anyone is going to know if I don't.

Besides, I don't know how I'm going to show my face in photography, for obvious reasons.

Collapsing onto my bed, I groan with my face in the pillows. My laptop digs into my side from where I've left it, and it takes me a moment to wrestle it free as I roll over onto my side. After a moment of hesitation I open it, navigating to *funxcams* to see if I've gotten any messages or reminders or even a verbal slap on the wrist for missing my scheduled stream today.

At this point, I don't know if I'm ever going to stream again.

There are four messages blinking at me, and two of them are random spam. The third is from *rob784*, moaning about how I've fucked up his day and ruined everything for him. But frankly. I can't bring myself to care. It's not like I'm a doctor or a therapist. I'm not a chef or some kind of general contractor coming to fix something in his house. I'm a fucking cam girl doing amateur porn. If he can't get over the fact that I didn't stream for a day, that's his problem and he should seek immediate help for what has to be some kind of addiction, clearly.

I don't bother to answer him, because fuck Rob, honestly.

The fourth message drags up a feeling of nausea that's quickly replaced with anxiety bubbling between my ribs. I shouldn't even look at it, let alone consider what it might say.

Because now that I know Rook is *thrillingterror*, I'm having a hard time coming to terms with the things I'd told him before I knew his identity.

Against my better judgment, I click the message open, surprised to see that a tip notification pops up on my screen as I do.

Three hundred dollars have been delivered to my account, and my heart nearly stops at the prospect of two shows worth of money given to me without me having to do anything at all.

Well, unless I count concussing myself at the house of two serial killers.

Belatedly, my eyes flick to the message, and my heart thrums in my chest as I read it.

I'm worried about you, Love. Having him say my last name like this suddenly has a much different connotation than it had before. Pressing my lips together, I keep reading. *I figured you wouldn't stream today. I don't want you to be low on money because of it. If you need anything else, you can just ask.*

The message was sent hours ago, right after I'd missed my stream. He's not online anymore, and that knowledge is the only thing that gives me the courage to type back and send, *I didn't ask for it. I don't need money from you.*

Before I can close my laptop lid, however, a message notification appears on my screen, and his reply appears under mine.

I know you didn't. But I don't think that's exactly true, either. I'm not buying your silence about Oliver, or paying you for anything. I just don't want you to struggle.

I barely hesitate before replying, and I still wonder why in the world I don't just shut up. *Juniper came home. I told her about finding a dead body.*

Again, his response is quick, and I want to ask why in the world he's still online this late. *Did you tell her that the bodies have an eerie resemblance to her? I don't know if she'd appreciate the knowledge, but it's not my place to tell you what you should or shouldn't say.*

Aren't you worried I told her about you two?

No, baby girl. I can't help the shiver that works its way up my spine at the nickname. *I know you didn't. And I'm not worried about it, or you. How are you feeling? Is your head still hurting?*

Does he really not care? Or rather, is he really not worried about me telling her? Surely, two of us going to the police would be more influential than me going alone.

It hurts, I say finally, not adding anything else.

It shouldn't for long. Take some ibuprofen. And let me know if you aren't coming to class tomorrow. I'll have Oliver send you a copy of his notes.

It's so... considerate that for a moment I can't even believe this is *Rook.* Or rather, Professor Solomon to me, up until this weekend.

I already took some. I know how to deal with a headache. And won't you be upset if I don't show up? You're never this nice to me, so I'm going to assume you're trying to get on my good side so I don't go to the cops about Oliver. It's risky, and stupid, but I'm much bolder here, behind a computer screen, than I was when I was in their house.

I might be a little disappointed. The response takes him a minute, and is followed quickly by another. *But I'm also not an idiot. I figure you most likely won't show up, and I can't exactly fault you for it. I'm also not worried about getting on your good side, but if you keep trying to push me into saying something cruel, then you're not going to love where it leads, Love.*

I'm not coming tomorrow. I send the message, not interested in addressing the rest of the message, or dragging out the conversation. Still, I hesitate, feeling suddenly guilty. *And thank you for the money.*

You're welcome. I'll have Oliver email you notes tomorrow night. Get some sleep. You probably need it.

I don't respond. Instead, I slam my laptop shut with a sigh and let it slide to the floor beside my bed. Then, without doing more than dragging a blanket up and over my body, I bury my face into my pillow with an exasperated moan and try to find sleep.

CHAPTER 19

E ven though I'd told Rook, and myself, that I wouldn't
go to photography on Monday, somehow my feet have
dragged me here, anyway.

It's last-minute, unlike my normal routine that gets me
here much earlier than this, and if I'd maybe planned it this
way in order to avoid Oliver, then it's certainly not something
I'm going to admit. Though realistically, it's pretty obvious.

I see Professor Solomon striding toward the door to slam it,
as he always does, when his eyes find mine and he pauses. His
brows climb a few centimeters, and if I wasn't sure he was too
proud to be impressed, I'd absolutely say he was. He stands
back, tilting his head toward the door, and I realize that I've
stopped walking to stare at him.

"Today, Love," he drawls, in the voice I know him best for.
The words seem to stiffen my spine, and I stride in like I hadn't
just been considering escaping down the hallway. It's not like
he would've stopped me, after all.

The room is as full as ever, and no one bothers to give me

more attention than usual as I breeze into the room and run a hand through my long blonde hair to untangle it from my hoodie. The door closes hard behind me, a rush of air hitting my bare thighs where my denim shorts end.

I don't bother to hesitate here, either. I sit down in my spot like I belong here. Like Oliver doesn't scare me to the edge of the universe and back, and like I still trust him to get me through this class. When I sit, I hear his soft intake of breath, but to my surprise, he behaves himself. He sits there, at a chaste distance, not looking up. It's as if I haven't come in at all.

Or, more likely, that he's worried about scaring me off. It would be cute if he wasn't a psychotic murderer who spends his free time killing women who look like my roommate.

What am I saying? It's still sweet of him. Still cute, too, but with a new undercurrent of blood and danger.

"As I was saying." Professor Solomon's voice is sharp, and he pays me no more attention than usual. "Group projects are due in two weeks. I'm not monitoring your progress, so I'm assuming you're all in a spot to be finished by then. Obviously, if you haven't even picked your subject, I would assume you're not doing well."

I suck in a breath, unable to stop thinking about the fact that *Oliver* is my partner for this project and to finish it, I'll need his help. We're long past deciding on what to photograph, however. While he'd suggested candid pictures of unsuspecting and unaware people downtown, I'd been adamant about wanting to do something different.

I want to photograph a cemetery.

Looking back, it definitely feels a little macabre, especially given the new circumstances of my relationship with him. It's unfortunate, as well, since more than anything I'd been excited to do it. Though... I drum my fingers silently on the table as our professor warns that not turning it in is an automatic failure. Do I really have to give up on this idea? There are some truly amazing cemeteries in St. Augustine, with interesting histories that have fascinated me for years. Why do I need to give up on it at all?

Just because Oliver is my partner, it doesn't mean he has to do the work with me. Especially since he's just auditing the class, not actually taking it. His working with me was a formality anyway, so that I wouldn't be doing it alone. At the time, it had been an extra way for me to spend time with him.

But I'm not afraid of hard work. Not in the slightest. I'll do it alone, enjoy it, and turn it in alone if I have to. If Oliver wants his name on it, I don't care.

"You're dismissed." Rook's voice is a long, disappointed sigh that drags me out of my thoughts. I've missed a lot of his lecture today, thanks to my own muddled thoughts that have brought me down like a whirlpool. From what I do remember, it was mostly group presentation details.

Which I definitely needed to hear.

Shit.

A notebook suddenly slides my way gently, and I can feel Oliver's eyes on me as I see that he's written down all of what's been said today in his neat penmanship, and even gone so far as to highlight certain parts of it.

I can't help it. I look up at him, eyes wide in surprise, and he offers me the smallest, sweetest grin known to man.

I also can't help the way it feels like some icy barrier around my heart is melting, just the tiniest bit, when he looks at me like that. But God, I wish it wouldn't. It's easier to hate him for what he is, than to accept it and roll with the details of him. Of *both* of them, really. Since it's now obvious that the two of them come as a package deal.

For a moment, I can't help but think of it. Images of having both of them pressed against me, kissing my throat and my mouth, flicker through my brain like a wavering candle flame. Imaginary touches stroke against my skin as I look at him, and I finally shove the inappropriate thoughts away as Oliver starts to speak.

"Professor Solomon said you weren't coming," he admits quietly, tapping a knuckle on the page. "I had these written out anyway, but I took them for you again. I wasn't going to, but then I noticed you weren't taking any." He looks down, pointedly, at my notebook that's still mostly blank. "So I thought you might need them."

He's so, so careful. Is he worried that he's hurt my feelings? Does he think I'll forgive him for what he's done? Or I suppose, if I'm being more realistic about the situation, what he *hasn't* done. After all, if he didn't like me, then he probably wouldn't be taking his anger out on Juniper's proxies, instead of her. He would've hurt her by now, or killed her.

But that doesn't make his murders okay, no matter how I look at it.

"Love." It's amazing that he always manages to sound so disappointed when he calls my name, and I tear my gaze away from Oliver's face to glare at our professor. It's a look he returns, and I see him roll his eyes while the others leave. "Stay. I need to talk to you about your project."

A nervous thrill flutters through my stomach like a bird seeking freedom, and I glance back at Oliver for safety. "Why?" I ask, not moving. Except when Oliver stands, I do the same, backpack slung over my shoulder with my notes and his.

"Because I said so." His voice holds just as much disdain as normal. No more, no less. But this isn't *normal*.

"Well, Oliver's my partner," I remind him, finding that I'm all but blocking the door from the brunet at my side so he can't leave. It's probably laughable that the spree killer is more of an ally to me than the controlled, seasoned murderer, but I can't help it. Oliver has never hurt me, exactly, and seems a lot more genuine and easy to read than Rook. "So he should stay too."

The last students leave, and Rook looks up to pin me with a glare. "No, he shouldn't," he says slowly, lifting a hand to crook his fingers in my direction. "It's not a death sentence, Love," he adds, glaring at two students who have the audacity to walk close to the door. "I literally just need to talk to you about your project."

I could run. He can't stop me, if I really tried to. This isn't their house. If I scream, then everyone is going to hear me.

"But"—he glances at the clock, calculating—"in my office, not here. Come on." It doesn't seem to occur to him for even a second that he won't be obeyed, and he sweeps out of the classroom and down the hall, long legs taking him to his office in less than twenty strides.

"He's not going to eat you," Oliver remarks, his shoulder brushing mine as I follow after him like a lost puppy.

"Can you come with me?" I ask, just as we reach his door as well.

"He just told you no," Oliver points out, a friendly and supportive grin stretching across his full lips.

"So? You disobey him all the time!" I hiss, my face feeling warm all of a sudden. "Why is now the time you suddenly decide to obey him without question?"

"Actually, he obeys me without question a lot." Rook's voice is just loud enough to carry to our ears, and he sits down at his desk, elbows coming down hard on top of it, and sighs. "It's only when he's very obsessed or wants me to play with him his way that he's not so sweet. Today's not either of those days, is it?" He pins Oliver with a look, and the younger man just shakes his head.

"It's not," he admits to me, sighing almost happily. "But seriously, it's fine. You're fine," he assures me, clapping a hand to my shoulder.

"I could leave," I remind both of them. "I didn't even have to come today." Suddenly the doorframe is more interesting than either of their faces, and I study it with fervor. "I don't have to go into your office. And if I scream—"

"If you're screaming, then it's because I'm going to fail you. Which, I'm not," Professor Solomon remarks. "You can either go home and take points off of your group project, or come in here and present the proposal to me."

I blink, completely perplexed. "What?"

"Love, you are the *only* one who hasn't made an appointment to deliver their group project proposal." He sounds irritated, and runs his hands through his dark brown hair. "I don't have a lot of free time to spend on office hours, thanks to someone." His eyes pin Oliver, who can't help but smile sweetly. "So this is what I'm making for you. If you don't present the proposal and have it accepted by me, then it's twenty percent off your grade."

"*What?*" I gasp, fingers tightening on my backpack. "What the *fuck*—"

"Or if you prefer to speak to me like that, we can just do thirty percent off now anyway," he continues. "I don't care what's going on in your home life. If you're going to take my class, you're going to complete the work like anyone else. Now, get in my office, and present your group project proposal, or leave. I don't care which."

I stare at him for a moment longer until finally stepping inside and allowing Oliver to close the door behind me. The room feels smaller than it did a second ago, and I suck in a breath as I drop into the chair sitting across from him, backpack in my lap.

"You're nicer when I'm talking to you over the internet," I mutter unhappily, digging through my bag for my photography notebook.

"I'd be nicer to you in person too, if you deserved it," he clarifies without missing a beat. I feel my cheeks flush at his words, but still drop my notebook onto the desk and let my backpack slide onto the floor beside me.

His office is colder than his classroom, I realize, and rub my bare arms. It hadn't been cool enough to wear more than a tee and shorts, but now I'm wishing I'd worn a hoodie. The problem, of course, is the only one that doesn't need to be thrown in the laundry is the one that *he* got me.

"I'm photographing the cemetery," I tell him, tapping the shot mockups in my notebook. "My plan is to go to Tolomato Cemetery tomorrow night to do it, since it's going to be clear and the new camera you got me is equipped to shoot at night. Hopefully, I can catch some sundown shots as well, but it depends on the tourist action at that time."

I sit back, eyes on his, as he pulls my notebook over to him and studies my notes and mockups for the project.

"Most people use people or animals," he tells me, glancing up from the pages. "Mind telling me why you aren't, since it would be an easier first project if you were? I'm sure Oliver suggested it."

"Because that's easy. A person or an animal is an obvious focal point. I thought, originally, about finding an *interesting* spot in a crowd or an object that would naturally pull the eye from a crowd of people," I admit with a small shrug. "But that wasn't what I wanted in the end."

"So what do you want?" He gets up and walks behind me, then opens a drawer by the door a few feet back. "I'm getting you a different lens," he says, both hands coming to rest on the top of the cabinet. "I know what I gave you, and I don't think it's going to do you the most justice. If you'd told me that this was your plan, I would've made sure you were better prepared for it."

My eyes flit from him to the drawer, and the doorknob that he's mostly obscuring. Had I heard the click of the lock? Or had it just been the drawer, as he'd explained? I sure as hell hadn't seen him lock it. "Lens," he repeats, showing the small cloth bag he's pulled out of the drawer before closing it. "You didn't answer. What are you going for?"

Tapping my fingers against the surface of his desk, I straighten so I can wait for him to come back around in a more comfortable position. "I want to create interest with a lack of a common focal point. In using the cemetery, I want to use the shapes, angles, and it would be nice to get some... shadows," I say, then swallow hard as he suddenly leans over me, his arms on either side of my shoulders as he places the lens on my notebook and scoots them closer to my side of the desk.

"Go on," he invites, warmth seeping into my body from the heat of his. "It's not a proposal until you finish the idea."

"You can't be serious about grading me on this," I snap, unable to go anywhere unless I'm willing to slam my chair back into him. "You're—"

"Completely serious," he assures me, jaw brushing my hair. "Go *on*, Love."

"I want to take the graves and tombstones—to use them as my focal points. Not just the easy, angel or human shaped tombs. But I want to use the more complex and unusual ones as well to draw the eye. I don't know. I just like weird things, okay?"

"I'm not condemning your ideas," he sighs, urging me up and out of the chair. I feel myself trembling, my body like a wire pulled tight as I wait for his touch with equal parts fear and anticipation. "While you might want to avoid him right now, you should really use Oliver. He's done projects similar to that before, and he'll be able to help." He pulls me around to his side of the desk, firmly enough that I can't refuse unless I'm willing to put up a fight, or scream. Both of which are viable options right now.

"How's your head?" he asks conversationally, turning me by my arm and forcing me to *sit* on the edge of his desk.

"I—what?" I ask, confused and unsure of what he's even asking. Then bring my hand up to grab his wrist when he reaches out, and his smile turns almost endearing.

"Your head, baby girl. Does it still hurt?"

"I guess, but it's more like a headache now." I don't know what else to say, or if I should be replying at all, frankly. But it isn't a crime for asking... yet.

His fingers smooth through my blonde hair, searching gently along my scalp for the knot I'd given myself at his place. When he finds it, I move to pull away, but he does so first. "I was worried I was wrong, and you were a little concussed," he admits, hands falling to my shoulders.

"Well, I'm not," I snap, eyes wide as I examine his face for any clue of what he wants. "I'm fine; I just have to go. I have another class, and—"

"No, you don't, Love," he sighs, reaching up to press a thumb against my lips as he grips my jaw in his hand. "The only place either of us have to go is home. I have twenty minutes to spare so I can still make Oliver's stream, and while I know he'd love for you to watch it too, I'm not going to tell you if you should or shouldn't."

"Maybe I don't want anything to do with either of you," I whisper, face hot as I work to speak around his grip on my face.

"Maybe that's not true." His voice isn't unkind, exactly, but there's definitely a note of arrogance in it. "If you didn't want anything to do with us, you would've gone to the cops. You would've told Juniper. At the very least, you would've dropped my class or not come in today. I was wondering if I'd still see you on the roster, truthfully. But you are, and you're here." He shoves his thigh between my knees, working them open until he can stand almost pressed against me.

"I didn't think you even liked me," I find myself accusing, my hands gripping the desk under me. "I thought it was just Oliver. You don't act like you want anything to do with me most of the time."

"Of course I like you." His smile is wider than I've seen before, and it doesn't reach his eyes. It makes my stomach twist, but his hands hold me steady. "I just don't show it like Oliver does. You'll get used to it."

"I don't trust you," I breathe like an accusation. "I trust Oliver more than you."

"I don't think it matters who you trust more, baby girl," Rook admits. "Not right now, at least. If you trust him, then you should trust I won't hurt you. Otherwise, he never would've let you in here with me alone, would he?"

That feels logical, but I can't say for sure that I trust it.

"Tell me something," he requests, his hands coming up to tug at the neck of my tee. I stare at him, like a deer in headlights, and find myself acquiescing to his silent request for me to remove my shirt, which ends up on the floor by my backpack. "Has Oliver fucked you yet?"

My stomach twists at the question, and I feel my face flush. "Don't you know?" I accuse nervously, shivering when he drags his nails up my sides.

"No," he admits. "I don't. And I don't want to take that

from him, if he hasn't. You were always *his* first, after all. So he deserves to—"

"I'm not anyone's," I interrupt, my words turning to a gasp when he grabs my hips roughly.

"That would've been true if you hadn't come back," he informs me, and unbuttons my shorts with quick, deft movements. "Has he fucked you, Love?" It's too easy for him to jerk both my shorts and underwear down in a few quick movements, until they hang precariously from one ankle.

"I-I mean, we've done some things," I admit in a breathy tone when he stands back up to loom over me.

"Sorry," Rook teases, almost cruelly. He unhooks my bra and slides it free, and when he tilts my chin up to his, my stomach clenches. "I'll be clearer. I know how much Oliver wants to fill that sweet cunt of yours. He talks about it all the time. He's invented all kinds of ways to fuck you, most of which take place *while* I'm fucking him. So what I'm asking is what you've given him. Has he tasted you yet?" He leans down to kiss me hard, his teeth sharp against mine. "Or has he just fucked you with his fingers?" He pushes my thighs wide, and I feel his fingers tease along my slit, causing my thighs to tremble. "Since you've made it clear he hasn't taken you properly yet."

I look at him with parted lips and heat staining my cheeks as he strokes along my inner thighs. They flex around his legs, but I can't close them, even if I'd wanted to. "He hasn't..." I lick my lips nervously, trying to gather my thoughts. *Why am I going to tell him this?* "He's only used his fingers."

"Good girl." The praise is rough and unexpected. So is being jerked off the corner of the desk, only so Rook can push me down into his leather office chair.

"What are you—"

"Hook your knees up and over, Love. Just like that." He

presses me back against the chair, helping me until my knees are hooked over the arms of it. "Don't make me find a way to keep you there," he threatens, sinking to his knees in front of me just as it registers in my brain what he's about to do.

My hand flies out to catch his arm, but I only manage to grip his hair instead. "Wait!" I hiss, panicking. "We're in your *office*."

"The door is locked."

"Someone could hear!"

"Oh, you should've told me you were loud." He gets to his feet with a warning look in my direction as I try to fathom an answer to that statement. "Don't move, Love," he warns, sounding much more like the professor I'm used to.

He walks away, only going so far as to pick up his bag, as I squirm in his chair and shiver at the feeling of the cool air finding every inch of me. It's embarrassing to be so open, so fucking vulnerable. Especially when he turns and just *looks* at me.

It's so hard to break my eyes away from his, that I don't notice what's in his hand until he's right in front of me and dangling it in my face.

"Oliver and I have a lot of disciplinary meetings," he informs me as the ball gag is held in front of my nose. "And he's not very quiet. I keep this with me for him, in case he's too antsy to wait until we're home."

"You aren't really going to—"

"Here's how this works." He carefully sets the gag against my teeth and buckles it at the back of my head. It's firm, and keeps my mouth open uncomfortably. My teeth press into the soft firmness of the red ball, and I stare at him, waiting on his next words. "You're going to try so, so hard not to make any noise. Or at least keep it *soft*. Do you hear me?" he says the last part as he leans over me, thumb on my chin again. I nod once, and the soft smile graces his lips once more. "Good girl."

He sinks to his knees in front of me a moment later, hands press against my shaking thighs. "I'll hold you still if I have to," he admits, not bothering to look up at my face. "But you'll like it more if I can use my fingers too."

I can't help but squirm in his grip, but he stops that with his fingers pressing into my inner thighs. Is he really about to do what I think he is?

The answer comes when his tongue swipes up my slit, teasing at my entrance as I yelp lightly against the gag and then flicking once over my clit. I shudder, the sensations new and maddening when all I can do is grip the armrests or his hair.

One of my hands curls in his hair when he licks me again, and I tense up, expecting him to say something. He doesn't. Instead, he nuzzles his face against my inner thigh, giving me a momentary reprieve from the sharp, heady sensation of his mouth.

Not able to do anything else, I lean my head back against the chair, eyes pressed tightly closed while he kisses along my inner thigh until he's back where he wants to be once more. This time his licks are short and targeted. He teases my entrance for a few seconds before moving to my clit where he can press and flick his tongue over it in earnest.

I squirm again, though it's not much more than a wiggle of my hips, and one of his arms unwraps from my thigh, disappearing from my body altogether. For a few seconds, at least. His fingers run the same path as his tongue, and he sits up so his hand can take the place of his mouth at my clit for a few seconds. Still, the new stimulation has me whimpering, my teeth sinking further into the gag.

It occurs to me that I have no idea how to fucking *swallow*. I can feel the uncomfortable wetness of my mouth, and I'm glad my head is tipped back so that I can't do something embarrassing like drool all over myself.

"Relax, Love," he murmurs, mouthing at my hip. "You're so gorgeous, aren't you? Such a sweet, *sick* little puppy." The more humiliating nickname sends a shiver down my spine. "And you're all mine right now, so you can just relax."

If only I could tell him that those words should elicit the opposite response.

He kisses my body again, and slowly I find myself relaxing, my thighs no longer shaking when the muscles aren't knotted with tension.

"There you go." His mouth returns to my clit, lapping over it lightly as his fingers tease my entrance simultaneously. I whine a question behind the gag, opening my eyes and tilting my head just enough that I can see his eyes are closed as he runs his tongue up my slit. When he flicks his tongue against my clit, two of his long fingers sink into my body and draw a long, low moan from me.

"Oh, how I want to take my time with you," he muses, thrusting his fingers deep into my body. "And I will, I promise. But not today. I told myself that if you showed up today, I'd reward you for being so good, and so brave. My brave, sweet girl." His fingers curl upward, finding a place inside of me that has my hips arching into his touch. "There you go. Ride my fingers, Love. Just like that." He encourages my movements for a few seconds before pressing me down again, his tongue replacing his hand as he presses his tongue into my body.

It's thicker than his fingers, and such a different sensation that I have to squeeze my eyes shut once again. My head falls back against the chair, and I focus on the feeling of his mouth and the way it draws me closer to my release.

When his fingers find my clit, my hand flies back down to

his hair, tangling in the coarse dark strands. He doesn't hesitate, however. Rook continues what he's doing, like he's trying to devour and taste every inch of me his tongue can reach.

When I'm dizzy and near my end, I tug on his hair, trying to tell him the same. He chuckles, his free hand curling tightly against my hip as he leans more of his weight against me to hold me in place. "Are you going to come, Love?" he purrs, his voice liquid silk and rough velvet. "You've been so good, and so quiet. You deserve this for being so good. Come for me. I want to taste you, Love." His mouth finds my entrance again, tongue thrusting into me as his fingers tease my clit with more purpose than before.

I can't help the whine building in my throat, or the way my hips writhe under him. He doesn't seem to mind either, based on how he's still going at this with such enjoyment that it almost feels like his favorite hobby. I try not to yell, managing a soft keen when my orgasm hits me in a dizzying wave, body clenching around him.

He doesn't move. His tongue laps against my inner walls, fingers still gingerly teasing me as I come. The wetness on my jaw is what draws me back, and I let out a groan of irritation when I smack my head back against the chair, realizing there's drool on my face from the gag.

Rook gets up and wipes his arm on his face, chuckling. "Don't move, Love," he orders, and presses my arm back down when I start to wipe the drool off my face.

I sigh and close my eyes, trying to figure out *why*, when a sudden *click* has my eyes snapping back open again.

The bastard has a camera. He takes another picture before I can think to move, and when I try to get up, he leans forward and pins me in place with a hand under my chin and his knee once more between mine.

"Don't pout," he purrs, bringing up the camera to take

another two pictures of my face at this close angle. "You're just so sexy like this that I couldn't help it." He lays the camera gingerly on the desk and helps me with the gag, and only then do I wipe the drool off my face with a sneer.

"That's disgusting," I pant, still eyeing him nervously. "I look—"

"Wrecked," Rook interrupts in agreement. "You looked wrecked. Here." He hands me my bra, and proceeds to find my clothes while I get dressed. He's so... *nice* about it. Like this wasn't the strangest, most frightening sexual encounter in my life. "Do you feel okay?" He smooths my hair down as I stare at him.

"You're so... strange," I murmur, all of my misgivings flooding back to me. "I don't get you."

"Why, Love?"

"Because sometimes you're so nice to me, and other times you're definitely not."

Rook chuckles, my backpack on his fingers. He sets it down hard on the desk, then slips the lens and my notebook into it. "I'm nice to you when you deserve it. And after *that*, you definitely deserve it. Remember that. You get what you earn from me, Love."

"That's..." I don't know what to say. Especially when he steps close and pins me to the wall with his arms on either side of my face.

"I don't need you to put me in a box, Love," he purrs against my lips. "But I do think it's time for you to go home. It's getting dark soon, and I need to go watch Oliver's stream." He kisses me hard, then pulls away and gathers up his own things as I stand there, debating on my next question.

Fuck it. I decide, and inhale sharply before asking, "Why?"

"Why what?" he doesn't look up, but does point to the door when his bag is over one shoulder.

205

"Why do you watch it? You're in the same house as him, and obviously he can take care of myself." I let him walk by, but instead of unlocking the door right away he turns, trapping me against the wall again.

"For the same reason that I watch yours, Love," he says, eyes dark. "Because you're both mine."

CHAPTER 20

I t's a coincidence that I waited until Friday to go to Tolomato Cemetery. I'd meant to go on Tuesday, like I'd told Professor Solomon I would. But it just hadn't been right, then the rain clouds had started rolling in.

The only thing I'd purposefully been vague about was inviting Oliver. Maybe he's right, and Oliver really would be a benefit to me here. But I'm not sure how I feel about him right now, except for the fact that he's a fucking serial killer, and I'm definitely not.

I stride through the cemetery in my leggings and hoodie, aware of how the night air is starting to cool off quickly now that we've hit late October. With Halloween tomorrow and my only plan being to possibly stream, the only thing I can hope for is to finish this tonight.

My eyes flick around the cemetery as I walk, looking for any tombs or structures that will make for good pictures. I need ten to present, but I obviously intend to take at least triple that.

As my feet scuff along the grass, I look up to see a tourist group weaving through the cemetery. I can tell it's one of St. Augustine's famous ghost tours by the way the guide's voice rises and falls, putting emphasis on certain parts of his story about the people that are buried there.

And here I had thought I wouldn't run into them until night had well and truly fallen. Don't they know that seeing ghosts works better once the sun has set?

Pausing, I realize that I'm feeling *watched*. I suck in a few breaths, closing my eyes hard, and turn to see if it's a ghost or just an unwelcome guest staring at me.

It's *Oliver*. I stare at him, taking in his hunched shoulders and his hands that are jammed into his pockets. He looks so apologetic that I almost believe it, and his face is full of concern that's plain to anyone in a ten-mile radius.

My eyes search his expression and his posture. I clench the gifted camera more tightly in one hand, surprised that he hasn't snuck up to grab me or start suggesting ideas for my shoot.

But he just watches me, half-forlorn and a little bit hopefully, like a puppy I've kicked that still comes back. The thought makes me frown, because I don't ever want to feel like that. I don't deserve to feel like that after what Oliver did. He's the one in the wrong.

So why do I feel so guilty?

"How did you know I was here?" I ask suspiciously, scuffing my foot along the ground.

A soft smile curls his lips. "Lucky guess?" he admits, raising his shoulders and letting them drop. "Well, I've been coming here every night. Except for last night, since it was raining. I figured that since you weren't in class today, you were coming here instead."

I hesitate, still unsure. "Aren't you supposed to be streaming?"

"I would, but you're more important." He takes a step toward me, looking like he's trying to be careful and nonchalant about it, then another. "Can I help you?"

I should tell him no. He's putting on an act for me right now, and I absolutely have every right to tell him to fuck right off. Especially until I figure out how I feel and what I'm going to do.

But I really want a good grade. The thought makes me wince, because I already know that I'm going to let him help me. And unfortunately, I can't quite convince myself that it's only because he's good at photography.

"Besides, you want some good sunset shots," Oliver adds, like he needs more of a selling point. "And you're about to miss it. I can help you frame them, and I have some ideas for your vision, if you want my help with it."

I let out a breath, close my eyes, and say, "Oliver, why are you acting like you're a six-month-old golden retriever I've punted across the kitchen?"

He takes a moment to respond, but when I open my eyes, I see the grin curling at his lips. "Because I'm willing to do anything to earn your forgiveness?"

"*Forgiveness?*" I stride closer to him so I can speak more quietly, so close that I'm almost pressed against his chest. "Oliver, you are going around and *murdering* people who look like my roommate."

Of course, he doesn't have the decency to look offended, but I hadn't really expected him to. "Yeah," he agrees, reaching out to tuck my hair behind my ear as he says, "But it's only so I don't kill your best friend. I'm doing my best here, wonder girl. I had to make some kind of compromise since I didn't want to hurt you."

That's certainly an interesting twist on it. I start to reply, but he leans forward so his lips brush my ear. "But if you wait much longer and yell at me instead of taking photos, you're going to miss about half your shots." He nudges my hand that's holding the camera, and I let out a frustrated breath.

It's unfortunate that he's right. I lift the camera toward him, eyes a little bit mournful, as I silently ask for his help, but Oliver just chuckles and shakes his head. "Oh, no, I don't think so. You're still taking them; I'm just here to assist you. I'm your sexy assistant, actually."

"If you were, you'd be wearing less," I mutter, watching as he walks toward the gazebo-like structure in the middle of the area we're in. When he hears me, he wiggles his hips, and I can't help but roll my eyes.

"Look at these." He points at the structure and the tombstone behind it, launching into an explanation about depth of field and how I can make things look more interesting. I nod along with what he says, taking pictures from the angles he suggests as the sun dips lower and lower over the horizon.

Finally, when it's dark, we end up using a combination of street lamps and our phones to set up some kind of dramatic lighting. It isn't cinema quality by any means, but that was never what I was going for.

"Last one?" I ask, lying on my stomach on the ground to take an upward shot of a towering obelisk. Our light and the shot angle make it look larger, more commanding than it is in real life, and the cracks along it are accentuated perfectly.

I barely notice Oliver moving until he lies down on the ground beside me and rolls over to his back with a sigh. "Are you okay?" he inquires, staring up at the sky as I look down at my camera. My body is tense where it presses against him, and I play the night I'd ended up at his apartment over and over in my head.

Somehow, when I'm just thinking about it, I no longer feel

as awful about the whole thing as I had, and that's a little worrying to me.

"Why?" I sigh, going through the pictures while being hyper aware of him beside me. "Why wouldn't I be, actually?"

"Well, I understand you're upset with me. I guess I can't really fault you for that, huh?" he chuckles the question into the cool air above our heads, and I don't think it requires an answer. "But it's more than that. You're quiet, and you aren't yourself. You haven't been streaming at all. But you don't have another job, do you?"

I pause and glance in his direction, eyes narrowed. "Are you stalking me?"

"Of course I am."

"That isn't as comforting as I think you mean it to be."

We're quiet for a few more seconds until I sit up and stare down at him. Oliver doesn't move, except to look at me with a wide emerald-eyed look of sweetness that looks so real that I want to believe it. But can a serial killer really be *sweet*? Or has this all been just an act?

"I don't have another job," I agree finally, letting out a long breath. "That's all I have. I was hoping to save up before I graduated, so maybe I don't have to work at a gas station."

"You could ask Rook for money," Oliver points out lazily. "He'd give it to you, if you aren't comfortable—"

"But that's part of the problem, Oliver. I'm nervous to stream, because you're both watching me. But it's not just that. I just feel like things have *changed*. Things aren't the same. I started streaming—" I break off and swallow my words before trying again. "I started streaming because I watched you, and you were so fucking hot. You are so good at it that it's unreal, and maybe I was a little in love with you the first time I saw you."

"Are you still?" he asks, blinking a few times as he shifts to get more comfortable on the cemetery grass.

"You kill people."

"Irrelevant."

"*What?*" I lean over him, as if he isn't hearing me or just isn't understanding. "What do you mean, irrelevant?! It's incredibly relevant, actually!" How can he not see that? How can he not understand that the whole crux of the issue balances on the fact that he, Oliver, is a fucking *murderer*.

"I would say I'd stop for you," Oliver admits, flicking his fingers dismissively in the air above his chest. "If I could, I would, I think. But I can't. It's not just something I *like* to do. It's something I *need* to do."

"It's weird that you're telling me this." I sit back on my hands nervously.

"Is it?" he hums, twisting his body like a cat. "I like you a lot. I've liked you since I saw you, but even more when I saw *you* stream. You're so much better at it than me. I'd also tell you I'll stop watching you. That I'll ask Rook to, as well. But..." He shakes his head. "We'd worry about you too much. I'm not *jealous* or anything like that. I love that you make men so horny for you it's unreal. But I see the way they bully you, and I'd worry too much not to step in. Sorry, Blair." He gives me a cocky half smile.

I let my shoulders fall. "Whatever. It's fine. I mean, it's not *just* you. I've been off this week, and with men demanding more and more of me, I'm not sure what to do. I love the money, but I don't know if I'm cut out for it. In order to make real money, I feel like I'd have to do something more. Or find a way to stick up for myself better. I can't *always* rely on you and Rook."

"You could," Oliver points out. "I'd let you." When I don't

reply, he sits up and leans over me, gesturing for the camera. "How did they turn out? I want to see."

Wordlessly, I pass over the camera, watching as he goes through the photos and shows me his top ten. Afterward we both stand, and Oliver stares at me, unashamed and not trying to hide it, as I fumble with my camera to get it back in my backpack.

"I'll help you," he says finally, reaching out to tuck my hair behind my ear again. "Can I help you with your stream?"

"Not if it's killing someone." I hesitate, and then add, "Unless it's *rob784*. Fuck, I can't *stand* him."

"He's pretty much in love with you," Oliver informs me gravely. But he hums thoughtfully and shakes his head. "No, I'm not sure. But give me time. I'll figure something out and get back to you tomorrow, okay? You're an excellent streamer. You're good at this, and you could make more money at it than you do now, I promise."

"You'd really give me some tips, or some help?" I ask, and before I finish, Oliver is already nodding enthusiastically.

"Absolutely. Consider it the first part of me making up the whole kidnapping thing to you." He *beams* at a couple that walks by, and they smile back uncomfortably. "Let me think about it, Blair. Tomorrow we'll have an awesome game plan that'll have you back on your game, come hell or high water."

"Okay," I agree slowly, letting him brush his fingers against my arm. "If you say so, Oliver." He leaves after that, wishing me a good night. For a while longer, I stand in the cemetery and think that maybe, perhaps, I'm getting myself into more trouble than I would've been in if I hadn't said a damn thing.

CHAPTER 21

T he knock on my door sends my stomach plummeting to the floor. It has to be Juniper; I figure. I'm certainly not expecting anyone else on Halloween, especially. As with most years, she's out at a costume party, and I'd told her I'd be home binging kids' Halloween movies instead.

That, of course, had been a lie. But not one I'd thought she'd catch me in.

When another knock comes, it registers that Juniper wouldn't be *knocking*. But I haven't ordered food or anything, so I still don't know who it could be. But I need to get rid of them if I'm going to stream in ten minutes.

I bolt to the door, barefoot and dressed in just my running shorts and tee over my usual lingerie. My fox mask is on my desk, ready to use, and I close the door to my room just in case my houseguest needs to come inside.

When I pull open the door, relief and nervousness both flood my system, and I suck in a breath.

Oliver stands there, grinning, with a backpack over one shoulder and his hair tousled like he's just rolled out of bed.

"Hello," he greets sweetly, stepping in without a direct invitation from me. "Sorry, I'm a little late. I wanted to be here a half hour ago, but Rook stopped me, and, well..." he trails off with a grin. "Better almost late than never?"

I follow him into the kitchen, confused. "What are you doing here at all? I thought you were going to call me with some ideas, or something?" I can't help the way my voice pitches upward as he walks right into my room and tosses his backpack on the bed.

"Oh, well, sure. I guess I could've called," he agrees. Oliver turns to me, closing the distance between us as he grins sharply with his teeth bared. "But that would've ruined the fun. You trust me, don't you?"

"Not on your life," I reply automatically, without thinking about it whatsoever. "I don't get it—Oliver, if I'm going to stream, I have to do it in *eight minutes*," I snap, gesturing to where my laptop is set up on my desk as well.

"Okay, well, I'm going to help you," he goes on sweetly, his voice like rich honey in my ears. "Just like I told you I would."

"I don't need a cinematographer."

"I'm not offering to be one." He reaches out to rest his hands on my hips, causing my breath to stutter in my lungs. "Let me stream with you."

"*What?*" I yelp, voice sounding high and strangled. "With me? You?" He nods. "Not just on your stream as well. You mean *with* me, like, same show and same webcam?"

He nods again, smile turning teasing and darkly amused.

"Will we be like? Umm... Sitting next to each other, or interacting, or—" I have a good feeling that isn't what he means at all. Especially when he cuts me off.

"No, wonder girl," he purrs, lips close to mine. "I want to fuck you on your stream for all those men that wish they could do it themselves."

My heart stops beating in my chest. That's the only explanation for the way my ribs contract just as his mouth brushes mine. "I don't know if I—"

"Come on," he continues. "What's the harm? They've seen everything before. They've seen you get yourself off. You aren't hiding anything from them. Let me help you take things up a level, won't you?"

The idea sounds equal parts enticing and terrifying. There's a big difference in controlling what I do while streaming, and letting Oliver fuck me during it.

"What if..." I trail off, biting my lip, and suck in a breath. "I don't know, Oliver. I mean, for one, I've never done that on my stream. What if my viewers hate it?"

"What if you gain more?"

"What if I do something I don't want to do?"

"What if you trust me not to let you?" He reaches up to cup my cheek in his warm palm, steady gaze finding mine.

I shouldn't. Not with everything I know about him. Not with everything that I'm still trying to figure out, and the way I'm trying to push him away from me. I need him to understand that I don't want him, *or* a relationship with a serial killer.

I need him to take me seriously.

"I won't hurt you," he promises in a soft purr. "I would never hurt you. Or let you do anything you'd regret. We'll shorten your stream, say it's a Halloween special before you go out tonight. We'll say I'm just a friendly trick-or-treater, coming to demand something so *sweet*." I shiver when he *licks* up my jaw.

"You'll never take me seriously again when I tell you I don't want to be in a relationship with you," I breathe, my eyes closed as I try not to focus on how much my body is responding to him.

"I'll always take you seriously. And this isn't you saying yes to *us*, Blair. This isn't you agreeing to anything more than hosting me on your stream."

"Somehow it feels like more than that." God, I wish I could believe him that this really is just me doing that. But how in the world could I?

"We'll go slow," he continues, still agonizingly understanding. "We'll go slow and if I see you aren't into it, I'll stop. Okay? Thirty minutes with me and you're going to have so many new viewers, it'll be insane, I promise."

"What if you're wrong?" My heart flutters in my chest as a smile curves his lips again.

"Then I'll give you ten grand to make up for it."

"No, you won't. You don't have ten grand."

"Then I better not be wrong, huh? Or Rook might kill me for going into debt for this." His teasing tone is infectious, intriguing, and frankly?

I want to.

It's curiosity more than anything, I tell myself as he tugs me over to the bed. He stops me when I start to take off my shirt, and shakes his head. "Let me do it on stream." When I hesitate, he adds, "What's wrong, Blair? Is there something else?"

"Well, I shouldn't be giving into this, so easily," I say, pointing out the obvious. "But more than that? We've never fucked before. You don't know if you'll like it, or if I'll like it. I don't know what you're like. What if I don't like it, and I can't fake it for my stream? What if *you* don't like it, and they know?"

"What if you like it so much that they see it on your face, even behind that pretty mask of yours?" he replies darkly. "I won't let you fail. I'm not going to let you embarrass yourself. And most of all, Blair?" He goes to my desk, scoops up my mask and laptop, and comes back to the bed to hand them to me.

"Don't you ever worry that I won't like it. I promise, that's nowhere in the realm of possibility. Okay? You're all right. Besides, if anyone says anything shitty, you know Rook is watching. He'll take care of us."

I don't know what he's going to do from the other side of a screen, but the argument dies in my throat as my alarm goes off, reminding me it's time to start my stream. I grab my phone and stop it, turning to see Oliver standing beside my bed and tugging off his shirt.

"Remember," he says, stepping far back from where the camera can see him while I drag off my shorts and chuck them across the room. "I'm a trick-or-treater. Make up the rest." His mask comes up, and he adjusts it against his face, moments before I scramble to do the same with mine.

This is a bad idea, I think, and click the button that will start my stream.

For a few moments, as usual, I don't do anything of interest. It takes that long for people to filter in, though I see Rook's name instantly, as *Framed_Failures* this time instead of *Thrillingterror*.

"Happy Halloween," I greet finally, unsure of how to sit to not look like I'm perched or hunched like some creature from Lord of the Rings looking to attack the hobbits. "First things first, today won't be as long of a stream as usual. Umm... My friend invited me out to go to a costume party. And you know, I'm already halfway set." I tap the mask on my face, and get a few remarks and greetings from the twenty or so viewers in my chat.

"But more than that..." I sit back, toying with my shirt. "I have a surprise for you guys. Right before I started the stream, there was a trick-or-treater at my door." My words tremble slightly, and I can *feel* Oliver at my back, his weight causing the bed to dip under me. "I don't have any candy," I admit, as he reaches up to wrap his long fingers around my throat.

He can't kiss me, but I hear the soft chuckle when his mask presses to my face. "But I told her that's okay," he tells the viewers, some of whom have erupted into greetings for him. Had he told them he'd be here? Is that why I have more than usual online so early? "I just want something sweet, but it doesn't have to be candy."

There's a smile in his voice, just as there usually is when he streams. "I'm *letsplayjay*," he goes on, his fingers tugging on my shirt. He takes it off teasingly, then settles me back against him on the bed. "In case any of you aren't familiar with my stream. I've been watching Envy since she started, and well, what a coincidence, don't you guys think?" He shifts to grip my throat lightly again, turning my face up to his behind the mask.

"Such a coincidence I ended up here, right before her stream, so I can get my treat while all of you watch." He guides my knees outward, hooking them over each of his, so that my viewers can see all of me. There's barely anything hidden under my purple, lacy lingerie, but he ghosts his fingers along my inner thighs as the first couple of tips start rolling in. "We'll let her stream work like mine tonight. The highest tipper always gets to request what they want. More than ten means you can have me do something to her... within reason, of course. We wouldn't want to scare poor, sweet Envy, would we?"

The excitement coming from my viewers is stronger than it ever has been, and when a tip comes in asking for Oliver to take off my mask, another one, this time from Rook, comes in telling Oliver to finger me instead.

Thanks, Professor, I think darkly in my head as Oliver chuckles against my skin. "They want to see your pretty pussy so bad, huh?" he teases, fingers sliding up and down my slit just over my panties. "Of course they do. Who wouldn't?"

Before I can think of any kind of reply, he shoves the material of my panties gently to one side, rubbing against me again before using his pinkie and pointer finger to spread me open.

I whimper, lips parted, and let him tilt my head back against his shoulder with his grip still firm on my throat as he slides two fingers into me.

"I think she started dripping when I came in," he tells our viewers sweetly. "But I think this is deserved, don't all of you? After all, I recognize some of you from my stream who've made me stop *right* when I want to come. Don't think I don't. Well, since this is Envy's stream, I won't stop with her until I'm satisfied and had my fill of her sweetness. Tell your viewers how you love my fingers, baby," he insists, gesturing for me to sit up.

"*Fuck*, I really do," I tell them, my hips nearly moving of their own accord while he thrusts deep and spreads his fingers wide inside me. "He's so good at this."

"Does it feel better than the toys you like to use?"

"So much better."

"I bet you'll love it even more when you're full of my cock, won't you?" he teases, then suddenly lets go of my throat to lean forward and drag the laptop closer.

I let out a gasp of surprise, and I feel my legs tense as my viewers are suddenly granted a closer view of my body and the way he's fingering me. He speeds up, still watching the screen as much as he can, until finally he pushes it back with a low laugh.

"Thought you guys might want to get a closer look, since she never gives us one. She's just so cruel like that. And for those of you more used to seeing me, well. I'll put it this way. I know how much you'd want me to fuck you, so now you're getting a live demo of just what I'd do to you."

His viewers get suddenly more invested in the chat as he continues to tease me, and I lose myself a little as he unhooks my bra to play with my nipples.

It's embarrassing, I think. Though not in a way that's necessarily awful. I can feel the fine tremble going through my body, and the soft gasps leaving my mouth aren't exactly staged.

"They're talking to you, Envy," Oliver teases. "You can't go all blissed out on us. *Whirled4x* wants to know if you like it when I play with your nipples like this. I mean, it's pretty obvious to me, but why don't you go on and tell them what your body is saying loud and clear?"

Righting myself so I can look at my laptop, I take a breath and fix a shaky smile on my lips. "Feels so sweet," I tell them, thankful that Oliver has nudged my mask back into place a few times. "He's so fucking *sweet*. But maybe some of you could tell him that I won't break, please? He could play a little rougher."

My hunch had been right, and just like when he'd asked for something, tips and suggestions roll in. A few want him to choke me, while others want him to just be more aggressive overall.

"Choke her?" Oliver laughs. "You want to see my hand wrapped around her throat like this?" His free hand is back at my neck, fingers digging lightly into me just under my jaw. "She does look pretty with my fingers around her throat, doesn't she? I agree with all of you about that. But we don't want to hurt sweet Envy, no matter if she says I can play rough with her."

There's a warning in his voice that might just be for me.

"Besides, sweet girl has a party to get to," he adds, voice goading. "How about I fuck her, hmm? I'm not sure I'm feeling very creative today, so why don't all of you tell me how you'd like me to take her. I could put her on her back and wrap her legs around my hips? What do you guys think?"

A few guys put in tips, begging Oliver to do this or that, or to show them my pussy again. He obliges those wordlessly, spreading me open once more and keeping me there for them to see. It's just as embarrassing as it was the first time, so I bite my lip and try not to bury my face in his throat.

Unfortunately, with my eyes mostly closed, all I hear is his laugh to know that someone has probably put in a large tip for a suggestion on how he should fuck me. "Why thank you, *Framed_Failures*. It's great to see you made it over here, by the way. And since he's the highest tipper by a mile, thanks to that three hundred dollars—"

What? Three hundred?

"It looks like we have a winner." I had expected him to tell me what it was. I thought he'd warn me, or tell me how to move. But instead, Oliver all but picks me up, just to shove me forward until my face is shoved against the mattress, just below my laptop. It's a wonder I hadn't knocked into the keyboard, but Oliver is better than that.

"Look at your viewers, sweet Envy," Oliver growls as he drags my hips up off the bed. I feel a yank, then the tearing sound of my lacy underwear that makes me want to hiss at him in irritation.

"Let them see all the pretty faces you make behind that mask while I fuck this pretty cunt." I hear him unzipping his jeans, and reach up to maneuver the laptop enough that not only can they see part of my face, but now Oliver is perfectly in frame, as well. It requires the shoving of some of my pillows, but the result is... shocking.

I get to watch as Oliver grips my hips and drags them up to

him. I shudder as he runs his nails down my curved spine as he nearly vibrates with excitement.

"Happy Halloween, everyone," he says, and rearranges his grip on my thighs.

I don't know what I'm expecting. For him to be gentle, maybe? But he's not. Maybe it's because of my goading, or maybe it's what Rook requested. Either way, Oliver slams into me until his hips are against my ass, and I cry out at the feel of him stretching my body.

"*Fuck*," I gasp, closing my eyes and burying my face against the pillows. He doesn't let me rest for long, though.

Oliver reaches out to thread his fingers in my hair, yanking my face up for my viewers to see. "Tell them how I feel," he orders, and when I only whimper, he lightly slaps my thigh. "Don't tease them, Envy, baby. That's not very nice."

Neither is he, and I worry that I've gotten in over my head this time. His grip on my hair causes my scalp to prickle and burn, but it's definitely not the worst feeling I've ever had.

"He's so big," I tell my viewers, my voice soft and trembling. "He's so fucking big and—" I trail off with a grasp as he pulls out just to thrust back in. I close my eyes and arch into him, letting out another breath as he sets a rhythm for my viewers.

While I'm having problems getting more than one word out, Oliver certainly isn't. He tells my viewers how hot I am, how tight I feel around him, and lets them know every fucking time my muscles clench around his cock. He basks in their attention and their questions, and indulges every fantasy about all the things I probably like.

Meanwhile, I can barely answer the most basic of questions for them. They don't seem to care, just like Oliver predicted. They care more about him telling them everything about me, and my uncontrolled reactions to his movements, than anything I might have to say.

"You really don't think I can feel how close she is?" The words drag me out of my haze, and it hits me that he's right. I want to come so badly, and not just because of how thoroughly he's fucking me.

It's the humiliation, too. The way he talks about me like I'm barely here for more than for him to fuck.

"I can feel it," Oliver assures them. "You don't know how well I can feel it. She's so expressive with her body. All right. One last question, and whichever answer gets the most tips, wins. Should I come all over her, or should I fill up her sweet cunt before I leave so she has to lie here and remember how good I felt while it drips out of her pussy?"

I know what I'd vote for, but I'm not exactly someone who has a vote.

"Hurry up now," Oliver urges. "Once she comes, I'm not going to last long. And she's so close, chat. She's begging me to make her come." He leans over me and watches the screen, setting his mask against my shoulder as he does.

"Better look up, Envy," he growls, close enough for both me and chat to hear him. "Your viewers have decided what they want."

I try to math through the small tips, but right now that's impossible. I can only make a high, questioning noise and wait for Oliver to tell me, or at least tell the chat what he's going to do, since my math skills have regressed to that of a first grader.

"Guess you'll be dripping cum for the next few hours," he laughs darkly, and grips my hips more tightly. "But you're going to come for me first, baby."

I swear softly, coming up off the bed on all fours until he shoves me back down with the palm of one hand.

"No, stay right there. They have a perfect view of your face and how I'm fucking you. Don't take that away from them," he taunts, switching the angle of his thrusts just enough that he rubs against the spot inside of me that makes me see stars every single time.

It's enough to slam me into an orgasm, and I cry out as I come, hands fisting the sheets and twisting them. I nearly lose my mask, though I manage to keep it from popping off just in time, as Oliver slams into me again and holds me in a grip that's bruising while he comes as well.

"So good. Such a good Halloween treat. We just don't deserve our Envy, do we chat?" His voice is rough, and trembles as he keeps himself deep in my body. Oliver moves his hips a few times, just enough to drag another whimper from me, before he finally pulls out and lets my hips fall to the bed.

"Seems she's a little fucked out right now," he tells the viewers, lifting my face up with his fingers tangled in my hair once more. "But I'm sure if she wasn't, she'd tell you all how happy she is that you've made this a great Halloween for her."

I stir, not wanting to let him take the whole burden of ending my stream. "He's right," I say, a smile curling over my lips. "And I'll have to apologize again to Jay for not having any candy, when he was coming here to trick-or-treat," I say, trying to match his savage enthusiasm.

"Nah, I got the sweetest thing for my trouble," he replies, and tilts his head to read the messages of envy and how much most of my viewers wish they could trade places with him. "Sorry guys," he apologizes, a cocky note entering his voice. "Maybe next year you'll knock on the right door too. But this year?" He shoves me back down flat, his knee pressed between my thighs. "This year, she's all mine. Remember her stream schedule, and mine, and we'll see you again."

He ends the stream and I groan, thankful when my laptop is closed and slid to the floor.

"Are you okay? You were so good for me," Oliver promises, pulling off my mask and then his. "Do you want anything?" From his backpack, he procures a bottle of water, which he holds out to me.

I eye him, surprised at the softness in his tone. "You're being really nice," I say finally, taking the water but not getting up. "I thought you'd... leave? Or, I don't know what I thought." My inhibitions are back in full force, reminding me of all the reasons this had been a bad idea.

"Not until I know you're okay. Here. Do you want to put these on? Would it make you more comfortable?" He stands and buttons his jeans, though I half wish I'd gotten a better view of his cock. I can tell how big it is, based on what it had felt like inside me, but I'd still like to *see* it as well.

I stomp down on that thought, trying to pretend it had never hit me as he sits back down with my clothes in his hands.

"Thanks," I murmur, tugging on my shorts and tee. "Do you think my viewers liked what we did?"

"I think you have so many new viewers you won't know what to do with them," Oliver replies. "Did you see how much you made today? Even without Rook?"

I shake my head.

"Over six hundred dollars with him. Without, around three fifty."

"Holy *shit*," I breathe, eyes wide. "That's so much."

"I know." He sounds thrilled for me, his eyes bright. "I'm glad I could help you," he tells me, leaning over to brush his lips so sweetly against mine. "I didn't hurt you, did I Blair?"

"No," I tell him honestly, only needing a second to think about it. "No, I'm really okay."

"Good. Rook would've killed me, if I had. And I would've been pretty upset too." He kisses my forehead and stands up, stretching. "I'll see you later? I have to go get some work done for my thesis, but next time, maybe?"

"Next time," I agree stupidly, not following my own creed on what I *should* be doing and saying. "Thank you, by the way. It was pretty unorthodox, but I appreciate it. And you."

"Anytime," he assures me, and hooks his backpack over his shoulder. "After all, it wasn't exactly a hardship. And I really am looking forward to next time." Without giving me a chance to do more than sit up, he breezes out of the room, whistling.

CHAPTER 22

I look up from my mug of hot chocolate, still staring at the darkening sky. Then I blink and suddenly tune in to the words on the tv behind me, where Juniper is lounging with her arm over her eyes on our long sofa.

"Turn it up," I request, spinning away from the window and falling onto the uninhabited part of the sofa.

She moves her arm enough to open her eyes to slits, hand groping for the remote so she can point it in the direction of the television and hit the volume button.

"*Another detective says that, even though they had been looking for a new suspect, the likely killer is someone they've looked into before.*" The news anchor sounds stern, and her face is set in a grim expression that I can't help but feel is pretty appropriate for the situation.

My heart catches in my throat as an unsteady camera comes around the edge of the news van, a voice yelling their innocence loudly. It sounds like a man, but past that, I can't tell.

Is it Oliver? Is it Rook? My stomach plummets at the

thought, my ribs tightening around my lungs. I should be happy that Oliver has been caught if it is him. I should be relieved... because he is a *murderer* and he's killing people that look like my roommate.

I shouldn't be a nervous wreck as my eyes search the screen for any sign of his face or their house. I shouldn't want to jump to my feet and call them to ask if they're all right.

I shouldn't care this much, or have any kind of need in my system for the cops to be wrong. Setting the hot chocolate down, I try not to sigh loudly in relief when the camera zooms in and focuses on the man's face.

It isn't Oliver, and it isn't Rook. It's someone I don't know, and my eyes narrow as I watch him howl and spit his innocence at the cops and the reporters both. How did they come to the conclusion that it was him?

Rook's unworried face flickers into my mind, and I frown. Was it him? Had he planted the evidence on some innocent guy to make him take the fall for Oliver? The thought is terrifying enough, but the one that comes after is even more so.

What if he's done this before? After all, an open case would probably point to Oliver, eventually. But if the case was closed, with a suspect that everyone believed had done it and reasonable motivations to do so, then no one would ever think it was Oliver, would they?

If the motivations were strong enough, even if the suspect couldn't be sent to jail, public opinion would still be against them.

"The suspect, Walter Mowes, has been convicted of two hate crimes against the Asian community in the past two years. Police are investigating further, but have found both evidence and motivation for the murders of Mikaela Hayes and a college student found earlier this autumn." I wonder why they haven't released her name yet, but the thought just rolls on off of me as I sigh.

They haven't been caught. Neither of them, even though it seems wild to me that they're getting away with this so cleanly. Is it Rook's talent to find someone to take the fall for them? One who has enough motive to keep the cops occupied for months, if not forever? Or is that just something they're good at getting lucky with?

Looking down at my hot chocolate, I'm surprised to find it's empty, and stand up. "I think I'm going to go for a walk," I tell Juniper, who's barely interested in the news, and is back to drowsing on the sofa. "I want to see if I can find anything to shoot for extra credit." Then wave my small camera bag at her, but she's barely paying attention.

"Just be careful," she drawls, tired from her long week. Mine has felt longer, but who am I to tell her that? It isn't a competition, and I'm just wired from nerves.

And from the fact that, even though it's been a week since Oliver broke in and 'helped' me with my stream on Halloween, I can't get the memory of him, of what we'd done, out of my head.

I've never had better sex before, but that's not really an accomplishment. What is one, in my opinion, is the fact that he's had a solid place in my thoughts every night since then. It's been to the point that I've thought about calling him, so I can use his voice to get off.

Luckily, however, the memory of him has been more than enough for that.

"I'll be fine," I assure her, sounding more confident than I feel. "I'm just going to walk down the block." Though, that has gotten me in trouble before, at least this time I *know* who the killer is and I'm not worried that the next victim is going to be me.

At least, I hope I won't. I guess there's always the chance if

Rook and Oliver decide they're done with me, but I can only hope that isn't going to be the case.

My sneakers are loud on the stairs as I take the long way down, and I'm gasping for air like my lungs are closing by the time I get to the sidewalk. Clearly I'm in pretty bad shape, as is obvious from the way my body is protesting a few flights of stairs so strongly. But I set off anyway and try not to gulp air like a dying fish.

I'm partly successful, I think, due to the fact no one is staring at me like a leper staggering around St. Augustine, and I walk past my favorite coffee shop to the quiet street with small, boutique style shops on the other side of it.

By the time I'm there, and my camera is up in my hands as I look around for something to shoot, I feel better. My lungs aren't burning in protest anymore, and I can actually walk without wanting to double over in pain. No more running stairs for me, unless it's absolutely necessary, of course.

I use the front of a small, religion-based boutique for a few shots, using the shadows of night falling to make things look ominous. I find an angle where I can get the praying hands sticking out of the door in a light that gives them a spooky shadow. I like the contrast, and do it again with a few more of their signs before moving on. It isn't that I'm focusing *specifically* on religion, or anything so dramatic.

It's just that I love the contrast, the depth. The irony, sometimes, of taking a thing that should be one way, and finding a way to make it another. Like the cross throwing shadows down to the street below menacingly. Or the praying hands glowing red in the dying sun. It feels like a conversation piece in my brain. A way to start a debate over the meaning of something, instead of just looking at a picture, appreciating it with a bland smile, and moving on.

But maybe that's just the art history major side of me. I'm a sucker for complexity, even if I have to create it myself. Even if I'm going too far, and these won't have the impact that I'm looking for, perhaps Professor Solomon will find it in the goodness of his black, withered heart to point out where I went wrong, or lend Oliver to me for my extra credit. Either is possible, though both are probably unlikely.

By the time I finish shooting a staircase behind a metal grate, the light is mostly gone. The streets are brightened only by the dirty, dingy street lamps, and I realize as I straighten that I feel *off*.

I feel like someone's watching me, or about to breathe on the back of my neck.

Whirling around, I expect to find Oliver there, like a ghost possessing me and able to find me at a moment's notice, but I don't.

I find someone else instead, and I realize instantly that his face is unknown to me, and nothing about him seems familiar.

The man, who might be in his late thirties and probably needs to be thrown into a shower for five days, appears nervous. He looks anywhere but at me, and when he does glance in my direction, it's with wide, almost frightened eyes. A hood covers his hair, though I can see greasy brown strands plastered to his forehead like his sweat can double for glue. His face is shiny with perspiration, and his hands are thrust so forcefully in his pockets I worry he'll tear the thin material of the worn hoodie.

"Hi," he greets, voice almost too soft for me to hear. "I didn't mean to, umm, bother you."

The admonition should put me at ease. I should feel better about him, or at least not feel so awful about the situation. But instead, I frown at him and step backward, my back hitting the grate.

"Do I know you?" I ask, not replying to his apology directly. "Have we met before?"

He opens his mouth to say something, closes it, and looks at me as if he's trying to figure out what to say. I half-think that *I'm* the idiot, and that we've met before or I should obviously know him. But I've definitely never talked to this man for a second in my life, let alone been so close to him.

"I don't think so," he says finally, his foot grinding against the pavement and causing his knee to jerk. "My friend and I..." He looks down at the other end of the street, his tongue darting out to lick at cracked lips. "He's not here or anything," the man assures me, like I had been worried he was.

Problem is, I am. I still am, because he's not so convincing that he's alone.

"I just thought you were someone else," he says finally, slowly and deliberately. His smile, when it's pulled onto his lips like a mask, is apologetic and wide. "I didn't mean to scare you."

"You didn't," I tell him, the words a lie. "I was startled, but I'm not scared. Sorry that I'm not who you're looking for." He doesn't move, so I do. I edge around him, the hair at the back of my neck still standing on end as I march back toward my apartment. I don't know him, and he says he doesn't know me, but somehow that's not quite good enough.

As if he's an unseen shield, I dial Oliver's number.

"*Hello Blair.*" It's Rook who picks up, his voice smooth and velvety. "*Oliver's a little busy—*"

"Can you just talk to me?" I hiss, more hurriedly than I'd meant to sound. "I mean, if you have time—"

"*What's wrong?*" he cuts me off quickly, voice turning sharp. "*Are you all right?*"

"Yeah," I assure him, sucking in a breath as I deliberately

slow my steps. It hits me that I could've called Juniper, and she would've been here in minutes.

So why didn't I?

"Yes, I'm fine. I just had someone startle me." I look over my shoulder, but the man isn't there anymore. Still, I can't shake the feeling that he is, or that he's hiding at the corners of my vision and if I keep looking around fast enough—

"*Where are you?*" He doesn't sound so worked up, and in the background, I think I hear Oliver's questioning voice. "*You promise me you're safe?*"

What an ironic question coming from him.

"Yeah," I breathe, closing my eyes hard for a moment and standing still in the street. "Yes, I'm okay and everything. Someone startled me. I don't know, I'm on edge lately. I think..." trailing off, I suck in a breath. "I just wanted someone to talk to on my way home. But I didn't mean to interrupt whatever you two were doing."

"*I'll talk to you, unless you'd prefer Oliver. He's a little out of it, but I can get him up for you, I believe.*" I'm not sure what 'out of it means' in this context, but I shake my head.

Realizing he can't see me, I smile ruefully and say, "I'm more than okay talking to you, Professor."

"*You can call me Rook outside of class, Love,*" he reminds me with a sniff. "*What have you been doing tonight?*"

"Oh, you know. Taking some pictures for extra credit. I'm taking this photography class with this professor who's kind of insane about grading, so I don't have an A+. Not sure he'll like these either, but maybe I can drag up that B of mine before the end of the semester."

"*Do you deserve an A, Love?*" he hums, making a soft shushing noise that I'm pretty sure isn't directed at me.

"Absolutely I do." It's much easier to talk like this when he isn't in front of me, I find. "I'm the best student ever. Umm..." I trail off, then ask, "Oliver's okay, right? He's not hurt or anything? I watched the news report earlier about, you know. But he's okay?"

Rook chuckles against the phone. *"Yes, Love. He's more than all right. He's just been a little frustrated with me for being so busy, so I was reminding him how much I love him."*

I've certainly never heard either of them use the strong L-Word before, outside of its connection to my name, and it takes me back slightly. "You love him?" The words come out without my permission, and I wince as I turn onto my street. "Sorry. I didn't mean to—"

"Of course I do. I've loved him for over a year, and I like to remind him of that. He's fine. He likes it when I'm rough with him, but I'm a big proponent of aftercare, even if he says he doesn't need it." In the background, Oliver says something I can't make out, though it draws a huffed chuckle from Rook. *"Maybe I'll tell you about it sometime, Love."*

"Oh." There's really nothing else to say, and I let out a tense breath I hadn't known I was holding as I reach the elevator of my building. "I'm. Umm, home now," I tell him, feeling the words fall from my mouth like stones. "I didn't mean to interrupt you—"

"You're always welcome to interrupt us. Do you want anything? Need anything?"

"No. I'm fine," I assure him, feeling small and vulnerable when he says shit like that. It isn't a bad feeling, exactly. Just incredibly strange. "I'm going to go." I'm suddenly uncomfortable, now that I'm not terrified. "Tell Oliver, uh, hi?" That's pretty lame, but I can't think of anything else.

"Will do. Text him to let him know you're all right in the morning, please." It's not a question or a request. But I agree and hang up, then step into the elevator and hit the button so I can lean hard against the far wall and close my eyes hard.

Why didn't I just call Juniper? I'm supposed to be proving to them that I want them to leave me alone. *Not* that I want them to stick around or to keep popping up in my life. I could've called her, and they never would've known.

I could cut them out, and they would leave me alone.

So why is it that the thought makes me nauseous, uncomfortable, and a bit sad?

CHAPTER 23

N o matter how much I want to avoid it, I can't. No matter if I want to stop any conversation from happening, or for Oliver to think I *need* him, I don't know how to get around it this time.

I don't have an eye for photography, and I don't know what to choose for my extra credit. More than that, I need him to read over the report I'd written alongside the group project. When I'd told Oliver after the *kidnapping* that I'd be doing it myself, he hadn't argued. He'd been completely fine with me doing it myself, if that's what I wanted.

Of course, now that's led me here.

I'm not a photography major. I'm not even that knowledgeable about the subject. He is, and he lives with the asshole professor who assigned this in the first place. If anyone can help me figure out what I'm doing so I don't fail the class, it's him.

I let out a breath and close my eyes hard, one hand already reaching for my phone. I don't know if we can do this over a call. More than likely, I'm going to invite him here, and I have a feeling it won't be a fifteen minute visit.

The problem, obviously, is that I don't *want* it to be. Flickers of him fucking me in front of my viewers continuously play through my brain. And while I want to be able to not think about it, maybe, I can't seem to stop.

The other problem is that I want to do it again. I want him to pin me down the moment he gets here, and—

"*Hello?*" My heart races. I'd forgotten I'd already tapped his contact name, and it takes me a moment to get my thoughts together after Oliver answers the phone.

"Hey. Um. Hi," I stammer, wincing at the sound of my own voice. "I'm really sorry. I should've texted you, or... something."

"*No, you can call me anytime,*" Oliver assures me sweetly. "*What's up, wonder girl? What would you like from me?*"

"Uh." I blink a few times, staring down at the photos and my laptop. "I have our project done. I think. But I'm not super sure on a few things, or which photos I should submit for extra credit. I was wondering if you'd help me, maybe? You could come over. I could order pizza, if that's your thing?" I know that I'm rambling now, but I can't help how nervous he makes me.

"*Nah, I'm not coming over,*" Oliver replies, his voice just as kind and enthusiastic as usual.

It takes me a moment to register what he'd said. "What?"

"*You can come over here. No offense, Blair?*" I hear him shift. "*But I kind of hate your roommate. So I hate being somewhere that she might show up, and where she lives. I'm really trying for you. In a lot of ways.*" I blink at my photos, barely able to register what he's really saying. "*I haven't killed anyone else, either. So I'd rather not be tempted to break the streak.*"

"Oh," I breathe lightly. It makes sense, unfortunately. It makes a lot of sense.

"We can do it over the phone, but I'd really prefer it if you just came over with your work. I'll help you with it as much as you want. As much as I'm allowed to, without betraying the whole boyfriend-privilege. And I'll get us dinner. I'll pay for the Uber, too. Since I doubt you want to ride with me again right now."

It's surprisingly thoughtful. Enough so that I sigh and feel my guard relaxing. "Okay," I say finally, thinking about what I'm doing and kicking myself for it. "That's umm. I can do that. You don't have to pay for the Uber, though. That's fine. What time do you want me to—"

"Now," he replies, unable to hide the thrill in his voice. *"I'll text you my address. What do you like to eat?"*

"I'm not picky," I lie. "But I really like chicken? I'll take pizza or whatever you prefer." I don't want to be a weird nuisance at his almost-mansion.

"I'll find something," he promises, my phone buzzing with a message. When I check, I find Oliver's address, and he goes on, *"Just let me know when you're a couple minutes away so I can come outside."*

"Okay. Hey, Oliver?" I ask, before he can hang up.

"Yes, Blair," he says, not waiting for my question. *"Rook is here, too."* With that, he hangs up, leaving me staring at my phone with my lips pressed together.

"I guess that's it then," I sigh, dropping my phone so I can gather up my things. "Maybe he'll be too busy to notice me." I pick up my phone once I'm ready to call an Uber, and do so quickly so I can't back out.

Maybe Rook will be too busy to notice my existence, and maybe my Uber driver will show up on a unicorn. Anything's possible, after all.

· · ·

"It's so nice not getting *dragged* in here and worried I'm about to be cut into kebabs," I remark as Oliver pushes the door open and ushers me inside.

He snorts, closing it behind me, and only the smallest tingle of trepidation crawls down my spine when he does. "I'd never hurt you, wonder girl," he reminds me, taking the lead. I follow him down a hallway, through the kitchen, and up the stairs I'd knocked myself out on. My heart thuds in my chest as I surreptitiously peek into any room for a sign of Professor Solomon, until Oliver adds, "Rook's office is on the other side of the house. You're not going to find him like that."

"I wasn't trying," I lie breezily, ignoring his snort. He pushes open a door and leads me into a large bedroom with a desk on one side. The room is huge, and when I peek through a door that isn't closed, I see that there's a large bathroom on the other side, complete with a glass-walled shower.

"Sure. If you want to email me your essay, or just airdrop it, I can look at it for you. We can look at your photos here, too." He drags a stool beside the impressive office chair, and flips on the desk light that illuminates the surface like a second sun.

It's certainly fancier than what I thought Oliver's room would look like. There are framed photographs on the walls, and the bed is made up neatly with darkly colored linens. The floor is hardwood, and I curl my toes in my flip-flops as I think about how underdressed I am to even exist in a house like this.

Not that it'll be for long, I don't think. A couple of hours, maybe, with dinner included.

I do as Oliver says, sending over the essay for him to read as I arrange the photos in lines on the desk. One for the project that's due, and one for my extra credit. He looks over them, simultaneously reading my essay as his eyes flick from the computer to the photos and back again.

It's quieter than I'd expected. Not only that, he's not

teasing or taunting me as he works. He picks up one photo and pulls it out of the pile, shaking his head, before moving onto the next while I fidget.

"Are they... okay?" I ask, after what has to be eight or ten minutes of him doing this.

"Hmm? Yeah, umm." He shows me the two piles he's made, explaining his picks and which ones he thinks would work best. I nod at his reasoning, not sure about half of the terms he uses, and only some of it really sinks in.

"But you can disagree with me," Oliver promises, sliding the photos back in my direction. "You're not like, bound to use the ones I think are best."

"I want to use them," I assure them as he leans closer to me, shoulder brushing mine so he can flick his eyes over the essay again. "I trust you." His mouth flicks upward in a smile, eyes never wavering, and I quickly add, "With photography, I mean. I don't know if I trust you... with other things."

"Your essay is okay. Just give it a once over before you turn it in, if you want. But I didn't see anything glaring. What other things *don't* you trust me with, Blair?" he asks, scooting closer. "The rest of your portfolio review you're turning in?"

I drop the folder of the other photos from the semester that I've chosen to turn in to Professor Solomon, and Oliver slides it open without looking away from me.

"You know," I say, barely able to move now that he's so close. His knee slides between both of mine, and even when he looks away, he doesn't pull it back.

This time, his review takes longer. He points out the flaws in my work, making me feel somewhat bad about not knowing enough about photography, but tells me that I should do well overall. When I glance at my phone, I'm surprised to see it's already been forty minutes since we'd started.

I like doing this, I realize. Oliver is intelligent and articulate. I like working with him, and the way he throws ideas back at me to make me think. It's just too bad about everything else.

Realizing he's asked me a question, I glance up, brows raised. "What?"

"I asked how your stream is going," Oliver replies easily, gathering up my other photos and putting them back into the folder. He puts that back into my backpack as well, then zips it up. "Since Halloween."

"I feel like people are disappointed you aren't there," I admit, shrugging my shoulders. "You made it exciting. I'm kind of boring."

"You're not boring," Oliver assures me, getting to his feet and leaving me in the office chair. "You're not boring at all. Do you want to figure out some ways to be more exciting? That's how I built an audience. Consistency, yes. They want to know what they're going to get from you. But, I hate to say it, sweet and shy isn't going to do it forever. Especially for your long time viewers. You have to take risks."

"Because you fucking me on stream wasn't a risk?"

He grins and takes a step back. "I have an idea for you, if you'll take it," he admits, almost shyly. "It's pretty popular when streamers do it. Especially women. *Especially* with your mask. But I'm not going to make you."

His attitude shift is... strange. I study Oliver, unsure of where he is heading with this. He hasn't led me astray before, and he *has* helped me grow my stream. Even if it was inspired by him originally, it's my thing now. And it's my *job*. I'll do anything to make more.

"Okay," I agree, getting to my feet.

"Just wait here. I'll be back." He escapes the room quickly, and I hear the sound of rummaging from further down the hallway.

Standing there, I tap my heels on the hardwood, looking

around the room again. This really isn't what I expected from Oliver, and when I creep to the bathroom and look inside, it just makes me more confused. It's just so... perfect. Oliver is such a chaotic mess, even at the best of times, that this feels a lot more like—

"What are you doing in my bathroom, Love?" The following sigh makes me jump, and I whirl around just as Rook leans back against the wall by the door.

"Your bathroom?" I repeat nervously, stepping away from the open door. "But Oliver said this was his room."

"His room looks like a tornado hit it at the best of times." Rook's eyes flick to the desk where my backpack sits. "He told me he was going to review your work today. Is that why you're here? Trying to get Oliver to help you not fail?"

I suck in a breath, my hands trembling. Oliver makes me nervous, sure, but Rook? He still frightens me when we're face to face. Especially when we're here, inside his home. "He's my project partner," I remind him coolly, keeping my gaze on his. "We were just going over everything to turn it in."

Oliver strides back in, brow quirked as he passes Rook. "I told you that we were using your room," he reminds him, tossing a black plastic bag on the bed.

"You didn't," Rook informs him smoothly. "You said she was coming over, but that was it. Why *did* you pick my room, exactly?"

When Oliver grins, Rook shakes his head and scoffs. "Careful, Oliver," he warns. "You're likely to chase her out that door again if you're not considerate of Blair's feelings, and her misgivings about you."

"I'd never hurt you," Oliver replies, though the words are directed at me instead of his professor and lover. "Come on." He sinks down onto the bed, but I hesitate beside it, looking back at my professor.

He inclines his head towards the mattress, then turns and walks right back out the door.

"Are you sure he doesn't hate me?" I breathe, wanting to be quiet in case he isn't gone.

"Rook?" Oliver looks up, and towards the door as well. "He likes you a lot. You'd know if he didn't." I don't know how that could be true, but my attention is stolen by the contents of the bag that he's dumped onto the bed.

"No." I state, making him snicker. Still, my hands reach out anyway, until I'm touching the soft fur of the *tail* that sits between us. As I do, I can't decide if I'm more appalled by the existence of the shiny plug that it's attached to, or the size.

Probably the size.

"Why not?" Oliver laughs, running his fingers over it as well. The purple fur curls around his fingers, and the black stripe on one side looks like it would be painting a runway straight to my body. "It's gorgeous. And it's unexpected. You'd shock them, wow them, and have them begging you for more."

"Okay, first off. I don't even know how to put it on. In," I correct, feeling my face blush. "Second, it's huge. There's literally no way. None."

"It's *really* not that bad," Oliver assures me, and picks up the small bottle of lube to show me, as if that's proving anything. "Whatever you're thinking is worse than it is."

"I don't believe you," I say, meeting his eyes. I don't mean it as a challenge, but I see the sparkle in the depths of his gaze that makes my stomach twist into knots.

Shit.

"If you don't believe me, then prove me wrong." His words come out as a low purr, and he leans closer to me on Rook's huge bed. "I promise, wonder girl. It wouldn't hurt a bit. Just let me show you."

"I don't know," I whisper, hating the way he's so good at

overwhelming me. God, I don't trust him. I have such good intentions when it comes to the two of them, but every time he leans in like this, his breath on my lips, I just... melt.

It's unfortunate, to say the least. Especially when Oliver takes advantage of my indecision and presses me back onto the comforter. He crawls over me, his thighs bracketing my hips, to lean down and press his lips sweetly to mine.

"I'd never hurt you," he purrs, his voice so sweet.

"I don't know," I say again, letting him roll us over until I'm the one on top, straddling him. His grin is wide, like he's done something so smart, but all I can see is that now I'll have an easier time escaping. "It's not you, Oliver," I lie, voice faltering once more. It is, a little. If I was going to have someone show me how to use one, I don't know if it would be him. Not with how rough he likes to play.

"Isn't it?" he asks, eyes dancing. "Aren't you worried that I'm too rough, too fast, and not patient enough to open you up to take that in your ass, wonder girl?"

I don't answer right away. His argument is exactly what I'm thinking, but I don't understand *why*. Unless he just doesn't want to do it, anyway, and this was all a joke to begin with to get me right here.

"It's a better idea not to trust him." The voice in my ear is accompanied by a hand running up my spine to curl around my neck. I gasp just as Oliver's arms wrap around my waist, not letting me go. Not that I could go anywhere when Rook's body slides against my back.

The bed dips under his weight as I try to squirm out of Oliver's hold, but Rook just chuckles and kisses the skin under my right ear. "You're fine," he urges, hand flat against my back. "You're fine, Love. We're just helping you."

"I don't know how this is helping me," I hiss. "It feels like you're tricking me."

"I don't need to trick you. Oliver's right, and I've seen it in your stream before. Some of your other viewers think you'd look good as their 'pet.' Why don't you want to capitalize on that?" His voice is warm and soothing, and sends shudders down my spine.

"I've never done that," I say, still meeting Oliver's eyes.

"That's why we're not going to let Oliver ruin it for you. You're at our house anyway, aren't you? And all three of us know how much you enjoy it when we play with you." I shiver at his words, and he makes an approving sound in his throat.

He's right, but he shouldn't be. I shouldn't be this willing to throw everything out the window.

"It doesn't mean anything," Oliver assures me, but I don't think I believe him. "We're just helping you with ideas for your stream. Whenever I want to do something new, he helps me, too."

"You're dating," I point out, already feeling Rook's fingers hooking in the hem of my running shorts.

"And you're in need of ideas," Rook answers, pulling them smoothly down. His fingers run back up my skin, massaging my calves and thighs as I try to at least pull away so I can see what he's doing.

"Stay with me," Oliver insists, dragging me down for a kiss. His arm wraps around my hips, fingers dragging over my skin as his other hand curls in my hair.

"Wait," I say, my voice soft as Rook's fingers find my thighs. "What if it hurts?"

"Then I'm doing it wrong," Rook replies almost kindly. "And Oliver never seems to have any complaints."

"None," Oliver agrees enthusiastically. "Absolutely zero."

Rook waits as I think it over, though his thumbs rub comforting circles against my hips. I can't help the small shudder that goes through me at the reassuring motions, and I take a deep breath, my heart pounding against my ribs. "You'll stop if I ask?" I demand, my eyes on Oliver's since I can't look at Rook.

"Of course I will," he agrees, and I can't decide if I hear a note of anticipation in his voice, or it's just my heart thumping in my ears.

"Okay," I whisper, mind racing. "Okay, umm. Do you need me to do something?"

"I need you to kiss Oliver," the man behind me says smoothly. "He's been dying to kiss you properly all day. Can't you tell?" As if on cue, Oliver tugs me back down to him, lips crushing against mine. He's intense, and his intentions are clear when he deepens the kiss as quickly as he can to explore every inch of my mouth with his tongue.

It's hard to focus on him, no matter how much I love kissing him. It's hard to do anything but be hyper aware of Rook's hands on my thighs, or the sound of a cap clicking open that makes me flinch.

"Just relax, Love," my professor soothes, smoothing a hand down my spine and shoving my t-shirt up my body. "Just relax. I'll make this good for you, I promise."

Still, I whimper into Oliver's mouth when Rook's fingers skim up my slit until he's teasing my hole. I tense, even though he murmurs his disapproval, as one finger slowly enters me, sending a light burning sensation up my spine.

But it isn't as painful as I thought it would be. Finally, when he sinks another finger into me and I don't fall into a thousand pieces, I let out a sigh into Oliver's mouth and feel my body relax around his fingers.

"Good girl," he soothes, other hand against my hip. "Just relax for me like that." His fingers move inside me, dragging a soft moan from my lips at the not-quite painful stretch.

"This is the worst part, baby," Oliver agrees when I turn my face away from his to hiss my discomfort. "When it's new and you don't know what comes next? It kind of sucks. But it's not *that* bad, right?"

"I don't know yet," I admit in a small voice. My body tries to tense when Rook spreads his fingers wide, dragging a whimper from me, but he stops the movement and holds his hand still, my brain registering confusion when he does.

At least until his other hand finds my slit. His fingers tease me, flicking over my clit, until once again I'm relaxed enough that he can keep going.

It's not long before he pulls away, however, surprising me and causing me to arch my back at the strange, empty sensation now that he's not touching me.

"Don't go anywhere, puppy," Rook chuckles, pushing me back down against Oliver. Being flush against him makes me realize just how much he loves me wiggling around against him, and I look away so he can't see my face flush at the realization. "Don't hold your breath," my professor advises, hand pressed against my skin at the base of my spine. "Just breathe. It's not much bigger than my fingers."

I feel the cold metal of the plug for just a second before he pushes it in, slowly, and I can't help the strangled sound that leaves me. "You're a liar," I mutter, face against Oliver's shoulder. "You're such a fucking liar."

"I am," Rook agrees. "It's bigger than my fingers, but that's okay. You're okay, Love. See?" He sits back, hand still on my back. "It's there, and you're fine. You're more than fine."

I sit up, unable to not reach behind me to feel the soft fur of the wolf-like tail. I gasp when it twists inside me, and quickly drop it, seeing Rook's grin when I do.

"You're not doing it right," he tells me, voice rough as he reaches forward. Before I can ask what he's doing, he runs his hand along the fur, then gives it a soft tug that brings a yelp to my lips. "There you go. That's how you do it right."

"*Fuck*," I snap, surprised at how sensitive I am just to something like that. "I don't know if I can wear this for a stream. It's too much."

"It's not," Oliver disagrees, rolling to his knees. When I meet his eyes, I'm surprised at the dark, excited look he wears, and I pause.

"Yeah?" I ask, unsure.

"Nah, Blair. It's not too much for you. Can I see? Please?"

I just stare at him, searching his gaze, and shrug one shoulder. "You can already see it."

"Okay, I want to play with it," he admits, just as Rook's hands catch at my shoulder and my throat. He kneels on the bed and pulls me against his thigh, one hand cupping my neck as Oliver kneels between my spread thighs.

"He's not going to hurt you," my professor promises, eyes catching mine. Rook feathers his fingers over my jaw, still holding me firmly in place, as Oliver strokes his hands up my thighs. Then teases the tail and tugs on it lightly, drawing soft sounds from me while Rook just fucking *watches*.

"You're such a fucking sweet little puppy, aren't you?" Oliver breathes. "Won't you stay the night? Please? You can keep your shirt; but all I want is to see you walk around like this. I'll get you a leash and the prettiest collar... let me keep you, wonder girl. Let me keep you for my very own little pet."

"I'm not—" I begin, but I don't get to finish. Not when Oliver shoves two fingers into me and I lean backward further, back arching, so Rook is forced to sit down on the bed and settle me more comfortably on his lap.

He moves his legs, one of them still under me while he stretches the other out against my side, as if to keep me right where I am. Thanks to both of them, I'm flat on my back now, hips off the bed to keep as much pressure off of the tail as I can while Oliver arranges himself between my thighs.

"If she's your puppy, you should take care of her," Rook says lazily, his free hand reaching down to tug on my tee. My heart races as he pulls it upward enough to unhook my bra, and my breasts spill free for him to touch.

He doesn't wait. With his hand still on my throat, he teases my breasts, fingers pinching and pulling at my nipples. It's hotter than it has any right to be, and I can't help writhing under him as Oliver fingers me somewhat impatiently.

"I would always take care of you, wonder girl," he informs me, meeting my eyes. "I'll give you everything you need. You know I would. *Fuck*, you don't know how much I want to. I bet you'd be so good for me. I bet you'd do *anything* for me, wouldn't you?" He wastes no time unzipping his jeans and pulling them down his thighs until his length is free, and my breath catches at the sight.

"Maybe it's a little cliche," he chuckles, as Rook wraps his arms around as much of my shoulders as he can reach. It still gives him access to my throat, and when I look up, I see that he's just as excited as Oliver, and his muscles are tight against me. "But God, wonder girl. I just want to fuck you like you're a bitch in heat."

"What—" I don't get to continue with whatever indignation I'd been going for. Oliver grips my hips and slides home, causing me to cry out under him.

"Wait," Rook growls, after about thirty seconds of Oliver's frenzy. "*Wait.* I'm going to move her. I'm going to hold her for you, Oliver."

Oliver pulls away, eyes nearly glowing with intensity, and his lips parted as he stares at me. I don't know what to say, and I certainly don't know what to do when Rook drags me up against him, hooking my knees over his to spread me wide for Oliver once more.

And Oliver doesn't waste a second, he just *lunges* forward. The new angle drives him even deeper and I shriek, surprised at the new feeling that has me reeling.

"Fuck, oh *fuck*," I cry out, not resisting when my head is yanked back so Rook can attack my throat with his teeth. Oliver joins him, his mouth on my jaw pressing sloppy kisses against my skin.

"She's so good," he growls, hands wandering up my body as he fucks me. "I told him you'd be so *fucking* perfect, Blair. Holy shit." He keens when Rook reaches up to tug on his hair, drawing his mouth away from me so he can slam their mouths together hard enough I can hear a click of teeth.

I can't help but watch. I don't think I could do anything else *but* watch the two of them devour each other on the spot as Oliver fucks me. Rook's other hand leaves my body, since he doesn't need to hold me anymore, and wraps around Oliver's hip to urge him forward, welcoming him to thrust even deeper into me.

A soft whine leaves my lips, though I don't know if it's protest or encouragement. Either way it draws their attention, and Rook turns to catch my lips this time, giving Oliver the perfect opportunity to fasten his teeth in my skin, at the juncture between my neck and shoulder.

He bites down, and I *scream* into Rook's mouth. His reaction is just to laugh, however, his lips curling against mine as he drinks in every soft, pained noise I make as Oliver leaves a mark in my skin.

"I'm gonna come," Oliver pants, fisting his hand in my hair as Rook's falls free. "Fucking *perfect*, gorgeous girl. I'm going to come so deep in your pussy you'll be dripping for days. Don't you fucking move, oh *fuck* don't you move." I can't, which he doesn't seem to consider, and finally after a few more thrusts, he buries himself deep inside me and presses his body flush to mine.

The fact that I haven't come yet barely registers in my own brain, so I doubt Oliver is thinking about it, either. And it isn't until he pulls back, leaving me empty, that I realize maybe, *maybe*, I'm not done.

Oliver tugs on me, guiding me into his lap as he falls backward onto the bed. I end up with my face against his stomach, lips grazing his skin.

Though it doesn't register until Rook's fingers find my hips why we're in this position.

"You can take me, too," Rook assures me, when I make a small noise of hesitation. "Look at you, so wrecked already. You can absolutely take me, too. I wish you could see yourself. Dripping Oliver's cum and your cunt begging for more. Look at you." I feel his length brush my slit seconds before he slides in as deeply as he can.

"Ready to beg for it, aren't you, my sick little puppy?" He holds me in place, and when I try to sit up, he grabs both of my hands and pins them behind me so I can't go anywhere at all. He's quieter than Oliver, who finally sits up enough to drag his fingers through my hair and watch Rook thrust into me.

He's slower, as well, though every thrust is as deep as possible and makes me see stars.

"I'm going to come," I whine, shuddering under Oliver's fingers in my hair. "Fuck, I'm going to come—"

"Not yet, you aren't," Rook sighs in contentment, finally letting go of my arms. "Don't get up. Don't make me pin you there." I try anyway, only for his hand to find my spine and press. "I'll give you this one, Love. But just this once. Don't you come. Not until I tell you to."

I shudder under him, body on edge. God, I *need* to come. "I can't—"

"Yes, you can. You'll wait until I tell you to." He tugs on the tail, causing me to cry out, and I hear his soft chuckle behind me. "Not yet, Love. Don't come yet."

I wait, trying so hard not to come, that I'm *sobbing* into Oliver's lap. My classmate comforts me with soft, sweet noises and his fingers in my hair. "You can do it," he promises. "You're so good, you look so amazing like this. Just behave for us and let us wreck you, baby."

I shake my head, though I don't know what I'm disagreeing with since I'm already in this position as it is.

"Thirty more seconds, Love," Rook promises, just as his thrusts pick up until he's slamming into me. I gasp, then shriek again when he continues to tug on the tail in time with his thrusts. "Good puppy. Good girl," he says, encouraging me ever so sweetly. "Are you ready to come for me?"

"Yes!" I yelp, squirming on the sheets. "Yes, a thousand times yes—"

"Then fucking *beg*." He snarls. "Beg me to come, Love."

For some reason, it doesn't even occur to me to hesitate. My lips fall open and I babble out a thousand pleas, a thousand variations of asking him to please, *please* let me come because I need it so badly.

He laughs again, darkly, and strokes a hand down my spine. "That's all I wanted. Come for me, my sick little puppy. Come for me while I fill you up."

As if trained like the puppy they're calling me, I come at his words. My eyes close hard, and he continues to stroke my hair as my body tenses around Rook's cock as he fills me up like he'd said he would. For a few moments I'm sure I'll pass out, but finally my orgasm finishes tearing through me, and instead, I go limp, my weight falling more completely against Oliver.

"Good girl," Rook praises, gently easing out of my body. "You're so good. Don't move for me, darling. Just stay still." With a hand on my hip, he slowly slides the tail plug out of me, causing me to whimper. "So good. Now you just need to let us take care of you."

CHAPTER 24

"What?" I finally ask, trying to blink away the fog that threatens to put me right to sleep after such mind blowing sex.

"You heard me," Rook replies, getting to his feet. He goes to the bathroom with the tail, and when he comes back, it's with a dark, damp towel in his hands. "Can you roll over for me? Let me clean you up, darling?"

"This is... weird?" I ask the ceiling, doing what he asks as he runs a towel over my inner thighs. "Like this just feels really strange. Why are you being so nice to me?" Then I watch as Rook cleans himself up as well, and gives the towel to Oliver, before he throws it back into the bathroom and comes to sit on the bed once more.

"This is aftercare," Oliver says, shifting to sit at the head of the bed. I'm not *particularly* sore, exactly. Though I feel like I could be. "Don't tell me you've never had aftercare before."

"No," I admit, shrugging one shoulder as Oliver tugs me up beside him. Rook moves to sit beside me, one leg outstretched and the other knee raised, so his foot is propped on the bed while he studies me.

"I guess with your past relationships, it wasn't strictly necessary," he says, reaching down to run his fingers through my hair. "But no matter what, even if it's just sex, I like for us to check in here, at the very least. And you did a lot for us."

Did I?

"You were so good," Oliver agrees, causing me even more confusion when he wraps his arm around my waist and kisses my shoulder gently. "Do you want a bottle of water?"

"I'm fine," I say, still wondering if this is still some part of their game. "You know you didn't hurt me, right?" Sure, I'd gotten carried away. It definitely wasn't my intention to come over here and let them fuck me like this. But I'm fine, and it's not like they've injured me or whatever they seem to think.

Rook's smile is soft and caring, and so out of place on his face it nearly convinces me I've gone crazy. "Just because I haven't hurt you, doesn't mean you don't deserve to be taken care of. Do you feel okay? Was the tail all right?"

"It was fine. It hurt a little, so clearly I've been lied to and traumatized, but it wasn't *terrible*." I should leave. I know I should leave, especially with Oliver curling tighter and tighter around me like a damn octopus.

The bigger problem is, I don't want to push him away.

Rook reaches down again to stroke a knuckle over my cheek, searching my face for something that I doubt he'll find. Hell, I don't even know what it is.

"Next time, I'll be better prepared," he tells me, leaning down enough to kiss my hair. "I like to keep a fridge stocked for him. He's starving after I play with him. And next time, you're drinking water as soon as we're done."

I don't *feel* dehydrated, if that's what he's getting at. But with the rush of adrenaline wearing off and Oliver's soft touches, I can't help but feel like I'm going to fall asleep.

"I can't stay the night," I murmur, fighting myself to stay awake as I remember how bad of an idea it would be. "I can't stay at all. All I came over for was for Oliver to look at my photography... stuff." It's a losing battle. Even with every reason that this is a bad idea marching through my brain in repetition, I just can't keep my eyes open.

"Sure, baby," Oliver murmurs in my ear. "It's just a little nap, wonder girl. It doesn't mean anything."

I'm drifting off, and I can feel my breathing change as sleep drags me down, yet I can still hear Rook's amused question as I go.

"You really think she believes that, Oliver?"

"No," comes Oliver's voice, just before I lose sense of everything around me. "But maybe we can keep convincing her, just for a little while."

When I wake up, it occurs to me I've been carried out to the couch. The smell of food drags me out of my coma, and I sit up with a groan and the realization I have my clothes back on, except for my bra.

"What time is it?" I mumble, staggering to my feet. No matter what time it is, I need to leave. I need to go home... and according to my sneering stomach, I need *food*.

"It's almost midnight," Oliver informs me lightly, smiling from the kitchen. Rook is standing at the stove, cooking something that looks like extra thick bread. "You seemed to be waking up, so Rook's making breakfast."

I look between them, a little confused, and ask, "Breakfast? Did you really just say breakfast?" The sense of caution is creeping back in, but hunger beats it back with a stick.

"Yeah," Rook says, turning to drop another piece of French toast on a plate. "And since I doubt you like your eggs burned, I cooked for you." He puts a plate in front of me, and one in front of Oliver, before getting both of us water out of the fridge.

It's entirely... domestic. Especially with how Oliver is drowning his sausage and French toast in maple syrup and acting like this is just a typical midnight. But it isn't. Not to me, anyway.

And Rook is never this nice to me.

"This doesn't mean anything," I say, staring down at the plate of food that looks amazing. "I don't—I can't stick around you. While I appreciate all of this, once I don't have a class with Oliver or you, that's it. I won't have a reason to keep coming over here."

Rook leans his hip against the counter, arms folded for a second before he reaches up to push his dark hair out of his eyes. "Is that so?" he asks, as if he doesn't want to argue with me but doesn't quite believe me.

Which is fair, since I'm not sure if I actually believe myself in this situation.

"You can't think I would stay around, right?" I stab into the French toast, tearing off a piece before bringing it to my mouth. My face must show how good it is, because Rook looks pleased. "I mean. Because... you know." My eyebrows raise as he studies me, and I feel a flush creeping up my cheeks.

Oliver doesn't say anything, though I don't know if it's because he's too engrossed in his food or because he wants to see me make a fool of myself.

"No, I don't think I do. Go on," Rook invites. "Tell me why you just *can't* make this a thing and give us a chance."

"Because you're serial killers!" I snap, my voice quieter than I mean it to be. "You kidnapped me!"

"Only barely. He's pretty bad at kidnapping, as I think we've both discovered. It's not in his future," Rook remarks, eyes sliding to Oliver before coming back to rest on mine. "Go on."

"No, that's it. That's the whole thing. *I'm not a serial killer.* This is..." I don't like using the word mistake, so I bite it back. This doesn't feel like a mistake, either. It feels, well, stupid. But not accidental. "I don't know what this is or was. I guess it's Oliver helping me and. Umm... I guess we all got carried away. How can I be okay with this, when you're killing women because you want to hurt my best friend so much?"

"I didn't get carried away," Oliver points out quietly, like his feelings are hurt. "What makes you think I did? Not to mention, I'm killing them *because* I don't want to hurt your feelings."

"She doesn't mean us, Oliver," Rook explains smoothly, gaze holding mine. "She means that *she* got carried away. Isn't that what you're trying to say, Love? That you came over here expecting just a little classwork and now you can't fathom why you let us fuck you like that?"

The heat climbs up my cheeks, and I can't hold his gaze any longer. Not when he looks at me with a mix of accusation and understanding. "It's okay to like it," he points out. "And it's okay to let me take care of you."

"No, it's not," I snap quietly, sliding to my feet. Even though I don't want to go, I have to make a point here. Even if my resolve is crumbling to shit, I can't let them believe that. "I can't; I told you that. I told you I didn't want you in my life like... that."

Still, I blink back frustration, and look around for my things. "Where's my backpack?" I ask, stepping away from Oliver when he slides off the stool. Needing to be cold. I *need* to act aloof, like it doesn't bother me.

Fuck, I really need it not to bother me.

"Right there." Rook doesn't sound perturbed, even though I

can't look at him or Oliver. "Everything is in it, including what you aren't wearing. Do you want me to call you an Uber?"

"No," I say. "I want to do it myself. I'm going to wait outside, too. Okay?" God, why am I asking for *permission*?

"Not okay," Rook denies, dragging my gaze up to his with surprise. He raises a brow, and shakes his head again. "Call an Uber, and wait in here. It's midnight in St. Augustine. I don't want anything happening to you."

What a bold thing to say, when he's the scariest thing here.

"You don't have to go," Oliver murmurs, disappointment lacing his words. "You could stay—"

"No." Meeting his eyes, with my own wide, and maybe a little afraid. "I have to go, Oliver. I just... have to go."

Thankfully, he doesn't argue. Neither of them do, while I stand by the door and wait for Bob the Uber driver to show up.

And when he does, I try very hard not to look back. Even if I do, I pretend not to see the hurt on Oliver's face, or the way Rook watches me with a misplaced concern that I never would've pictured him wearing.

They're serial killers, I remind myself with every single step. They're bad, dreadful even. And everything that's wrong with the world, and I can't keep doing this.

So why is it, then, that I can't convince myself that *they're* the real problem? Or that I don't want to stride back in, pull up my chair, and have another piece of French toast before falling asleep in Oliver's bed?

CHAPTER 25

Getting them out of my head is difficult. So is not running everything through my head that had happened, and instead I try to take a pointed interest the weather.

St. Augustine, after all, is nothing like indiana.

In November, back home, the temperature can be anywhere from seventy to twenty. Sometimes lower, quite frankly, since Indiana has a mind of its own and can't be controlled by something so trivial as seasons or averages. I've seen snow, ice storms, and people snowboarding in t-shirts in November, and none of it has me bat an eye anymore.

But St. Augustine is different. It's *warm* here, and only marginally cooler than it was a month ago, or even two months ago. The weather is just as muggy, just as rainy, and just as humid. If not even more so, honestly. The one thing I won't miss about this place is the humidity, even if I enjoy the storms that hit the city on a much more frequent basis than the ones back home.

After all, I much prefer a thunderstorm to three inches of snow covered by an impenetrable layer of literal ice.

Delivering the end of my farewell, I smile sweetly at my webcam and end my stream. I've been steadily gaining viewers since I picked up streaming again, though I have a feeling that's due to Oliver, or *letsplayjay* to the masses, promoting me on his channel and talking about how much fun it had been to work with me. I'm pretty sure he'd said something along the lines of joining me for my stream again to his viewers, or suggesting I might show up on his stream instead.

But if those are his intentions, he hasn't said anything to me about them. Nor has he made any kind of formal invite, or anything else.

Maybe they're just words to tease his viewers. He's good at that. He's good at doing things that make people want more of him, instead of like me, when all I can do is act the shy, inexperienced camgirl who plays on the emotions of guys who like that kind of thing.

Somehow, when I try to smoosh Oliver and Rook into that category, it makes my nose curl in disgust, and I immediately chase the thoughts away. They don't seem to like me for those reasons. They don't make comments about my innocence, my vulnerability, or about how unsure I am. Not like my viewers do when they suggest and tease and sometimes taunt.

I'm thankful. Because if they did, I doubt I'd want to be around either of them very much.

Then again, if they did, it would be easier to do what I need to. It would be that much less of a challenge to shove Oliver away from me, which I know would push Rook away as well. I have to, I think, because of what they are.

Serial killers can't love anyone. And Oliver is insane sometimes. Getting the look on his face from the night he'd basically kidnapped me out of my head is impossible, even though he didn't hurt me. Getting the idea out of my head that he killed proxies to make up for not wanting to kill Juniper is terrifying. Normal people don't do that. Surely you have to be born that way, with a propensity for killing people. People like Juniper, or definitely me, aren't capable of being *monsters*.

Right?

The phone rings, surprising me, and I nearly fall out of my chair as I rip off my mask and pull my t-shirt on before looking at the name.

It's my mom. Of course it is, when I know she has a fun habit of calling at the absolute worst time ever. Maybe she doesn't mean to, and maybe it's just a magical sense she was born with. Either way, it's her gift to bestow upon this world, and I can't think of a worse time for her to call, except in the middle of my stream.

"Hey, mom," I greet after I've scooped the phone up to my ear. I pad, barefoot, to my bed and flop down onto it, groaning audibly at the relaxation that clouds my brain from the change in position. "I've missed you. Looking forward to having me home for almost two months?" With the end of the semester only two more weeks from now, the last thing to do is to get my exams done and get my group project grade back from Rook. Is it terrifying that he only has one major assignment, along with a few minor ones, to see if we've passed? Absolutely.

But he's also clearly a sadist, so there's that.

"*I've got your bedroom back in order for you, in case you finish your exams early and come home sooner than you planned,*" my mom says, a smile in her voice and her tone warm. "*I'll be so excited to have you home. There's a few new shops in that old strip mall they've been sprucing up that I want to take you to. We'll get you a new spring wardrobe. Maybe something that makes you look like a professional young woman, hmm?*"

I roll my eyes at her good intentions, though I'm not offended by them. As a lawyer who owns her own practice, my mom is very aware at all times of the impression someone is making based on their makeup or how they dress. She used to be worse with me, while I was a child, but after I had a phase of goth clothes, black makeup running down my face, and my hair dyed box-black, she'd learned to lighten up with me. In return, I'd promised to moderate my tastes a little. I had no problem tempering them for her when that was the goal of my social experiment in the first place. Not that she's ever heard that from my lips, if she knows at all.

"I don't need to look professional, mom," I point out with a snicker. "I need to look like an eccentric artist. You know, I took a photography class this semester. We could look for 'successful but strange photographer' outfits, too."

"*Sure. Just remind me how they dress, exactly? I can't say I've paid much attention to any eccentric, successful, talented photographers in the last few years,*" my mother replies, full of good humor. I love her for the way we can carry on a light conversation full of inane banter like this.

"Oh, lots of blacks, for sure. Cute little hats. Plaid pants in all neutral colors and a turtleneck."

"*I thought you hated turtlenecks.*"

"Well, yeah. But we can make do." She laughs at my words, and I can't help the small huff of a giggle that leaves me as well. "How are you? How's Dad?"

"*Just as excited as I am to see you,*" mom assures me. "*He dragged down the Christmas boxes last week. I've never seen him itching so much to put up the tree. But you know how disappointed he was last year when he was in the hospital and we didn't get to celebrate properly. Between you and me, I think it's his intention to do double the decorating to make up for it.*"

"It's only November!" I protest, even though I can see my

dad doing exactly as she's described. He's always loved Christmas more than any other holiday, and takes pains to make sure our house, which sits at the end of a subdivision, looks like Santa personally uses it as a vacation home. At first, he'd maintained that it was because I was a kid and therefore deserved all the Christmas cheer in the world.

But now that I'm an adult, we all know it's just because he likes doing it so much. I smile when I think about what the house will look like in two weeks when I'm home, and also at the fact that home is my safe haven.

Nothing there presents me with difficult moral dilemmas wrapped up in pretty packages, either.

"*I just wanted to call and tell you I'm looking forward to you being home,*" my mom goes on, once we've had a laugh about Dad's decorating. "*I know you're probably preparing for exams, and I don't want to interrupt you. If Juniper's there, tell her I say hi.*"

"She isn't, but I'll tell her when she's back," I assure Mom, not remarking on the comment about what I could be doing right now. "I'm so excited to come home. I haven't seen the snow in ages, and I miss it."

"*You hate the cold and the snow.*"

"Well, yeah, but it's nostalgic," I agree with a laugh. "Tell Dad I said hi? And that I expect a twelve foot tree to be in the living room when I'm home."

"*I don't think I will,*" my mom replies dryly. "*Or he'll take it to heart. Have a good week, Blair. I love you.*"

"I love you too, Mom." I can't disguise the warmth in my voice, and I would never want to. My mother has always been my biggest supporter, and she's one of my best friends. "Have a good night."

She repeats the sentiment and hangs up, prompting me to get to my feet and drag my laptop over to the bed with a sigh. I look at the amount that was dropped into my account thanks to my stream, and thank Rook for contributing over half of it. Just like he does with Oliver's stream, I've noticed that he has to be the top tipper in mine as well.

And even though I've brought up that he doesn't have to give me money, it doesn't seem to make a difference or to sink in. He sends it anyway, and I don't know what to say anymore to stop him. It's also unfortunate that part of me doesn't *want* him to stop. Thanks to Rook, I've been able to set aside some money in a savings account, and use the rest for things like more coffee, pancakes, and small things just for me.

Another message catches my attention, and I groan at the sight of *rob784* flashing in my inbox. He's never done anything wrong, exactly, but I just don't like him. He doesn't tip well, if at all, and he never contributes anything to the stream except weird, filthy fantasies about me written out in long form in the chat box for everyone else to see.

It gives me the ick, honestly.

Still, I roll my eyes and open the message, expecting some generic line about how he enjoyed my stream or whatever. I'll tell him thanks, move on with my day, and won't have to deal with him until the next time.

Only, that's not what I find. My eyes narrow as I read the message again, tapping my fingers on the desk beside my laptop.

Your streams are better without that guy from halloween, and watching you getting fucked like a whore isn't what I signed up for. Besides, you could do better.

I read it again, unable to really process what he's said for a few moments. Shame tries to bubble up in my chest, but anger wins out. I don't care about keeping him as a fan. Frankly, I never have.

If you don't like him, you don't have to watch any of my streams at all. He's my friend, and we'll probably collaborate again. There are plenty of women who never work with a man, and you're welcome to their streams at any time. If he hadn't called me a whore, I wouldn't have been so shitty. But I don't deserve the insult and I'm not going to take it politely.

His response comes faster than I expect, or want it to.

Sorry for looking out for you. I've put a lot of dedication into your stream, you know. I don't have to be here.

Dedication, my ass.

Then don't, I reply, and slam my laptop lid shut. I'm not looking into getting into some stupid argument with a man I don't give a shit about. I'm not looking for an argument at all, today. Whatever else he has to say won't be any nicer, and I'm half-tempted to block him from my stream altogether.

"Don't get so worked up," I tell myself, sitting back against my headboard. "Don't let him get to you. It's just a stupid man, with a stupid opinion." The words are ones I live by. I give myself a few minutes, trying to figure out what I want for dinner, before I decide I need to move again.

He's not worth even half of my attention for the next five minutes, and I'm not going to let him take up space in my brain if I can help it.

CHAPTER 26

I've never hated project reviews for any class until this moment.

I shuffle on the sofa, wondering why Oliver isn't here. Normally he's on the couch, waiting for me or waiting for class to start. Though I suppose since there is no class, and he has no review to do, that it makes sense for him to *not* be here. Plus, I hadn't been particularly nice the last time we'd spoken.

But maybe, selfishly, I'd hoped he would be here anyway.

My fingers drum on the end table sitting beside the sofa, nails making soft, sharp noises against the glass top. I'm surprised it's survived this year, let alone however long it's been here. Some people aren't very careful coming through the building, and it shows in the mess I've seen made of the arts department before.

Though, with it facing Rook's office, I guess that's reason enough for people not to bother it. Knowing him, he'd fail a student for making it teeter, let alone fall outright.

The thought makes me grin, and I'm still wearing the stupid look when Professor Solomon's door opens and one of the other students, a girl who's been trying to get into his pants all semester, storms off.

He looks at me, boredom etched into every part of his face, while I grin like an idiot.

It's awkward, to say the least.

I can see the strength it takes for him not to roll his eyes, and he leans against the doorframe with raised brows in a small expression that just screams, *really?* But I don't know what to say or do except sit there, hand on the end table, and fucking grin.

"Let's get this over with," he sighs, crooking two fingers in my direction. "Since we're already late for your appointment."

Checking my phone, I realize that he's right, though not by much. My review was supposed to start three whole minutes ago. But clearly, I won't survive. By the look on his face, he definitely won't either.

"Okay," I sigh, getting to my feet and shoving my hands into the pockets of my hoodie. I don't need my backpack today, or anything else, so all I have with me are my keys, phone, and cards that slot into the case wrapped around it.

I take four long strides before another door opens, a voice interrupting me as I start to close in on his small office.

"I thought I saw you earlier, Love." The cold, feminine voice could match Rook's for disinterest, and I know it well. My weird grin changes, becoming genuine as I turn to see Professor Carmine coming out of a staff lounge. She closes the door, her thin, wrinkled hands moving slowly but gracefully at her task. "You'll be happy to know that I've graded exams."

My heart constricts as she walks over, just as it always does every time she's finished with one of our exams. While Professor Carmine, in all her dismissive, impolite glory, may be my favorite professor of all time, it hasn't stopped her from failing an essay I wrote once or twice.

"Hello Professor," I greet, throwing a quick look at Rook. He leans against the frame of his door still, a lazy smile on his lips. "I hope you aren't about to tell me I'll be repeating your class next semester."

"Well, I can't give you much right now, but it's safe to say that you'll only be seeing me next year for your senior seminar. I trust you'll book early for a session, since I am your advisor as far as I remember." Her gaze slides to Professor Solomon, still unimpressed. "Unless you're trying to steal my favorite student from me? I'd prefer you didn't. She's got a promising career in the historical aspects of study, along with anything else she wants to do. Has Miss Love told you about her senior thesis yet?"

I turn to look at him, eyes widening by increments. I don't know what he *could* say to get me in trouble with her, but I'm scared he'll find a way, even if I beg him not to.

"She's one of the best students I've had who isn't a photography major," Rook admits, hands in his pockets. "But you're in luck, as it's too late to convert her to my major now. I guess I'm stuck wishing I'd got to her sooner." He eyes me as he says it, and part of me is sure he means more than in the academic sense. "If her thesis has any photography related elements, however, I hope you'll advise her to come see me next year. Even if she doesn't decide to sign up for another of my classes."

I don't think I'll be doing that.

"Miss Love is adept at using her resources wisely." It's not quite a compliment when it sounds so... reprimanding. "She learned so much from her first semester in my class that I almost think she's a different person." I don't wince at the words, but she's right. The first time I'd taken a class from Professor Carmine, I'd nearly failed it.

"I appreciate you saying so, Professor Carmine," I say, trying to look grateful.

"Well, whether or not that's true, I won't hold you up. I just wanted to let you know that I found it brave to tackle *Laocoön and His Sons* for your final essay. Have a good day, Love. Professor Solomon." She nods her head, tightly curled grey-blonde hair never moving.

"You as well, Professor," I reply, and Rook echoes the sentiment as she turns and leaves.

"Come on then, Love." Rook sighs my name, and there's something to it when he says *Love* that isn't there with anyone else. He beckons me into the office and I follow, sinking into the chair in front of his desk with another sigh while he closes the door.

"She speaks particularly highly of you," he remarks, sitting in his chair. "She hates most of her students. Did something happen your first semester with her?"

"I almost failed," I admit. "I was a freshman coming in from a high school that had convinced me I was smart enough not to try. She broke me of that misconception by Halloween." I tap my knuckles against the chair arm. "She's pretty harsh when she grades. But I love her class, and the way she lectures, so here we are." I shrug one shoulder at him as he pulls out a folder.

"What's Laocoön and His Sons?" I'm surprised he cares enough to ask, but the art history major in me brightens at the question.

"You can't ask me that if you don't want me to ramble," I inform him, sitting back. "Seriously. You'll get an earful."

"Go for it." He meets my eyes with a lazy look of his own, hands flat on the folder. "Give me an earful."

"Laocoön and His Sons is a statue. It's Hellenistic in origin, and is in the Vatican Museums for display. There's some debate on whether it was a copy of the Greek design and subject, but I like the story of it more. That Laocoön tried to warn the Trojans about the horse being dangerous. There are a few different endings to the story, past his warning. One version is that Athena sent snakes to kill him and his sons. That's, obviously, what the sculpture implies. Another version tells that Laocoön watched them die, and had to spend the rest of his life alone in punishment." I blink, sucking in a breath, and say, "Please don't tell me you're just trying to distract me from the fact that *you* failed me."

A smile curves across his lips, but he wipes it away with a flick of his wrist before I can do more than notice that it's there.

"I haven't failed you, Love," Rook assures me. "Though, you might not like your grade."

I hate the way he says it, and I shift a little in my chair. "If you've failed me, I'm telling Oliver," I say, and he just shrugs.

"I just said I haven't failed you. And so what if you do tell him? What will he do, Love? *What will he do,* exactly?" He pins me with a half-glare, then opens the folder to my project and final grades.

"Wow," I mutter, staring at the B that glares up at me for my semester grade. "*Wow.*" This will be the only class I have a B in, to my knowledge, and it frustrates me more than I want to say. Tears burn at the corners of my eyes, and I blink them away quickly.

I don't like not being good at things. This is reminding me that I can't always live up to the perfection I strive for, and I definitely don't like it. Worse, it's a B *minus.* Barely higher than a C.

Professor Solomon sighs and lifts his hand to rub his eyes. "Don't cry," he says, with only a touch more kindness than he'd used seconds before. "You didn't fail."

"You shouldn't have lied to Professor Carmine about me," I snap, not meaning to.

"What do you mean?"

"You said I was a good student."

"You are a good student."

I gesture at the B- for being the clear evidence of him lying about it. Obviously I'm not. Not with that grade. It makes my stomach twist, and drags up my inferiority issues that I've worked to put a stop to for years. Had I thought, just for a moment, that I really was some great photography student that he'd like to have in another class? Yeah. I had.

"We're really doing this. You're really upset over a B." He sounds half like he can't believe it, and the other half, somewhat confused.

"Yes!" I snap, closing my eyes hard so I don't meet his eyes and let him know just how upset I am. If I cry, then I've lost. I haven't cried in front of a professor since my freshman year, and I *certainly* don't want my second time doing it to be right now.

"You weren't even this upset when you learned what Oliver was doing," Rook points out, elbows on the table as he leans his chin on his hands to watch me like I'm suddenly just so interesting. But clearly, not interesting enough to warrant more than a B-.

"Maybe I should've been!" I snap, feeling irritated. "I just... This is *class* and everything is separate, okay? But I thought, just maybe, that you would've had some fucking understanding for how this semester has gone." Under any other circumstance, I would never have spoken to him like this, but I'm so frustrated and stressed, and I just want this semester to be finished. "You can't tell me in class what I need to improve on, but the both of you find the extra time in the day to stalk me?"

He blinks, eyes narrowing. "Stalk you?"

"Follow. Stare at. Watch. What else would you want to call

it? I can feel when I'm being watched, just like I have been all the time since the beginning of the semester. I know you're still doing it, Professor. It's not like I'm an idiot. You, or Oliver, or both of you. I don't care."

"Blair." With a frown, he lets his hands fall to the desk so he can lean on his arms. "You think we're stalking you?"

"You've always been stalking me. Ever since the night at the party with Oliver. I've seen you outside my apartment, like that night Oliver went down to see who was watching. I know it was you, so drop it. I just thought—"

"I've never stood outside your apartment, Blair Love." His voice is firm, and he cuts me off without room for argument. "And Oliver only followed you a couple of times before I told him to stop. That's not what we do. We don't need to. You're in class twice a week, and we watch you stream. Plus, Oliver knows where you live, and has your number. Why would we be stalking you?"

The floor drops out from under me, sending me reeling, and all I can do is stare at him. "What?" I whisper finally, his words barely computing in my brain.

Professor Solomon looks back to my folder, spreading out photos and his analysis of them. "Let me just go through this with you while I think," he requests, launching into an explanation of why I didn't get more than a B minus.

I'm barely listening, however. I'm too busy running *his* confusion through my brain. If it wasn't him, or if he didn't know about it, could it really have been someone else? Or am I just crazy?

"Maybe I'm just misunderstanding," I interrupt, clearly not listening to what he's saying. "Maybe it's because of how on edge I am. I've been crazy lately because of you two. Like with that guy who scared me when I called you." I tap my fingers against the arm of the chair, matching the rhythm with my foot on the floor.

"Blair." The word is sharp and pulls my attention back to Professor Solomon. "Have you heard a word I've said to you about this?"

I shake my head and frown apologetically. "No. But it's fine. You gave me a B *minus*, I wasn't as good in your class as I thought, it's fine."

"You should still take another one of my classes next semester."

"No, nope. That's okay," I assure him, itching to get to my feet. "I work really hard for my average. I had to after freshman year. Call me a coward, but I take classes I'm good at. I..." I bite my lip, sigh, and continue. "Sorry, I guess. I wanted to do better—"

"God *damn it*, Blair." Rook stands up suddenly, causing me to stumble, and while I try to regain my balance, he comes around to my side of the desk. "Stop it. Do you know how many As I gave out this semester?" He crowds me back against the filing cabinets until he can reach out and grip them on either side of my face.

My heart pounds as I stare at him, lips parted as I shake my head.

"None. *None*. Oliver didn't even get one from me back when he actually took my classes. You're not bad at this, and you're not being punished. If you would *listen* with your ears, you might actually hear that I liked the direction of your project, and the way you handled it. It's your technique that needs work, and your choice of focus."

It's impossible not to listen to him when I'm this close to him and his breath is warm against my lips.

"You're so *frustrating*," he adds, eyes narrowed. "You remind me so much of Oliver sometimes, it's unreal. Except he wouldn't be in my office crying. He'd be trying to throw my shit out the window, or planning to key my car. *Yes*, Blair. He keyed my fucking car."

I don't want to laugh. It's inappropriate, and I clap my hand over my mouth when I let out a soft snort of a snicker.

Rook reaches up to peel my hand away, and I press my lips together as he glares down at me, finally letting go of my hand and replacing his on the cabinet.

"You are *not* going to cry over a passing grade," he threatens, like I've committed a sin. "Are you?"

"Probably."

He sighs. "Go home, Love. Go home, and just... *stay* home."

"Oh yeah? Why? Are you grounding me for getting a B?" I snap, eyes narrowed in anger at the idea of him being able to tell me what to do with my hours outside of class.

"No." He leans in closer until his lips are brushing mine. "Because I need to take the rest of the night to figure out who's stalking you." The words pull a gasp from me, and my eyes widen. I'm about to reply when he kisses me, teeth sharp against my lips and not giving me a chance to do more than lean back as he crowds against me to keep me there.

He's the best kisser I've ever met. That much is very clear. He deepens it, teeth and tongue teasing my own as he keeps me guessing as to what he'll do next. It's not until I've let out a soft whine that he pulls away, eyes dark.

"Go home," he repeats, pulling me to the door. "Before it gets dark. I'll have Oliver call you."

"It's really not you?" I ask, not sure if I believe him as the door opens.

He shakes his head. "It's not, Love. It's really not."

CHAPTER 27

S lamming my apartment door behind me as I step out into the hallway feels like a small, vindictive victory.

Hitting the elevator door button six times with more force than could ever be necessary feels like another.

I step into the elevator, sneakers making a soft double tap on the floor as I jab my finger into the button for the first floor. I don't feel like gasping for air in a mimicry of tuberculosis today like the time I hit the stairs. Plus, I'm more interested in pacing out my frustration in the elevator and getting out the door as fast as I can.

Last night, I believed Rook. I'd gone home like a good girl, called in dinner with Juniper, and helped her pack for her flight this morning. She left today, though had offered to stay for three more days with me, since I hadn't found a reasonably priced flight until then. Being nice and considerate, I'd assured her it was fine, and that rebooking her flight would be too much trouble.

I'd also waited on a call from Rook or Oliver to tell me everything was fine, but that never came.

And it's taken me this long to realize they're playing me for an idiot. No one else would be looking for me, stalking me, or following me. No one else would make me feel watched like them. There's no other possible culprit for me being on edge and feeling off whenever I'm out, and I'm stupid to think that he wasn't lying to me in his office just to get me to leave.

Admittedly, I'm not thrilled with myself for how I reacted to being given a shittier grade than I feel like I'd earned, but it's not like I'll ever be in a class with him again. And honestly, he's now made 'proving' that I don't want to be around them really easy.

So fuck you, Rook, I think to myself as I hit the sidewalk and walk toward the small shops I like. I'm not planning to buy anything, though a petty part of me wants to blow as much of Rook's money as I can on something that I know he won't like. I haven't, because money is money and I really am trying to save, but the compulsion to do it is there.

All I want is to walk and grab something for dinner. I'm not asking for much, especially since I'm equal parts embarrassed and hurt. Sure, Rook is a dick. He's literally the worst person I've probably ever met, but Oliver?

I hadn't expected this from Oliver. Even if he is a serial killer, I thought he really liked me. His absence hurts more than it has a right to, and tears burn at the corners of my eyes. I wasn't going to stay for them. For either or both of them. I'm well on my way to proving I want nothing to do with them no matter what. But I'd thought Oliver would keep trying until the very end to change my mind.

Not agree to humiliate and lie to me with our professor.

I'm too worked up to even window-shop. I'd planned to pace around a few shops, look for Christmas gifts I don't need, and finally go home with food. I'd thought I could calm my nerves that way, but every time I try to settle down enough to go into a store for something, I can't do it. I just need to *walk*. To try to outpace my problems, and walking around this part of St. Augustine is the best way to do so.

The sun falls beneath the buildings before I realize it, until I'm eventually relying on the street lamps to light my way. I shudder, glad I'd put on a purple hoodie over my tee and running shorts before coming out tonight. It's not cold enough for me to freeze by any means. It's nothing like Indiana. But there's enough of a chill that I'm grateful for the warmth and the ability to curl my fingers into the sleeves of my hoodie and pick at any loose threads.

I shiver, wrapping my arms around myself as I walk. I need to figure out what I'm doing before it gets too late, but all I can do is just walk around the block yet again. The door to the coffee shop catches my eye, and I snort at the notion of a sandwich and coffee for dinner. It wouldn't be the first time, but I am *trying* to eat a little better and consume less than a gallon of caffeine a day. It's a work in progress. Early progress.

My steps take me along the street, and I can't help but glance up at the same place I did the day I'd found the body of Mikaela Hayes.

This isn't something I should be thinking about. The warning to myself rings loud and clear in my head, but I still find myself following the path toward the less-populated street, until I'm standing where I'd found her purse and her plastic cup, ice splattered and crushed all over the ground.

This is where Oliver killed her. Where he'd looked for a person that had a similar appearance to my best friend, dragged her into an alley, and murdered her. And where I'd found her.

My feet drag, but I feel almost like I'm being pulled down

the alleyway by invisible magnets, until finally I'm standing almost exactly where I'd found her.

It's then that I realize why I've been rubbing the goose-bumps on my arms for the past few minutes, and why the hair on the back of my neck has been standing up as my body tried to warn me of what I've been aware of for at least ten minutes.

Someone has been following me.

I turn to face the street, my heart jumping into my throat when I see someone standing at the end of the alley, the light at their back obscuring the details of their face from me.

"What are you doing?" I ask, loudly enough that they have to hear me. The body shape is unfamiliar, but it has to be Oliver or Rook. There's no one else that would bother trailing me around my neighborhood, or over here. Is it Oliver, come to relive his crime? Or Rook, to lecture me about not doing exactly what he says.

Arguments for both bubble to my lips, and I'm prepared to let loose with either option as the person stalks closer. As they do, they push their hood back from their face so I can see their features in the dim light from the lamp against the wall behind me.

It's neither of them. I search the face, confused by the strange man who stands there looking expectant. I've never met him...have I? My eyes narrow, and I finally realize I *have* seen this man before.

He's the one who scared me when I'd been walking around before.

Coldness inks into my bones, and I can't help but pause and search my mind for any reason he might be following me now. He looks out of place here, somehow. Like he doesn't belong in St. Augustine at all. "Do I know you?" I ask, turning to face him and scrubbing my clammy hands against my shorts. "I've seen you before, when—"

"When I came up behind you by those shops," the man agrees expectantly. He looks excited, like I'm about to announce that I do remember him as some childhood friend. But really, I don't know him. He's not someone whose face I recognize from any aspect of my life.

"Okay. Umm." I curl my hands into fists at my sides, still utterly confused. "But I've never met you before that."

"We talk all the time," he refutes, shaking his head. "I thought you'd recognize me."

I stare at him, perplexed, and wrack my brain yet again for something that will give me any clue as to who he is. "Could you give me a hint?" I request finally. "I'm stupid, maybe? Are we in a class together?" I swear we aren't, but still. I could be mistaken. Sometimes I don't pay attention that well. "Do you work in the arts department?"

He rolls his eyes, frowning as he does. He looks irritated with me, exasperation tinging his expression. It's as though he really doesn't understand why I don't know him, and I really *don't* have any idea who he is. "No," he says at last, shaking his head. "I'm not associated with your school."

The man stares at me, as if he's giving me one more chance to recognize him. Like the knowledge is going to just strike me like a bolt of lightning.

Unfortunately today, there are no thunderstorms in the St. Augustine area.

At last he shifts, moving his weight from foot to foot as he looks down enough for the bald spot of his head to look shiny in the bad lighting. "I'm Rob," he says at last, slowly and condescendingly.

What?

I don't move. Somehow my expression doesn't change, and I feel the bemusement still etched into my own features.

Rob.

Like, of the *fuck Rob* fame? *Rob784* who I hate more than most people I've ever met? The things he'd said to me, like calling me a whore not so long ago, skitter through my head like spiders. I don't know what to do, and I just look at him, trying not to let the nervousness show on my face as my heart picks up in my chest.

This can't be promising. Has he been following me since he came to town?

A worse thought enters my brain. Has he been the one following me for *months*? Surely not, since a stalker does more than just *stalk*, right? But if Rook had been right, and the reason he'd told me to stay home is this one right here...

Then I really may have fucked up tonight. Not just by leaving my apartment, but by being *here*, in the alley where Mikaela had died. The street was bad enough, but back here, I'd have to really make a scene for someone to notice and help me. Especially since the street beyond is never that busy, and especially not at night.

"Oh," I say finally, after too long of a time. "Sorry, I just had never expected anyone from my stream to try to find me." I pull a smile onto my face that I'm positive doesn't reach my eyes. "That's why I wear the mask. I'm not very social in my real life, and it seemed like the best way to preserve that." I'm rambling, sure, but I don't know what else to do.

"Really?" He looks disbelieving. "Even though you let *letsplayjay* find out who you really are and come fuck you on camera?" I don't like the words being thrown at me like that, and I fight not to recoil as I shake my head.

"I've known him for a while," I lie. "He's a student at my school, and his stream was the inspiration for mine. I needed some help with my stream, and he offered to come over." God, here I am rambling again, trying to come up with an explanation that will make sense and make him go away. Should I lie and say he's my boyfriend?

"Shame." Rob seems disappointed. "You know, I thought the way you spoke to me the other day was really rude. And you don't seem apologetic about it. I was going to apologize to you, actually. I thought maybe I'd been rude, until I watched that stream with Jay again. I record all of yours, just in case."

Just in case *what*?

"I mean, it's for you," he explains, like I'd asked or somehow indicated that I was curious. "Just in case I need to go back through them for any reason. You were really into how he was treating you. It was disgusting."

My heart twists in my chest, ribs constricting around it as I unclench my hands and shove them in my pockets. "It was just a stream," I tell him, trying to maintain my composure and confidence. "It's just—"

"An act?" he snorts, with more venom in his words than I'd expected. I take a step back at the unfriendliness, and he steps forward as his face contorts into something less friendly. "Don't fuck with me, Envy." He doesn't even know my *name*. "You loved the way he acted. And the shit he said to you?" The incredulous look on his face is evident, even in the dim light. "It's borderline abuse, you know? You don't deserve that."

"Okay, umm. This is making me uncomfortable," I admit, barely able to suck in a full breath through my anxiety. I raise my hands in surrender, refusing to take another step back. "I don't like how you're talking to me, Rob. I'm sorry that you don't like Jay. I probably won't share my stream with anyone again. But this isn't really appropriate, you know?" With way more confidence than I feel, I walk forward to pass around him. "Why don't we go somewhere else—"

I see the flash of metal before my brain registers what it is. And by the time the gun is at chest level, glinting in the dim light, I'm close enough to him that the barrel is pressed to my arm.

A moment passes as I drag my gaze up to his, mouth open to say something or plead with him to point the gun somewhere else. It's such a short amount of time, yet it feels so long as his eyes darken and he takes a lurching step closer to me.

"Don't you fucking go anywhere," Rob snarls, waving the gun into my face. "I'm not *done*, Envy! You're going to hear me out." He shoves me backwards, until I hit the wall behind me hard enough to pull a gasp from my body. The gun is suddenly back in my face, and when I try to move, he hits me with it, pulling a louder sound from my throat.

"Don't you *fucking move!*" he shouts, showering my face with spittle. "I told you I'm not *done*. I've given you everything lately. I watch all of your streams. I've been here since the beginning, and this is how you treat me? You-you let some other man break into your bedroom! I saw you that night he came upstairs with you. What were you doing? Practicing?" He moves like he's going to hit me again and I flinch. Already my face is throbbing, and my cheekbone feels like it's on fire.

"You let him fuck you like a whore on camera so that, what? We'd all think that's what you are?" I whimper when he shoves the gun barrel into my face, my hands uselessly pressed against my face and close my eyes hard.

"Please don't shoot me," I whisper, feeling myself trembling. "Please, I'm sorry, I—"

"Sorry for what?" he asks cruelly, not moving the gun. "Sorry for *what*, Envy?"

"I don't know. Whatever you want!" I cry, feeling tears burning in my eyes.

"Are you sorry for being a whore? Are you sorry for wasting my time? Huh? Are you—"

"I don't think she has anything at all to be sorry for." The voice is firm and silky, and as cold as the Arctic Circle. "And actually, I'd love it if you'd stop calling her a whore."

I open my eyes, barely believing them when I see that Oliver is there, his hand on the gun barrel by my face as he smiles sweetly at Rob.

"Otherwise, I might just shoot *you*."

CHAPTER 28

"Oliver?" His name leaves my lips in a whisper, but he doesn't look at me. Instead, he rips the gun from Rob's hold, instantly yanking it away from my face as if he might be afraid it'll go off accidentally. He pulls again, easily disarming Rob and chucking the gun to the ground behind him.

"Hi," he greets, stalking forward as Rob stumbles back. "I don't think we've met. My name's Oliver, but I don't think you'd know me by that name, *friend*," he snarls savagely.

Rob's eyebrows lower, pinching a question in his full face. "I've never met you—"

"Right, you haven't. But you've sure as shit seen me. I'm the one you seem to be so jealous of. Oh, sorry. I mean, the one you're calling abusive and awful. It's nice to meet you." Oliver sticks a hand out in front of him, causing Rob to jerk back into a wall. "I'm *letsplayjay*. Welcome to my *fucking stream*." His words turn savage as he says them, the smile on his face morphing into something much less friendly. "And boy, do I hate the way you're talking to her."

I slide to the ground against the wall, unable to look away from them as new footsteps register in my brain. I pull back when dark boots and jeans enter my vision, looking up and up until I find Rook's face.

My breath catches in my throat, and I search his face for the anger and disapproval that I expect to be there. I know what he must think. I know that he has to be disappointed I didn't just fucking listen.

But instead, I find concern. He looks down at me with true consideration in his eyes, along with the anger that dances there like a flickering flame. From the look of him, Oliver isn't the only one who's upset with how Rob has acted.

"I don't..." Rob looks between the two of them, not looking particularly afraid. More incredulous than anything, though his eyes dart regretfully for the gun. "I wasn't going to shoot her. I was just—"

Oliver *slams* a hand into the brick over his head, leaning in close with that savage grin back in place. "What were you *just* going to do?" he sneers. "Scare her a little? Make her promise you all kinds of things? Were you going to *hurt* her?" He reaches into his back pocket, and in the light I see the glint of metal. For a terrifying moment, I think he's pulled out another gun. It's not though, I realize, when he twists the switchblade in the air and flicks it open.

"Tell you what, Rob," he drawls, not looking into the man's terrified face or paying attention to the small noises he's making. "How about you apologize to Blair? That's her name, by the way. Since I'm pretty sure the only thing you know about her is how much you want to fuck her. Not that you ever, in your wildest dreams, would've gotten a chance to."

"I didn't mean it," Rob says again, his confidence faltering, though his tone says he doesn't think Oliver is going to really hurt him. "Look, maybe I went a little overboard, but—"

AJ MERLIN

Oliver's movement is almost too fast for me to see. His arm is a blur as he moves, and the next thing I know, Rob is screaming and doubled over to hold his hand.

Two dark shapes fall to the ground, but my brain refuses to register what that means.

"That didn't sound like an apology to me!" Oliver yells joyfully, stepping back with a dramatic sweep of his arms. "Also, it was smart of you to wait until she was here to make your move. This place is dead after five pm, and you figured no one would hear her screaming. Too bad for you, it works in my favor as well. So let's try again, okay?" He gestures toward me. "She's over there. *Apologize.*"

Rob's eyes find mine. I stare at him, eyes wide, and he holds one hand in his other as darkness drips from his skin. "I'm sorry!" he says finally. "Really! I wasn't going to do anything. I just wanted to scare you a little. You just don't get it. Women like you are all the same to guys like me and—" His words cut off with a scream when Oliver's hand comes down once more, and Rob hits the ground hard on his knees.

More blood spatters the ground, though I can't tell from where. But right now, I don't think I want to know.

"Let's try that *again*," Oliver sneers, and kicks him. "Your apologies suck, and someone should've taught you better. But that's okay, Rob. That's just totally, completely okay. Let me help you!" He kicks him hard, throwing Rob to his side on the ground.

"Less is more, Oliver," Rook remarks, leaning against the wall on my other side. "I don't want to spend all night cleaning up his blood."

I shudder at the words, and Rob's face contorts into fear.

"Well, he hasn't apologized yet," Oliver points out, and turns to look at me. The expression on his face sends a tremor down my spine, and I can't look away from him when he just stares at me, his features unreadable apart from the scorn and violence.

"I'm trying, I'm *trying*," Rob sobs, still holding his hand. "I said I was sorry. I'm *sorry*. I wasn't going to hurt her. I wasn't going to do anything awful. I just wanted her to appreciate me."

Oliver makes a show of rolling his eyes; and leisurely picks up his foot to *smash* it into Rob's face. The latter screams, staying sprawled on the ground while Oliver looms over him. "That's okay," he soothes, a purr in his voice. "We can start over. We have all night—"

"Oliver." Rook's voice is a warning, and when the younger man looks up at him, Rook pointedly draws his attention back to me.

I fight the urge to hide my eyes, but fail to keep his gaze. Still, I hear Oliver sigh.

"Okay, you're right," he says, sounding partially apologetic and mostly petulant. "I'm overdoing it. I get it." I glance up at him in confusion at the words, just in time to see him kick Rob over onto his back. He falls down to his knees beside him, a look of disgust on his face. "You're not worth this," he sneers, and drags the knife against his throat.

Rob yells, cries, and gurgles a last defiance as his hand lifts, streaming blood from the stumps of his fingers. My stomach turns and Rook pushes away from the wall to kick Rob's hand down and lean down as well.

"You should've learned not to touch what doesn't belong to you," he murmurs to the dying man, as I scoot further down the alleyway. "Especially when it may belong to someone that doesn't like anyone to touch what's theirs." He reaches down quickly, and for a second I think he's grabbing Rob's throat and trying to staunch the blood.

It's not until Rob's eyes widen and he lets out a mostly

airless keen, that I realize that Rook's fingers are pushing *into* the open wound. Oliver grins, and blood pours to the ground from the newly widened wound. My stomach churns, but I can't bring myself to feel bad for Rob as I move again.

My hand bumps something on the ground, and I look down to see that my fingers have found Rob's gun. Trembling, I wrap my hand around it and pull the gun close, only half aware of what I'm doing.

Oliver stands and I do as well, watching him as he strides toward me with long, sweeping strides and wide arms. There's still a psychotic gleam in his eyes, and he lets the knife clatter to the ground, hands still bloody, as he reaches me.

"Blair—"

"Don't touch me," I whisper, drawing the gun up between us. From the corner of my eye, I see Rook tense and get to his feet as well, but Oliver doesn't even flinch.

"Blair," he breathes, concern on his face. "Are you okay? Your face—"

"You killed him," I reply, in just as soft of a tone. "Oliver, you *killed* him."

"Of course I did." Is he sorry? He doesn't seem sorry. He doesn't seem *anything* except concerned about me and probably crazy. "Of course I fucking killed him. He *hurt* you, wonder girl." He reminds me of a kicked puppy again when he says it, but I shake my head and hold the gun between us.

"I don't know. I don't *know, I don't know* what you want from me!" I scream, my hand that holds the gun trembling. "You're crazy. Fuck, you're *insane!* Look what you did to him!" Tears stream down my face as my cheek throbs, and I find it hard to breathe.

Oliver does look, his eyes flicking over Rob's body like it's always been there. "He hurt you," Oliver says again, turning to look at me. "What else would I have done?"

"What if I didn't want you to kill him? What if I don't want you here? What if I just want *you* to leave?" I murmur, unsure of the words or how much I mean them. Especially right now, when I can barely breathe and feel detached from my own body

Suddenly, Oliver does the most unexpected thing. He steps forward, and grabs my hand so that the gun is pressed against his temple. Before I can do more than whimper, Oliver's body is pressed to mine, and with his free hand, he reaches out to cup my face.

"Then shoot me," he whispers, eyes wide and terrifyingly calm. "Shoot me, Blair. If you don't want me, then you'll have to kill me. Otherwise, I don't know if I can ever get over you. I don't think I'd even want to."

"Don't." I've never heard concern in Rook's voice before. He doesn't come any closer, but I hear the fear he has for Oliver, just as surely as I know I never would've shot him.

"I can't," I say, tears cascading down my face. "I can't. I'm not going to—"

"I know you won't," he purrs, eyes still wide and full of a kind of madness that threatens to overwhelm me. "But if you don't shoot me, then you're telling me that I still have the chance to make you *ours*."

It isn't the time for love declarations, if this is what that is. My vision is tunneling, though when I blink, I see double of him. My grip on the gun slackens, and Oliver takes it from me to hand it off to Rook before closing back in against me to brush his lips to mine.

"I think I'm going to pass out," I tell him, nausea rolling in my stomach. "I-I don't know why, I just—"

"That's okay, Blair," he promises, hand cradling my face gently. "You can go on and fall. I'll catch you, wonder girl. I'll help you, and I won't let anything happen to you."

"I don't want to."

"I know, baby, I know." The madness is fading, leaving the sweet, endearing boy my heart can't help but love. "But by the way you're barely breathing and can't focus, I don't think you have much of a choice." He's so gentle. So kind, but I hate that he's right.

My knees buckle and I fall forward, right into his waiting arms.

CHAPTER 29

"What do you mean you don't know what her favorite food is?" The disappointment in Rook's tone is palpable, even when consciousness is still a question for me. "You've been trying to get to know her for months."

"She likes breakfast foods." Oliver sounds defensive, and a little embarrassed. "I'm *sorry* that I can't remember more than that."

"Whatever." Rook lets out a long-suffering sigh. "I'll make... something. French toast, I guess. Bacon, eggs. You need to eat too, so I know it won't go to waste..." His words trail off as the dark waters of sleep claim me once again, though this time not nearly so violently.

"Hey, wonder girl." The soft voice in my ear is unmistakably Oliver's, but it's the coldness against my cheek that yanks me out of the ocean of sleep and makes me groan in dislike. "I know, baby. But your cheek and jaw are swollen. I just want to make you feel better. What do you prefer, Tylenol or ibuprofen?" He's so kind. So fucking sweet, it's teeth-rotting, and I want to hit him.

Instead, I crack open my eyes, not surprised to see Oliver right in front of my face and holding an ice pack to my cheek.

"Hi," he greets, his smile widening. "How do you feel?"

"Like a B minus student who just got kidnapped by a serial killer and her asshole professor," I mumble, unable to stop the rather candid word vomit from escaping my lips.

Oliver snorts, and flicks his eyes toward where I presume Rook is standing. "He really gave you a B *minus*? That's criminal."

"Literally deserving of jail time," I agree lightly, still trying to focus on his face. It's getting easier, even as my stomach lets me know that it's prepared to cannibalize itself for the greater good. Slowly, I sit up, not complaining when Oliver helps me to do so.

Rook strides by, tossing me a couple of pieces of clothing as he does. "We're burning what you have on," he informs me, eyes level.

I tense, shaking my head. "No way. I'm out of hoodies," I protest, meaning that I'm out of *clean* hoodies. "And I really like this shirt."

"That's a shame, but there's blood on it. And evidence all over it." He stops, sighs, and adds, "Don't make me take your clothes off of you, Love. You don't look up to a fight. Also, I heard what you were both talking about. If you don't change, I'll give *him* the lecture as to why your work deserved a B *minus*." He walks away before I can think of anything to say, and Oliver eases himself onto the sofa next to me.

My mind feels fuzzy, and I shiver in spite of myself. I'm confused, especially because I know exactly what I'd said to Oliver while I'd been hyperventilating and close to passing out. Not that I'm sure how much differently I feel right now, but it's worth noting that I don't want to put a gun to his head anymore.

"Are you mad at me?" I ask, promising myself it's a question for curiosity's sake. "For the alley?"

His eyes narrow, brows furrowing in his confusion. "Mad at you? Why would I be?" There's no trace of the crazed psycho from what feels like a few hours ago. It's like that part of him has sunk deep down into his chest, far too deep for me to see.

"Uh, I put a gun to your head," I remind him quietly, taking off my hoodie and the tee under it. Oliver shakes out the new clothes, which include a shirt and jacket that look like they might belong to him. He hands them to me one by one, as if dealing with both is more than I can handle.

"It happens," he shrugs, not looking at all upset about it.

"I could've shot you," I point out, eyes widening. "Oliver, I had a gun to your head."

"You had an empty gun to my head," Oliver replies sweetly. "Seems like Rob really wasn't going to shoot you. He just wanted the threat to be there so you'd think he had the power. You weren't going to shoot me, either."

"But you didn't know that. I saw Rook's face. You both thought the gun was loaded, and—" I break off as he reaches out to cup the uninjured side of my face.

"You weren't going to shoot me," he promises with all the confidence in the universe. "You were never going to pull the trigger, wonder girl." Before I can ask him how he knows, how he *really* knows, he leans forward to gently kiss me.

I'm ready for my body and mind to shrink back. I'm waiting for the fear of what he's done to hit me, just like it has so many times before. Or maybe I'll recoil; smack his hand off of my face or bite his lip and remind him that I'm *done*.

But I'm not at all prepared for the way that I sigh into his mouth and lean into him until he can wrap an arm around my waist. He groans with satisfaction, deepening the kiss until it feels like he's trying to devour me. Oliver barely gives me time to breathe, let alone think, and my body sparks with approval and arousal as my hands catch and slide against his skin.

Belatedly, as he finally pulls away with pupils blown and the look of absolute pleasure on his face, I realize just how *fucked* I am. I haven't proven that I want to be away from him.

I've proven just the opposite to him. To both of them, judging by the way Rook is leaning in the doorframe and watching us.

"Hey, next time I pass out, could I wake up somewhere else?" I demand, eyes on Rook as he saunters through the living room to sit down behind me. I try to move, or at least to turn, but Rook yanks me back against him with a growl against my lips as he picks up where Oliver left off.

God, it's so hard to deny the things they make me feel. He wraps his arms around my shoulders, and the sensation of Oliver stroking his hands up my thighs isn't lost on me as Rook explores my mouth with ease.

"If you do me the favor of never putting a gun to Oliver's head again, I suppose it could be arranged," Rook purrs against my lips. "Where would you like to wake up, Love?"

"Do you have a solarium?"

"No."

"A pagoda?"

He lets out a sigh, eyeing me dryly.

"Okay, okay. A grand ballroom? Surely this place has a grand ballroom."

"Would you like us to build you a bedroom?" he replies in a smooth, sarcasm-laden tone.

"A wing," I reply, meeting his eyes and holding them. My heart flutters in my chest, and he must sense the unease warring inside me, because he leans forward to kiss my throat again.

My breathing picks up and I pull away from him after a moment, unable to shake my nerves and misgivings. "I don't know about this," I mumble, shaking my head. "It's pretty obvious I didn't prove anything. I know I didn't tell you to fuck off enough times or throw onion bombs at you from the window. I know that I give mixed signals..." Wrapping my arms around myself, still shaking my head, I continue, "But you can't expect me to be okay with... this."

Rook runs a hand through my hair and gets to his feet smoothly, exiting the room while Oliver just... watches me.

"Is he upset?" I ask, nodding to the doorway.

Oliver shakes his head. "No. He doesn't really get mad. And he thought we'd have to tie you down, so I'd say you're exceeding expectations." He flashes me a bright grin. "And you're wrong, by the way. You've shown me *exactly* what you want."

That's news to me, and I blink at him in surprise.

"You've shown me that I have all the time in the world to make you ours."

"Good luck, since I'm not in any of Rook's classes next semester," I say after a moment, once I have my feelings under control. But Oliver just shrugs and drags me to my feet, citing the fact that dinner is probably ready as he pulls me out of the room.

"Do you understand me, Love?" Rook's voice is sharp as he speaks, and I can feel his eyes on mine even though I'm staring at the remains of eggs and French toast on my plate. "The police shouldn't ask you anything. If they do, you give them nothing. You *have* nothing to give them."

Except, that isn't exactly true.

"So you're just, what, keeping his body in some kind of storage so you can dump it?" I ask lightly, not wanting a real answer.

The two of them trade looks, and Oliver just shrugs.

"I'm cleaning it up, and that's all either of you need to worry about. I've cleaned up a thousand other messes of his. This won't be the last one, will it?" Oliver just grins at the words, causing the other man to shake his head. "But don't make things worse. Get on your plane. Go home. Don't tell anyone, do you understand?"

That part hurts, but I figured he'd say it. Not to mention, if I tell my parents what happened, they'd want to know *why*. I'm not ready to tell the why, and I don't think I ever will be. "Great. Sure. Fine," I mutter, rubbing the heels of my palms against my stinging eyes while trying to avoid my bruised cheek. "I'll just write it in a diary if I need some support or someone to talk to. Or I'll just tell my smart phone and hope the government isn't listening."

"You tell *us*," Rook states firmly, his voice hard. "You ask *us* if you need help. I would've thought it was obvious by now."

It isn't, but who am I to burst his bubble? Instead, I chase a few dredges of maple syrup around my plate, unsure if I'm nauseous or amazed at how good of a cook he is.

Probably both, truth be told.

"Let Oliver know if you need anything. If you need money, I can send it to you. Though, it would be easier if you'd give me an actual account for me to deposit it into, instead of having to go through funxcams," he remarks, making me stiffen.

"No," I say sharply, lifting my eyes to his. "No. You're not getting access to my bank account. Absolutely not. And I'm not streaming over break, so you don't have to *pay* me for anything. I'm fine, Rook." I shoot Oliver a look as well, who raises his hands in surrender with his fork in one and his mouth full of bacon.

"I didn't do anything," he remarks, but I glare balefully anyway. "I'm just eating."

"I just don't want either of you to get the wrong idea. I'm not-you're not..." I suck in a deep breath. "I don't want to owe you. You're not my parents or my..." I trail off. What *are* they, even?

"We're not your boyfriends?" Rook supplies, his tone unimpressed. "We're just the serial killers who like to fuck you. I know, Love." He doesn't sound angry, per se, but I still eye him just to look for any micro-change in his already unreadable expression.

"Is that a problem for you?" I don't want to challenge him, his authority, or anything else. I just want him to see that I'm not giving in. That he hasn't won, and I don't belong to either of them.

Slowly, he shakes his head, looking as unperturbed as he's claiming to be. "Not at all, darling girl. The best prize is one that's earned, not the one that's given. Oliver's worked to win you over, but he's not the only one who'd like for you to accept where you belong." His words send a shiver down my spine that's from both anticipation and a healthy dose of fear. "You still have a semester to go, and I've barely given you any of my attention. That'll change when you come back, now that I know what I'm working with."

I want to remind him, again, that he won't have me in class at all so I don't know how he'll make my life miserable, but I manage not to. Instead, I go back to my food, wanting to get myself under control before I say something that has them stuffing me in the freezer next to *rob784*.

CHAPTER 30

While the airport is busy and my mom won't stop calling me, it isn't either of those things that has me standing perfectly still in the lobby, hand clutched around the handle of my duffel bag. People weave in and out of the doors, some of them throwing me irritated looks as I block the path with all the grace of a raccoon, and twice the audacity.

But I can't move. Not when Oliver is standing inside the atrium, hands shoved into his pockets as he stares up at the lazily spinning mobile above him. He doesn't twitch, he doesn't even look down at me as I step inside and cross the distance between us, heart thumping in my chest.

What is he doing here?

For a wild moment I think, suddenly, that he's gotten a ticket to come home with me and expects me to introduce him to my parents.

"I don't like flying," he admits, not looking anywhere but up at the ceiling. "It makes me nervous." Finally, he tilts his head down, one hand coming up to cup my jaw. "Good morning, wonder girl. Are you surprised to see me?"

"I'm surprised you know how to get out of bed before six am," I concede, not bothering to hide my exhausted yawn. The sun isn't up yet, and I don't want to be either, but here I am anyway. "What are you doing here, Oliver?"

"I just came to see you off." He kisses me on the cheek before I can pull away, and does so himself like he knows I'll jump away if he doesn't allow some space between us. "I wanted to get you a present, but honestly, I have no idea what to get you. Next Christmas, though, I'll do better."

"I'll have graduated by next Christmas," I point out unsurely.

"So will I." He flashes me that sweet smile once again. "Rook says not to be mad at him, but he's deposited five hundred into your account by way of funxcams." His smile widens. "Well, he didn't say the first part. He doesn't care if you're angry about it, truth be told."

My eyes widen as I stare at him, mouth open. "Five *hundred*?" I ask, voice rising by octaves until I'm basically squeaking. "Oliver, that's *ridiculous*."

"He worries," Oliver explains, as if that's supposed to assure me. "Let him worry *less*. He just wants you to be okay. And to be able to get what you need."

"I'm visiting my parents!" I remind him in a hiss, heart pounding against my ribs. "There's nothing to worry *about*."

"Well..." He shrugs his shoulders, obviously bored with the conversation. "Look, he told me not to come. And he'll be *pissed* at me when I get home." Oliver flashes me a quick grin. "He said we should give you space. That you need to consider everything before next semester."

I stare at Oliver, unimpressed with the explanation, and he snorts. "I don't know, though. I think this is kind of romantic, don't you? I'd offer to buy you coffee, but it's on the other side of the gate, and I don't want to make you late. Really, I'm not here to bother you or whatever you're thinking."

He steps closer, until his presence is blocking out everyone else's, and leans in once more so his lips brush mine. "Merry Christmas, Blair." He reaches out and slips something into my pocket. "I know I probably won't hear from you over break, but that's okay. That's fine, because I'll be right here to pick you up the moment you're back in town. You're *mine,* wonder girl." He kisses me softly, and I'm too stunned to move. "You're ours. And I can't wait for you to realize it."

Oliver kisses me once more, barely seeming to notice that I don't respond, before he pulls away and beams. "Have a good Christmas," he says again, loud enough for the people around us to hear. "See you in a few weeks."

He doesn't wait for my reply, whether or not I'm going to give one. I don't even know if I am, and it's a relief that he doesn't demand it. Instead, Oliver turns on his heel, a bounce in his step as he heads for the door and holds it open for an older man before exiting himself, and disappearing after a few steps.

It's then that I reach into my pocket and pull out the Polaroid there. I don't make a sound; though my lips press together and my hands tremble as I look it over.

Rob's face is displayed clearly by the flash. There's blood on his pale, bluish skin, and the wound in his throat reminds me of a grin. It's been pressed and torn wide, like someone stuck a screwdriver in it and twisted.

Or maybe just used their fingers.

My other hand comes up to trace the letters that read *Winter Parting Gift* at the bottom, scrawled in Oliver's graceful handwriting, and I wonder if I'm going to throw up.

A voice from nearby draws my attention, however, and I

look up as the older woman with greying hair and glasses perched on her nose says, clearly, "What a *nice* looking young man. He reminds me of my husband when we were your age. I bet you thank your lucky stars every night for such a polite and handsome fellow, isn't that right dear?" She winks jovially at me, knobby hands gripping an old purse.

My smile is slow to form, and I glance back down at the picture before shoving it back into the pocket of my jacket. "Yeah," I agree, trying not to let my voice shake. "He's really something. I don't know what I'd do without him."

"You have a good Christmas," the woman goes on, still smiling. "And I hope your boyfriend has the same."

"Absolutely," I say finally, the words tasting like copper on my tongue. "I hope he does too. I'll be thinking about him every single day."

ABOUT AJ MERLIN

AJ merlin is an author, crazy bird lady, and rampant horror movie enthusiast. Born and raised in the midwest United States, AJ is lucky to be right in the middle of people who support her and a menagerie of animals to keep her somewhat sane. Connect with her on facebook or social media to see updates, giveaways, and be bombarded with dog, cat, and pigeon pictures.